MOON REGARDLESS

NICK MANZOLILLO

This is a work of fiction. Names, characters, places, and incidents are products of the author's imagination or are used fictitiously and are not to be construed as real. Any resemblance to actual events, locations, organizations, or persons, living or dead, is entirely coincidental.

World Castle Publishing, LLC
Pensacola, Florida
Copyright © Nick Manzolillo 2021
Paperback ISBN: 9781953271792
eBook ISBN: 9781953271808
First Edition World Castle Publishing, LLC, March 22, 2021
http://www.worldcastlepublishing.com

Licensing Notes

Cover: Karen Fuller
Editor: Maxine Bringenberg

"I AM PROVIDENCE"- H. P. Lovecraft

For my wife, Brittany Grace, who showed me how to love Providence.

For my mom and dad, Denise and Lou, and my grandparents, James, Sheila, Steven, Mike and Carol, for their endless love and support.

Special Thanks

This novel wouldn't have been possible without the incredible guidance and inspiration from my teachers and peers at Western Connecticut State's Creative and Professional Writing MFA program; to everybody involved in the program, thank you for giving an awkward and introverted storyteller a place to feel accepted. May bad poetry night live on forever.

Thank you to the late Professor Robert Leuci and his highly energetic creative writing advice at the University of Rhode Island.

Thank you to Thuglit and the New England Horror Writers for my first professional short story publications.

Thank you to Mrs. Stormont and Mrs. Willison from Scituate High School for inspiring me to take writing seriously.

Thank you to Karen Fuller, Maxine Bringenberg, and everybody involved with World Castle Publishing for giving this strange novel a wonderful home.

CHAPTER 1
THE GIRL PERSUADED BY THE STARS

The more Hap digs, the more he bleeds. The early summer heat percolates from the rusted walls of the dumpster, creating an oven that roasts rancid meat and soiled kitty litter. As he heaves through the sacks of plastic, talons of glass, and cracked slabs of plaster, they seem to come alive to mince Hap into something more digestible. "No, no, no," he mumbles, sweat accumulating with his blood, searing his eyes. He's thrown out the only lead he has. The only chance he might have at finding Tiffany.

Hap has been telling anybody who will listen that he has a girlfriend and he can't find her. Either she has been raped, murdered, and dumped down a well, or she ran off with some backwoods carnie and is up in the White Mountains of New Hampshire. Either way, Hap has to know for certain. From outside the dumpster, men are yelling—a group of construction workers, remodeling yet another ancient Federal Hill building. He won't be able to evade them for much longer, but he has to find it. The totem. His taut and bleeding fingers have only found the winding threads to what may be his own sanity.

"Hey, buddy, what the hell are you doing?" Someone who doesn't understand has heard Hap's rummaging. Nobody wants to help him. The police have done nothing. Tiffany's parents and friends are spinning in circles that are warping into spirals of paranoia. Hap's own folks want him to come back to Pennsylvania. He lied, told them he wanted to finish up the year, hand in those last final papers, and earn his filthy media and communications degree, so he has something that makes this all worth it.

The worker who's found him whistles over his buddies. Gloved hands snatch Hap by the back of his shirt, hauling him out of the sea of filth like a grime-clad fish. The sun blinds him as he's laid down on the sidewalk. Men in vests of neon orange peer over him. One of them, a Hispanic guy wearing a hardhat, asks, "What are you on, kid?" But Hap doesn't care what they think. Clutched in his hand and speckled in blood is the totem. Carved in the vaguest of details and small enough to be swallowed up by Hap's fist, the obsidian totem is of a toad; it's squat and lumpy, with several humanoid arms blossoming out of its back.

He doesn't remember grabbing it. How long did he search with the totem clenched in his hand, as if there were something else to find in that stink bin of waste? Tiffany....

Hap springs to his feet, causing the workers to back away, eyes wide. Is Hap grinning? He works his jaw, roves his tongue behind his teeth. His mouth is open. Shit, he must look like a lunatic, bloody and snarling. "I...," he begins to say, but he's got nothing but a whole bunch of half-formed excuses he doesn't have the heart to spew. All these men see is a dark-skinned boy, probably on drugs.

"Do you need a phone?" an older guy with a graying beard and some kind of badge on his vest asks.

If something can happen to a girl like Tiff, then you have no friends, just varying degrees of enemy. Hap presses the totem to his chest, spots an opening between the men, and takes off running. Nobody chases after him.

Federal Hill, an old Italian district full of restaurants and bars and only a twenty-minute walk away from the Johnson and Wales campus, has become just another noisy distraction. Weaving through the twisting roads, he wishes that the buildings in his way were sheets he could pull and throw aside.

Nobody greets Hap when he enters the apartment. One of the girls, Erin, is lying on the couch, her eyes puffy, red, and glued to her laptop screen. Tiff has been gone for four days. By the end of that second day, when the idea of what happened to her began to grow dark, the other girls stopped acknowledging Hap's grief. He remembers how hopeful they were when he first told them he hadn't seen her. That she hadn't come home from her event at the downtown Miskatonic Hotel, where she was helping to organize a ball for the weekend-long astronomy convention. These girls, with their eyes now run red and raw from all their tears, once told Hap not to worry and that everything would be fine.

Of course, Tiff's parents were the first to *really* worry, but that's their job as parents. They were the ones who called the cops the first night of Tiff's disappearance. Tiff's mother had yelled at Hap because he slept until three in the afternoon that day, even though he had no idea she was missing at the time. The cops were full of the annoying kind of questions. They asked Hap if he and Tiff had any big fights, if she was depressed, if anyone was bothering her. No, no, and no.

In his poster-strewn bedroom, Hap sets the totem back where Tiff first placed it on his Xbox. What an ugly thing. He gave it the nickname *The Lord Over Joy* because there it sat, an outsider in the mix of Hap and Tiffany's personalities scattered around the room. His original painted Jimi Hendrix and Star Wars portraits mesh with a map of the (real) galaxy and Tiff's Native American dream catchers. The apartment may be one thing, but their room, however small, is precisely connected to each of them. The totem is an invader.

Tiff got the damn thing as some sort of party favor for helping set up the ball. It's not something you would expect to get from what's essentially a geek convention honoring Charles McKinley, a relatively obscure astrophysicist. Tiffany used to go on about him being the next Galileo when his theories about the elemental charging of the universe and parallel dimensions start being proven in the next ten years; Hap didn't know enough to dispute any of that. The people hosting the ball were more spiritual than scientific, according to Tiffany. A lot of the costumes and dresses for the ball were "grotesque," in her own words, and she only elaborated that there were a lot of awkward leather and masquerade masks. Hap was only half listening at the time. She always seemed to tell him about her day when he was playing *Halo*. There's no real explanation for the toad of a totem, *The Lord Over Joy*, except that maybe art and science should respect a well-defined line.

The totem sits on his Xbox, gloating over his grief once more. At night it eyes him through the orange streetlight-striped darkness of the bedroom, which, despite being nearly closet sized, now feels massive. He couldn't help throwing the damn totem away after that first night with Tiff gone. He didn't tell the cops about it. It didn't seem to matter, but now he remembers the little legends about the Miskatonic Hotel. Rumors about ghosts haunting the place. The cops tune out the moment they hear the word *ghost*, but there's a philosophy to myth and how it blurs reality. It makes no difference to him whether a dead thing or a man in a white sheet stole Tiffany away. All that matters is that something about the Miskatonic was off to begin with.

Hap sifts through his leather briefcase and retrieves his camera. He will not open it and look through album upon album of digitally stored photographs until he sees her again. Not until he can get down on one knee and do what he was meant to. A black box tumbles out of his bag, nearly rolling under the bed.

The day Tiff didn't come home from work, Hap had been practicing his proposal. He'd been taking a knee in front of his mirror and laughing at himself uncontrollably. He had gone over every possible way he could propose to her. Inside a bowl of chicken wings at the rather contradictory Federal Hill New York Pizza parlor? Under her pillow? At the downtown water fires? He had to get it right because, according to his younger sister,

Tiff probably had been imagining this proposal business since she was a little girl.

The night that Tiffany should have been home, there was a full moon, and even though Hap's never been one to send his wishes to the stars, he originally took that as a good sign. The plan evolved to include meeting Tiff at a pub on College Hill near Brown University, eating wings, and *then* walking three blocks over to Prospect Terrace, a humble little East Side park with a view overlooking the entire city. The proposal would have been perfect bathed in moonlight.

He had pictured her saying, "I just sent my graduation robes to get resized, and now you want me to buy a fucking wedding dress?" But Hap knew she would've said yes. Hell, she's the one who was supposed to be making near sixty grand a year right after graduation, probably at some international hotel. Hap figured he'd be lucky if the *Providence Journal* even considered him for an internship come winter. Hap and Tiff have already signed a lease for an apartment between Atwells Avenue and the beginning of Federal Hill. Hap had been planning on paying for his share of the rent and every other expense with the credit card his mother still covers the bills for back home in Pennsylvania.

Hap tucks the wedding ring back into his briefcase and falls onto the mattress, holding his camera, a top-of-the-line Canon his dad got him for high school graduation, up to the ceiling. The girls who worked the Astronomer's Ball with Tiffany told the police they never noticed her leave. The people who ran the event were artsy and relaxed, letting the girls come and go when they wished to, especially on that last night. Tiff must have hated how loosely structured it was. She would have stayed until the event was over, doing everything she could to stick out as a motivated employee.

The Astronomer's Ball wasn't the first event she coordinated from Providence to Newport, being a hospitality major and all, but it was the first event she seemed passionate about. If Hap's head is in the clouds, he's always imagined hers being in the stars. He's never used the two-thousand-dollar telescope in their bedroom, but for every cosmic event streaking across the sky, Tiffany always made sure he gets an eyeful, city lights be damned.

Hap aims his camera at the telescope in the corner of the bedroom and snaps a picture. The lighting's off, but he's too lazy to get up and flick a switch. Fuck, he's getting dumpster grime all over the bedsheets. Right now, Hap can't get behind the idea of showering, of being naked and all the more exposed. He kicks his shoes off, and that's good enough. There were many nights when he passed out to the fine sight of Tiff's squeezable thighs poking through her shorts, her blonde hair streaked across the silver of the scope while she hunched over, motionless, gazing onto other worlds. He has the totem. He has nothing left he can possibly do but dream and wait, and, with that thought, Hap closes his eyes and sees Tiffany again.

When he opens them, the totem is watching. A flurry of rapid, childlike knocks rattles against the bedroom door, startling Hap fully awake just as the group of girls comes barging in. Most concerning of all is that one of Tiff's roommates, Lexi, is hiding behind Erin and holding a baseball bat. "We need you to go," Erin speaks up as if it's such a simple request. It's only been a few hours, but he took his clothes off at some murky, dream clogged point, and now he's under the covers in only his underwear.

The girls have discussed their decision without him. He'd been dreading this. When the girlfriend of a twenty-two-year-old boy goes missing, the world knows who to blame.

"All right, but what if she comes back?" Hap begs.

"We don't know if you had something to do with it. Our parents…." Erin's trying to explain. Given that she's the loudest one of the bunch, the other girls have clearly put her up to this.

"You really think I did something? You seriously think I'd hurt her?" Hap could cry for them if they really needed to see some sincerity.

"We don't know you. We haven't gotten to know you for how long now? You don't talk," Lexi says from behind Erin, and there it is. He tries to be quiet and respectful as Tiff's boyfriend and all, and they think he's a freak. It's like they've never met an introvert before.

"We don't know if you're telling the truth, and this room doesn't belong to you. Your name's not on the lease, which me and Lex and Rachel are planning on renewing," Erin says, and go figure, three out of the four other girls aren't graduating on time. "We've called Cort," Erin says. Cort, the landlord, a punk in his thirties who often shows up unannounced and hasn't done anything about the mice problem the building's had for the past three years. "Your name is not on the lease. With her gone…you shouldn't be here. You should go home."

Hap tries to swallow with a throat gone dry, and in as neutral a tone as possible, tells the group of girls to fuck off. They back out of the room, not wanting to turn their backs to him. It's not until they slam the door shut that Hap realizes he's still flaked in dried blood and dumpster dung.

They want him gone? Good. He's done here. He…the totem catches Hap's eye, and why did he set it back onto the Xbox? He slaps it to the floor, tosses his backpack onto the bed, and begins packing. The girls are yelling at one another. One of them is crying. Through all of the dramatic chaos they've experienced over the past three years, from cheating boyfriends to failing grades to fights amongst one another and their dirty cats, their wrath is now set upon Hap.

Cort, the landlord, a skinny ginger man, shows up before Hap can even begin emptying Tiff's room of his stuff. The guy walks right into the bedroom wearing a baby blue golf polo and points a finger at Hap. "I'm calling the cops if you're not out of here in five minutes." Five minutes? He hasn't even had a chance to book a bus or call his brother to pick him up tomorrow morning.

"That's bullshit. I haven't done anything wrong. I can't even get home." Hap hates the panic that tinges his words, making him seem unstable. He hates the sobs that linger at the back of his throat, weakening his argument.

"Do I need to get the lease? You're harassing my tenants," Cort sneers. Allegedly, he has ties to the mob. That's supposedly a thing on Federal Hill, it being the chief Italian neighborhood in Rhode Island and all. If some kind of mob still exists, Hap figures they probably use people like Cort as a tampon.

The little moments are vanishing. Too many days have gone by already. There's no arguing with Cort. Getting arrested won't do. Hap emerges onto Federal Hill with his backpack and a duffel bag, thankful he remembered to grab his Xbox and camera. As soon as he hears Cort tell the girls, "Everything is going to be okay," he kicks over a pair of trash bins. If he knew what kind of car Cort drove, he'd kick that too.

Hap leaves the hill for Broadway, one of those classic primary streets that run through the heart of Providence. His heart is beating loud enough to dull the world around him. When he calls his mother, he's practically in a trance.

The voice of the woman who reared him and his four siblings is a loudspeaker over several distant hills behind him. He tells her he has no place to stay. She tells him to just come home, that she'll order him a bus ticket right this minute, that all he needs to focus on is heading home. When Hap hangs up, he can't remember what he's told her. His soothing bullshit seemed to comfort her, but it's lost to him. He can't think of a good lie that will stop him from doing something stupid.

He recalls that special something about the Miskatonic Hotel, that little bit of nonsense he heard kids repeat both his freshman year and while he was a hall advisor. The out-of-town students were quick to demand, eat up, and then regurgitate the stories about the one mad thing every city has: ghost stories.

There is something whispered about the Miskatonic Hotel that Hap begins to remember.

Rhode Island took Prohibition in stride despite its Puritan hierarchy, and it was notorious for being its own little booze-soaked plain of rebellion. According to kids newly exposed to the private exclusivity of frat parties and sorority socials, the Miskatonic is the grandfather of private events. Government men and their law enforcement spawn would drink for free in private rooms and ballrooms, sheltered by the enclosed privileges of the hotel. Complete with complimentary prostitutes and rooms where cigars were manufactured, one English professor mused that the hotel was probably a paradise out of *The Great Gatsby*. Like any other criminal watering hole, violence came in heavy chalices.

Any real details are bogged down by time and legend, but there were shootings, murders by police, and pedophile politicians. One poor prostitute was apparently drowned in a bathtub. Since the twenties, there have been numerous exciting reports of hauntings scattered throughout the hotel's corridors. Typical New England stuff like weeping women in ancient dresses wandering down hallways and vanishing into a wall, ghosts knocking, smiling, flickering out of focus, and little children asking for help in finding their parents before disappearing around a corner. Hap took an October ghost tour of the city with Tiff once. While they didn't set foot inside the actual hotel, they were given a briefing of its history. Back then, it was all a fine joke.

Providence is summed up by Broadway. There are colonial houses right next to gas stations. Pieces of the distant past and the mortar for the start of this country are scattered about the modern agenda like warts that never fade. The colonials all achieve a sense of alienation, loneliness. None of them really looks the same, though they can be summed up by their spiraling rooftops and pointed Victorian spliced windows. Many of them have been turned into law or government offices, masquerading as homes.

Hap's hands grow clammy and, oh, those miserable roommates of Tiff's—can't he linger in the bed that still smells of her? He's been huffing that for days, feeling her next to him when the rays of sunlight hit him. Sure, his name wasn't on the lease, but he paid his share for groceries and toilet paper. He was always polite, always lifted the toilet seat in the bathroom, and shut all the lights off when he left the living room. Nobody asked anything more from him.

The slope of Federal Hill over downtown is a gradual one, almost unnoticeable depending on where you're standing. Hap tries to imagine a time when there was grass instead of asphalt, but then he figures maybe the concept of there being a hill in the first place is artificial, and everything is built on manmade junk to begin with. The world gets taller as it builds upon the old and the fallen. Who will truly remember Tiffany in ten years?

The tears are coming now, which he considers good at first. Maybe crying will soothe this ache he can't scratch. He passes a sign that says "Manzolillo Chiropractic," and the overabundance of the letter L starts to seem like black vines emerging from the white backdrop of the sign. Hap starts to run, hefting his bags as hard as he can, leaking hot tears like fuel.

Downtown has always been a more petite scale model of something you'd find in New York. Being small, it has a fresh significance to it. How many meaningless corners and buildings are there in the bigger cities like New York and Philly? In Providence, each one of them matters.

A semicircle of broken unity forms the roundabout at the hotel's drop off/pick up zone. Within its center, beside a copse of weedy plants and a gold lettered sign proclaiming Miskatonic, there is a great black orb carved of marble. Hap has seen such decorations in front of semi-important buildings before, but something about that ball of darkness draws his chest tight. Out of context, it's sinister and haunting, like something from *Lord of The Rings*. It doesn't belong here, out in the open, hiding as art.

The Miskatonic's exterior brings to mind the reek of the stuffy, perfume-preserved walls of Hap's grandmother's house. Flat brick walls jut from the earth, and hundreds of black windows are symmetrically aligned like the many eyes of some microscopic insect. Completing its place outside of time's decay, the hotel's main iconic feature is a gold-tinged glass elevator. Hap rode it once with Tiff, and from the top, you get one of the best views of the entire city—aside from Prospect Park, that is.

Along the rooftop, the name Miskatonic continuously glows in dulled purple neon, reiterating its title, its dominance across the Providence skyline. Beneath the neon letters is an accompanying five-sided star, glowing with an orange center while its edges are black, as if from a creeping decay. Its dominance as what? Hap wonders. As a place for people to sleep, shit, and pop out of existence?

His sweat's stinging his eyes. Eyeing the suspicious black orb behind the ground sign, Hap is startled by an abrupt crack at his feet, as if the cement is trembling back from his weight. Wiping his aching eyes clean, Hap lifts his four-month-old sneakers, and he's stepped on the strangest little twig. It has five appendages like maybe it's some kind of lightning bolt stuck across his shoe. As he scrapes it off, it cracks and shatters. How is he stepping on the waste of a tree downtown? Nausea rises from his gut, low and bubbling. Is this how the world collapses? One weird little moment at a time?

Avoiding the eyes of a couple of valet boys dressed like they're from the sixties, Hap stumbles through the glass doors. He enters a realm of gold-embroidered walls reflecting what may as well be an Egyptian tomb. There are even sphinxes adorning the ceiling above the Miskatonic's revolving doors. As Hap's eyes adjust from all the maddening yellow, there are other amorphous, gold-flaked flowers that seep toward the center of the lobby, where a dangling stalactite of a chandelier hangs over a number of purple leather couches. Someone grabs Hap by the wrist, and he leaves the void of decoration and nonsensically placed art.

A bellhop gets in Hap's face. "Is there any way I can help you?" the bellhop asks, his voice gravel. Hap can't even come up with a good enough response. The sickness dancing in his stomach starts climbing up his esophagus.

"I'm looking for my girlfriend," Hap mumbles.

"What's her room number? How about we call up to her room, see if she's expecting you?" The man's pulling Hap toward the front desk, where there sits an elite, perky blonde woman with hair much more golden than that of *his* blonde girl. None of these people can help Hap. They are a part of this place.

"No, no, I can find her on my own."

The only time Hap has struggled for breath in the past four years is from furious tickling matches with Tiffany and headlocks from his drunken older brother. Hap pulls away from the sentinel in a funny bellhop hat, craning to look across the lobby, as if Tiff could merely be sitting in one of the plush velvet chairs and reading a *Home* magazine off one of the coffee tables.

"Sir!" The bellhop snarls in Hap's ears, and he pumps his arms, propelling himself into a run he only reserves for sudden rainstorms and pre-departing buses. He makes it halfway up a staircase with more flowery designs enmeshed into each step. His legs are grabbed, and he's falling forward as his chin smacks across the itchy carpet. The flower designs are two near-symmetrical roses that look as if they could be eyes. Everything in this building is watching him.

Hap is dragged out of the hotel by men made of dead flesh and a hive mind as he thrashes and begs for someone to bring him his girlfriend. The encroaching sirens of a city's disease-killing white blood cells beckon as the faintly flickering purple of the Miskatonic's neon sign brands Hap's eyes.

CHAPTER 2
THE PRINCE OF THE CANDLE LIGHTERS

Politician Paul traces his fingers over the fabric of the antique rolling chair, staring into his closed office door as if at any moment somebody important could come bursting through. As if. These Miskatonic guys, they aren't one for front doors. That's why that unspectacular side door pretending to be a part of the wall behind him is where a visitor is more likely to emerge. Next to a bookshelf riddled with random ink-dabbed word containers that were here before he moved in, there's no way for him to open the side panel. They can only visit him from their little halls within the walls. It's only on special occasions he gets a tap on the shoulder or, if he's lucky, a polite knock on the wall.

It hasn't gotten to the point where Paul's having whiskey for breakfast and an OxyContin cocktail before bed. He's got a more than modest apartment by the East Providence Bridge that overlooks a boat of his that most people can't afford. Just last Tuesday, he showed a woman from Boston that he is on the right side of fifty. Regardless, when Paul lifts his head and gazes over his rounding belly, he can plainly see that he's on a hill that's as big as it's ever going to get, save for any untold seismic eruptions. He's at his life's crescendo, and all that's left for him is to get so fat from his ninety-grand-a-year salary that he rolls off that sweet, prickly grass.

Feeling up for flirting with the front desk girls, Paul hears the confrontation before he leaves his office. Someone with an accent is complaining. A foreigner in Providence is more of an anomaly than in most cities. Paul rounds the hallway bend behind the front desk, and is this what he gets to look forward to for the rest of his life? The unknowable game of who will show up at your hotel next?

Cassandra's hands form white knuckles as she grips the front desk, her eyebrows doing this cute little curling trick while she stares at the man, trying to digest what he's saying. The guest is a bald fellow with a sloppy white beard and an icy blue halo tattooed around his skull, anywhere between thirty and sixty years old. It's impossible to tell with eyes as worn as his. A strand of golden hair is cast over Cassandra's cheek, surely irritating her eye. Paul wouldn't mind brushing it back for her. If there's one lesson he learned back when he was grooming himself for governor, it was that you can't date anyone five years below your age and within two miles of where you do your business.

"Sir, there aren't any events scheduled for tonight, and no animals are allowed in the hotel. For that matter, I — " Paul's hand on Cassandra's shoulder is a hushing of the teapot. He brushes past her, flicking a finger across the purple of his tie so as to signal to the man their mutual affiliation. Cassandra's still standing astute by Paul's side, and Lindsey, speaking with another guest on the far side of the reception stand, has her eye slanted his way as well. Now he has to choose his words carefully, and, on top of the other fuck ups, this is the last thing he wants to deal with. How hard is it for these people to follow the custom of secrecy?

"I'm sure you can figure out the mix-up when you get to your room. Maybe you're looking for a private event going on somewhere else." Paul shrugs. The guest doesn't lack intelligence, but he is missing an aptitude for discretion, and that means he'll state his intentions to attend "the honoring of the black goat" to the first inquisitor he comes across. This isn't the first candle lighter to spout his nonsense in public. It's as if these people think the threshold of the Miskatonic means they can drop their disguises of civility and normalcy.

"I've come a long way for unity. I don't need a bed or walls. I'm here for the—," the guest says, but Paul cuts him off.

"Listen." Paul leans forward, flicking his tie. Purple is important to them, like the flashy skin of some poisonous beast. Paul disregards his trained professionalism and says, "Shack up here for the night, and you'll find what you're looking for." His teeth are clenched as his words force their way through enamel.

The candle lighter's face is unchanged save for the slightest wavering of his head. Paul twists to Cassandra and takes the key still dangling from her fingertips, her confusion rightfully plastered all over her face.

"Room six three one." Paul places the keys on the counter, not wanting to touch the candle lighter's hands. The man snatches the keys away with a jangle.

"Paul, he never paid!" Cassandra says. What an honest and naïve creature. It's beyond her to even dream of peeking behind the curtain.

"We'll get him on the way out. Hey." Paul's smile is his most loyal and effective weapon. His father's ever-circulating rotation of girlfriends would always poke and prod at him, pinching his cheeks and telling him that, with a smile like that, he could get anything he wants. He once took one of them up on that offer. "Don't worry about anything. I've got all your backs." Cassandra and Lindsey smile at Paul like he's their savior. Somebody ought to take a picture. He's actually capable of making people happy.

The front desk phone rings, so why not answer it? "Paul, I never mistook you for the old-fashioned type, not with that Apple gadget in your pocket. Generals don't stick to the frontlines anymore. I don't believe they have since the North and South woke up and found themselves lost in the strange." The voice is familiar. A big fish in a small pond is nothing when compared to the people who own that pond and keep the algae levels from turning that fish into a bacteria-ridden husk.

"Candle lighter was asking about a goat, out loud." Paul clicks his teeth. "Shit, and now I am. One sec." Paul clicks the phone down. Cassandra hasn't heard him. She's talking with Lindsey about a country concert at Lupo's down the street, wondering out loud about where the lead singer is staying. Not here, honey, Paul thinks. Definitely not at the Miskatonic, with its fantastic sixty-inch box TVs that still have a channel for overpriced nineties porn. Paul will have to remember to tap his connection at the venue's box office and get the girls tickets.

The office door is firmly closed, yet Paul clearly remembers leaving it half ajar. He debates knocking, but it's supposed to be his office, isn't it? From the crack at the bottom of the door, he notices that the lights are on, and only now does Paul realize he was sitting in the dark earlier. How hadn't he noticed that?

Within, a hazy glow is cast over Johan Weissekopf, who is sitting at Paul's desk, leafing through a book on ancient astronomy, taking an extra moment to turn a final page before looking up and smiling at Paul. The man is like a priest without a white collar. In addition to being upper management at the Miskatonic, he's in charge of a certain group that often frequents the hotel, a group rife with its dim-eyed men of mumbling words and sudden outbursts of inarticulacy; the Candle Lighters.

Johan slides the textbook across the desk, and Paul wasn't aware he even had such a thing on the bookshelf. He thinks of Johan as a priest because of the softness of his eyes. His face is round, not quite fat but thick as if he has extra layers of skin. His rosy cheeks and light brown hair cast him almost as a boy, but he's only a few years younger than Paul at best. He is a priest because there is that gentle sluggishness to him that's still ripe in Paul's memory from his days in Catholic school. Unlike the witch-like nuns, the priests always seemed like less colorful Santa Clauses.

Johan's hand extends, and you would think Paul wouldn't be awkward about handshakes. By now, his political experience withstanding, it's the one chip in his armor that no amount of refining can overcome. Paul's grip never seems to fully join up with the other hand, and, of course, it's all mental, all a result of fear. Knowing that doesn't make life any easier. For Politician Paul, all he figures he needs in life are his words.

"I wanted you to hear this from me. There's been a murder that you aren't going to read about in the papers. It's one of us." The way Johan says "us" makes Paul start to feel the dampness of his armpits. He's not going to wear that tinfoil hat, not just yet. *Us.* Wasn't that his golden campaign word? *Us* and we and all of us, together, blah, blah, blah, Paul's a liar. Don't vote for him, ha-ha-ha; screw you, Paul.

"Who?" Paul knows everybody. Everybody in Providence, at least. He can make most of them smile, too. He was class president like nobody's business. He wasn't valedictorian or even always on the honor roll, but everybody liked him. He made sure of it.

"Boren Clementine." Johan's voice is like melted chocolate; he had to work for it to sound that way, Paul's almost sure of that. Even the devil had to forge his silver tongue.

"And I'm not supposed to ask why you're gonna leave it out of the papers?" Boren owned a restaurant on Broadway. They share the same black star insignia as the Miskatonic, except the restaurant's insignia has a tinge of red bordering those five points.

"Ask, and I'll tell." Johan folds his hands.

"Yeah, I'll leave it to the experts." Paul taps a finger along the corner of his desk. He wouldn't feel right sitting down while Johan's in the room. He still doesn't know how to really consider the man, but the guy commands more than a tone of respect. He's a vacuum of attention, of high-strung focus. Once you talk to Johan, you don't ask him to repeat himself. You pick up what he's saying, what he's actually saying, in between the duality of his words, and, if you don't fully understand, then you let him carry off any faith you've got. Now that — that's what makes the man a priest.

"The killer is no man or woman that has any degree of... communion...with us. It's strictly why I'm informing you. We don't know who it is." There's something new to Johan's lips, the way his precisely aligned teeth are showing.

"This isn't like the last mix-up, is what you're saying?" Paul asks. Somebody made a mistake not too long ago that brought cops to the hotel, however briefly.

"This is an outsider whose eye may have lingered over the right spot for too long. Settle yourself because you need to be aware of the kind of man we're talking about," Johan begins, looking Paul up and down, measuring him over and over. "Boren's eyes were missing. A half-moon was carved into his forehead, but most importantly, he was tortured. With a lighter or a cigar, I'm not sure on the details. I doubt Boren talked. There is an outsider in Providence looking at us. What may be even more unsettling for us all to come to grips with, Paul, is that this man is sane. He has heard the word of the Moon Shack, and he not only covers his ears, but he speaks over it." Johan leans over Paul's desk, smiling like a doctor delivering a treatable diagnosis.

The sweat's trying to change him into something else; Paul could use a seat, a fan blowing in his face and a gun against his temple. The hill is upside down; he's been hanging by the thinnest strands of grass for how long now? What the hell has he done to himself? He should be mentoring a law school pup fresh from Roger Williams. Even if he has to be like one of those guys on Broadway with his billboards all over I-95, that would be just fine. He'd have none of what this is. None of these promises and half hopes. He'd be semi-retired, joking and bragging that he's semi-retired or semi-retarded, living as he does with no worry other than the looming blackness of heart disease or ass cancer. Why is he here?

"Paul?" Johan's curiosity is on the borders of a merry bout of laughter as if Paul's pulling some kind of ditzy space out. Meanwhile, Paul can hear his heartbeat, louder than Johan's words, and it is singing a berating tune of its own. How could he allow the pressure and failure to bring him here?

"I have a gun I could keep...." He tries to mention the revolver he keeps under his mattress at home. Fuck Johan, Paul's taking a seat, leaving one hand on his desk to support him. No Catholic man could claim to be this blind, but murder...at what point is this now some real and tangible shit he's got himself caught up in?

"Paul, you're not one of us. You're above who we are, respectably. You will live your whole life without firing that thing at another living, breathing being. I'm merely informing you that there is a potentiality for...sloppiness, and, not that you have anything to be afraid of, but concerning our guests, there are going to be a few unfamiliar faces that will be loitering in the lounge, walking around the hallways at the most dismal of hours, watching us from the Omni Hotel across the street."

"Then why even tell me about a...." Paul keeps his voice in check. Johan is in control because there is no other alternative. The anomaly is over. Everything is already handled. He needs to welcome Johan's affirmations.

"Because you deserve to know what's going on. I want you to know that you're valued and safe," Johan says. The menace, hanging over the air like a translucent gas cloud, evaporates. Paul knows bullshit. If an expert in nothing else, he is versed in the universal truth of politics and human maneuverability.

"I'm flattered, but I don't mind riding this all out, back here, until the next election if you'll have me," Paul says. The "maybe" that Johan keeps promising him is something special that helps him fall asleep at night.

Johan's nodding, as if a child's guessed his birthday present. He's making his way to the corner of the room. He is beyond all political merits, to the point that it's clear he has one thing and one thing only that he thinks about, that he spends every idle thought slipping into: the Moon Shack. If only Paul knew anything about that damned thing. His best guess is that it's sort of like reaching Nirvana, only, instead of fat jolly monks, you get oddly tattooed and socially awkward men who pretty much have the word *occult* branded into their foreheads.

"So, what you're basically saying, in the most complicated and gruesome way, is that I might have to deal with something like a couple of bored cops asking questions about why they had to detain a hysterical college boy or two?" Paul asks.

"I'm only leaving the cards you refuse to touch face down on the table. People like you and me have to be careful with our mistakes because when we do make them, we create ripples that form tidal waves; candles could be extinguished."

"My mistake...." He's already regretting talking back to Johan to the extent that he has.

"Paul, how about you follow me into the next room? In addition to the wonderful people I could introduce you to, I could also tell you a fine story about why you don't want to be anything like Mayor Franco." Johan's slipping behind Paul's chair, and the hairs on the back of his neck are spiraling into goosebumps as Johan lowers his lips to Paul's ear. He can feel the hot moisture from his breath. "I'd say it'd be worth your time just to hear about what I, personally, make her do." And Johan's so close, Paul can feel his lips molding into a wicked grin.

Franco was the one who came up with that jagged little campaign, the one about how Paul's smile was "too" big. There was that whole thirty second commercial on a certified FBI technique on how to tell a liar, accompanied by pictures of Paul giving speeches that he spent weeks, sunset to dream-scorched sunrise, writing. Johan isn't the mob. He's a part of something stranger. If Providence has claim to anything, it's the right of its inhabitants to follow their religious pursuits, wherever their faith may take them. If anybody's to blame, it's Roger Williams, for not specifying his Puritan-hating scope and encouraging religious diversity.

"You're telling me there's somebody who hates your organization enough to, ah — to mutilate somebody, and you just get through telling me that I'm not in danger because I'm not actually involved, which is all true, hopefully, but now you're offering me a peek behind your curtain? Come on now! I mean...," Paul says, before Johan raises his hand from his shadowy corner of the room and cuts him off.

"This constant air of secrecy has you in pieces, and I'm sorry, Paul. You are one of the finest men I've ever met. You represent what makes being a man...a human being, so comprehensively true. Above all things, people trust you. If one man is to truly lead Providence, it is going to be you, and here's the part you don't want to hear. When the time is right, when those...." Johan's heading toward the wall, raising his hand to the ceiling. "...beady little eyes in the sky are aligned, you will be that man who will lead an entire city."

If this is all shit coming out of Johan's mouth, then Paul can't even pick through it for the nuggets of gold anymore. "Thanks for your vote, I guess, but I can't take any more promises."

Offbeat piping, like a flute or a wheezy bagpipe, begins tinkling from behind the hidden door Johan is about to enter. Something about that piping and its chaotic lack of synchrony starts to chip away at Paul's lucidness.

"Paul." Johan reaches back for him. Droplets of Paul's sweat are glistening all over the desk, his legs are shaking, and there is a shame akin to perhaps pissing his own pants or crying in the middle of a crowded room. Another man's hand is clasping his own, pulling him along, and Johan's soft and nauseatingly warm embrace is awkwardly pulling him close. "I'm going to show you the perspective you've been looking for. You'll sleep well tonight. You'll believe in something at last, I swear."

Johan takes Paul's hand and leads him to the half ajar panel along the faded wood. The sliding wall opens with a click, locking in place with a shudder. Paul's foot dips over the threshold. The mess of wind instruments spouting like frightened geese becomes an echo. The odor of burning meat drifts down a cold stone corridor. There is the drawling whine of metal dragging upon metal, incalculable clapping hands, and then the distant, weakened cry of an infant goat.

"Come now, my man of the Miskatonic. I'm going to give you a real tour." Johan's voice becomes a snicker in the darkness as the world of schedules, appointments, and plans for the future becomes irrelevant.

CHAPTER 3
THE PROVIDENCE DETECTIVE AGENCY

As the weeks pass, Hap stops crying, quits glancing at his phone, and finds that he can't bring himself to sleep in past eleven. The last semi-decent dream he has of Tiff involves him lying in their bed at the old apartment. He could hear the familiar jingling of keys in the hallway outside the apartment and prayed that it was somehow Tiff returning home, as she'd done so many times before. As if summoned by his lucid will, there was a clink from the front door popping open. "Babe, what are you doing?" she said, from just outside the bedroom door. He opened his eyes before she could enter, and there was no reeling that dream back in. From there, all of Hap's dreams have become formless nightmares, and with their oozing dominion, he knows he has to go back to Providence.

The Miskatonic didn't press charges. The cop who met him and that prick bellhop outside the hotel's front doors ended up driving him right to the bus station. They all felt bad for the crazy kid.

A four-hour drive in the Ford Focus he got as a high school graduation present somehow offers more therapy than every conversation he's had with his parents, his brother Doran, and the wise-cracking therapist he was sent to. There is a numbing effect to the endless lanes of the highway. Providence, inching closer mile by mile, is better than sleep.

His parents' grand response to his moving back to Rhode

Island is to give him extra money for the apartment for which he and Tiff had already put down a deposit. Her name is still on the lease, but there's little more he technically has to do besides pay every month. Of course, his mom tried every which way to get him to reconsider going back, but Hap has led her to believe he actually has a position at the *Providence Journal*. Short of a Google search, she doesn't know how small and selective the newspaper branch actually is. Meanwhile, Hap's resume only has three months of valet work and a college-level education, like a sole spine and femur with little else to explain why he can even stand on his own two feet in the adult world.

A phone call to Tiff's parents' house goes straight to a voicemail they may not even check. Without Tiff, there remains no way for Hap to even have the slightest inkling as to their cell phone numbers. The information flow that was always filed away right beside him in Tiff's phone has been severed, proving just how fragile his perfect world was.

Hap doesn't need the GPS once he takes an exit that dumps him onto Broadway. A shirtless kid on a bike holding some kind of metal pole cuts Hap off just as he's crossing a left lane to turn onto his new one-way street. Horns blare behind Hap, jostling up an instinctual road rage like a Taser prod to the stomach. The kid's pole makes him as wide as a garbage truck, and the Ford can't pass him. This is why Hap originally left his car at home. At least Tiff had a single parking spot behind her building. In a city this small with as many one-ways as it has and a nightly parking ban between 3AM and 6AM, owning a car in Providence is a nightmare he never thought he'd experience.

As prepared for the move back as he is, go figure, Hap forgot the Xbox, and for that, he can only blame the all-consuming idea of death. Each virtual soldier he killed in *Halo* seemed to matter. Life is something bright and near infinite in its impossibilities until the moment it shuts off with a click.

After squeezing into a parking spot, Hap finds the

sidewalks on either side of his building empty. Typical little Providence. At best, you'll see somebody smoking on their front stoop, and even then, they're usually still and silently blending into the loneliness around you.

The key Hap was sent in the mail fits; the apartment becomes real as he steps into a near-blinding, white-walled living space that's partially furnished with unwanted relics from prior tenants. How many other couples have lived here? Hap dumps everything but his backpack into the bedroom, taking note that he needs to buy bedding unless he wants to sleep on a naked and potentially piss-stained mattress. It's nothing he needs to worry about for tonight, though.

There is a single moment when Hap glances at the couch and finds it hard to breathe. The couch is just big enough that all six feet of Tiff could lie on it without having to curl up. Tall people are often neglected such comforts. If they were moving in together...hah. Well, their clothes would be on the floor, and everything would still be unpacked, save for a couple of bed sheets.

Tiff liked running things. Churning onwards since freshman year, she had been the one making all the plans, and Hap was more than happy to oblige. She was only his second girlfriend; he barely ever got past a few make-out sessions and one overenthusiastic hand job in high school. Tiff would have had this new apartment in tiptop shape, fully decorated.

Hap sighs, leans his head against the door, welcoming a brief shower of hot, useless tears. He debates punching the door, but then he's thinking about it instead of doing it. He's always hated those kinds of people who yell and hit shit and then walk around with a cheap athletic cast for a couple of weeks. "Fuck you," Hap mutters. Whether he's talking to Tiff or to himself, he's not sure.

If you can kiss somebody before they leave and feel fully satisfied with that last kiss until the next time you meet, then you don't love them. It was morning, the last he saw of her, and he was only a quarter awake when she brushed her mouth across his and wished him a nice day. Where did his lips send her?

Hap slinks a backpack over his shoulders and leaves his new apartment behind. Stepping out onto Broadway once more, the Miskatonic, his true destination, looms in the distance.

The night's sweeping in by the time he gets downtown, his day drained by last-minute packing and driving. How many Indian-looking boys are there in Providence? School's out, so already the city's population is more homogenous. Sure, combine the Indian-boy category with any Arabic or dark-skinned Spanish-speaking guys, and maybe there're enough young men walking around who look like Hap, which buys him a little anonymity. Six weeks of diluted memory should help, too. Or maybe that stone-faced employee of the Miskatonic will recognize him and have him in the arms of another cop on foot patrol. Could be after the month and a half that Hap's been away, they'll just check him into his damned room.

Either way, he took one of his dad's surplus Phillies caps to tilt partially over his eyes. He paid for the room online with his own credit card. His mom will see the charge if she looks, but Hap has plenty of bullshit explanations to choose from.

Readjusting his cap and keeping his head low, Hap avoids making eye contact with the valet guys lingering near the main entrance. Waiting months, even a year, would be better than hoping he's been forgotten after six weeks, but by then, this thing in his chest, swimming up through his blood and into his head every night, this gnawing thing inside of him would be starved and weakened if Hap let any more time pass. He needs this hurt if he wants to find any trace of her.

He makes it to the front desk, where there's a pretty girl his age with curly blonde hair. It takes an awkward moment longer than he'd like to come up with a comprehensible combination of words to let her know he's ready to check into his room. He catches a whiff of the blonde's perfume. He and Tiff would hook up twice a day most days, sometimes more, sometimes less, but nearly two months into this nightmare, and he can't think about even nuzzling somebody. Every morning he wakes up with that usual biological arousal, but then he's paralyzed. If Tiff's out there somewhere, hurt and incapacitated, thinking about him, crying constantly, pleading for him to find her, how could he even fantasize about anything but freeing her?

The blonde, forever typecast by the keratin proteins sprouting from her scalp, calls Hap "sir," and after looking up his information on a computer too sleek for a building this old, she makes eye contact with him and frowns. Hap readies himself to bolt right out of the room. This is taking too long. She sighs and obnoxiously pokes a button on her keyboard. "Here we go," she finally says, smiling. "Thank you so much for being patient. We've had a lot of crazy and rude guests lately."

"Glad to not be one of them." Hap slips into convenience-store-style pleasantry before realizing this is his chance to actually talk to a reasonable employee who may know something. "What do you mean by crazy? Anything interesting?" His words come out too quickly. He knows he's onto something. The gold of this girl's hair is treasure.

"Oh no. I mean, everybody's nice enough, just impatient people in a rush to get to their rooms, you know? Here ya go." She gives him a plastic card with the Miskatonic's dark-edged star emblem blazoned across its face, nested in a little paper slip labeled 347 in scrawling red ink. "Let me know if you need anything else," she says quickly, dismissing him.

With his head down, Hap resists the urge to gaze up at the golden, flowery designs across the ceiling alongside those two sphinxes and their vase. He will study them later, perhaps around three in the morning when the building is practically shut down. He plans on scrutinizing every stray portrait, anomalous doorknob, and spare room in this place. Already he notes a strange absence of security cameras in the lobby.

There are several people waiting for the glass elevator, and Hap wonders if they're even staying at the hotel. For that matter, a hotel in the city probably sees all manner of non-guests coming in or out. When he went down to New York City for a weekend with Tiffany, they couldn't use the elevator without swiping their room keys, which seemed to be a deterrent to keep the homeless away from the upper floors and maid carts. The Miskatonic has none of that. Anybody can walk into the building whenever they please. Hell, Hap caused a big scene, and even he made it past the front desk with a little friendly banter and a working credit card.

His main purpose for riding the glass elevator comes with the closing of its doors, as he presses his forehead against the glass, scanning the front lobby while trying hard not to appear suspicious. He keeps his eyes off the blonde girl and her equally attractive partner at the front desk, instead eyeing some of the people sitting down in the plush lounge chairs. As he glances at some of the men and the way they're dressed, he can't trust the pulsing paranoia throbbing through his cardiovascular system.

There are strange rings, suspicious tattoos, funny hats and suits and ties that are too removed from context to be anything but alien. You always catch your odd types when people watching. Thing is, the most normal guy in the lobby could become a perverse howling thing when the lights are dimmed. Hap scans the dark glasses of what may be a blind man, sitting in the farthest corner of the lobby with a buttered bagel on a napkin across his lap; it seems as if he's looking right at the elevator. As the elevator rises, the lobby is cut away by the cement separation between floors, and the rising view of Providence consumes the viewing panel of the elevator. As the other passengers gasp with delight, Hap looks away. He loved this city. In return, it ate his heart.

Overlooking the predictable pattern of a bed, a plain desk

with scraps of notebook paper, an ancient TV stand, and a half ajar bathroom door that leads to a trove of easy-to-steal soaps and lotions, Hap is left with the dim feeling that he should be excited for something. Hotel rooms remind him of the few Caribbean vacations he went on with Tiff and his family.

The bed of the enemy is soft. After kicking away the surely semen-tainted bedspread, Hap finds himself battling a coaxing temptation to curl up and shut his eyes. Like a vampire waiting for true night, he sets the alarm for later, when he'll emerge to wander the hotel in the early morning gloom. He's unable to rest, though, because there is the idea that Tiff is somehow in a room just like this, maybe a few floors away, tied up, beaten, and crying out for him. Assaulted by the what ifs, Hap kicks himself off the bed and does a half circle in the middle of the room.

What can the hotel really be guilty of? A haunted building can only be the problem to a fault. If ghosts are real and there are mystical forces and hungry half-alive things creeping around, then how can that really factor into Tiff disappearing? Aliens are the ones who abduct people. Somebody probably drugged her, dragged her away, and now she's tied up, being subjected to humankind gone warped. Despite being in the middle of the Miskatonic, Hap is still too far away. Every one of those rooms on each of the eleven floors is a secret that hides behind the mere idea that they are all identical. Identical beds, dressers, old TVs, bathrooms. If a hotel's got something to hide, then that would be the first lie it leads you to believe.

Apparently, people claim to still hear the sounds of uproarious toasting from secret 1920s parties spitting in the face of Prohibition, echoing through the hallways. There's also an allegedly fat ghost that follows people around, rattling empty room service trays. The Miskatonic was the subject of one of those paranormal TV shows a couple of years ago, and before coming back to Providence, Hap watched the episode. Twice. The show glossed over the hotel's history, offering nothing more than Wikipedia facts. Google searches for a toad totem revealed nothing. Hap also tried to look up modern Rhode Island gangs and New England crime families, but really, there aren't any. Not the *Godfather* kind, anyway.

Throughout his schooling, Hap's read a couple of nonfiction accounts of investigative journalists, but did they even take pictures? What's he thinking, that he'll go around the Miskatonic with a camera too big for his pocket and put together a big wall chart in his apartment of everything suspicious he finds? No, art and productivity hardly get to mix. Hap's Canon is a beautiful tool, but it's too noticeable. He'll have to use his smartphone for anything he wants to document in crappy, soulless resolution. Maybe a ghost will turn up. God, what if Tiff turns up, pale and shrieking over Hap's shoulder if he were to take a selfie? He's got to keep his paranoia in check.

The complimentary stack of notepaper on the dresser has *Miskatonic Hotel* sprawled across it, and given the way the hotel likes to put its name on trinkets, you'd think it was a Hilton or a Marriott. Beneath the nametag is a logo Hap hasn't noticed before: *Reserve your place in history.* Hap shivers as a result of what his imagination can do with those little words. Tiff is gone, and anything can be made sinister. This whole night could be a sign that Hap is getting sick in the way orange juice and Nyquil can't do a thing to solve.

There is no such thing as a Providence detective agency, but that's what Hap needs. Why couldn't the police just trace Tiff's phone? He tries typing online: *Where is Tiffany Lorice?* He winces when her picture pops up next to a brief article in the *Providence Journal*.

Wait a second. Would the *Journal* be interested in his story? The opinion of the missing boyfriend and his suspicions about the Miskatonic. Hap could get a real reporter, a real investigator, to look into this. Maybe he could even get in touch with a detective from Boston or someplace. Hap flicks over to the

Journal's website, bumping out an email to their "Got a Story?" section. As a paranoid backup plan, he sends an email to himself that states he is spending the night at the Miskatonic. If he joins Tiff in the land of the missing, then maybe somebody will find it.

As if in answer, there is a thump and a strangled cry from the room adjacent to Hap's. Finally, what he's been waiting for. In his excitement, Hap knocks his camera to the floor before he realizes it's just some couple having sex. His heart is pounding for nothing, and this is nothing. It sounds like rough sex, but that's definitely pleasure that he's hearing. Old walls must be thin.

Mixing passion and a paycheck was something Hap always wanted. Tiff lucked out both managing an event and attending much of the Astro-con scattered across the convention halls throughout the city. He attended a few events with her during the day, preferring the slideshow presentations to the discussion panels, if only for the kinds of pictures where content holds more power than anything. He asked Tiff if there was some way he could shoot the event and slap the pictures together on a blog to add flesh to his boney resume, but she told him the people running the show had their own camera crew for some exclusive magazine. Of course, Hap called her out on how stupid it was that she couldn't even ask for him. And Tiff, when you piss her off…oh boy. Hap's pillow wasn't thick enough to hold over his ears as she cussed him out.

Hap's watch chimes one thirty, and he can't wait another minute. It's a Wednesday; the city's hardly alive on weekends, let alone now. If someone catches him, then he'll tell whoever asks that he was looking for a maid's closet to find some pillows. Nothing suspicious about a fool in search of comfort.

As his door clicks shut behind him, he runs his hands over his room key, looking down the hallway first to his left, then his right—no men hauling unconscious girls over their shoulders, no wispy spirit orbs dipping behind a corner. So far, the worst part about the Miskatonic is a faint fishy smell in the bathroom, the origins of which Hap is happier not knowing.

In the elevator, there's the heart-swelling word *Ballroom* next to the button for the fourteenth floor. His finger can't press the button hard enough. What is he looking for, a bloodstain? Fingernail scrapings along the walls? Strands of blonde hair?

As the elevator slowly rises, Hap eyes a button marked *Service Station,* and another marked *The Garden Room.* The elevator comes to a stop, and the doors creak open—he will do this floor by floor and room by room if he has to. Before him stands a pair of grand double doors. Above them is a gold plaque with *Ballroom* scrawled across it in fancy, cursive lettering. What's behind door number one?

Hap nearly slips across an oddly moist carpet embroidered with an ornate pair of eyes, similar to the decorations scattered throughout the lobby. The doors are surprisingly unlocked. His eyes meet a vast expanse of darkness, save for the ever-burning bulbs of the picturesque city beyond a number of massive windows. Hap flicks out his phone, using its light to find a switch along the closest wall.

Illumination beams down, revealing a number of red-cloaked dining tables. The blood would blend in here. The domed walls of the ballroom are of carved and oaken wood, splashed with a faded green paint that almost looks like moss. Dancing, horned men with goat legs are carved into the wood. The men have furry, bare chests; some even hold flutes to their lips, while others play harps. Between every seven goat-men bleeds a gnarled, drooping face with curling antlers and tight, yet peaceful, lips slashed across its jaw. Hap tries to imagine the sprawling parties this room has seen over the past century. People back then wanted to be gods more than ever, maybe because their collective imagination was limited to fables and religion. Now rich people stroke their egos instead with tennis courts, Corvettes, and Gucci. The Miskatonic is immune to the effects of time.

Hap snaps off several pictures, even though the multi-purpose room would surely have been less of a dining room during the ball when Tiff disappeared. There's a massive chandelier with light bulbs shaped like triangles. It's worth a few smartphone shots as well. Should he check the floor for trapdoors, blood stains? There is no way Tiff was taken here; someone didn't pull her through the floor in the middle of a crowded room. Where could she have gone next? Will one of the rooms in this hotel have along its walls a black toad with humanoid arms clawing out of its back? What demented mythology is that thing even from?

When Hap calls the elevator with every intention of exploring the Garden Room, the doors slink open, and he finds himself face to face with a grinning bellhop clad in the royal attire of the Miskatonic. The velvet bucket hat and matching purple vest look like they might better suit the queen's guard in Britain.

"You lost, man?" The pimple-faced bellhop grins; he is just a kid Hap's age, carrying a mostly empty black trash bag by his side. He's nothing like the stone-eyed punk that dragged Hap out of the lobby a month ago.

"Ah, yeah, I thought there was a bar up here." Hap feels his face growing hot. If college prepared him for one thing, it's slipping into bullshit mode on autopilot.

"Shit outta luck. The one downstairs is the best we got, and you're three hours too late. First thing I learned here was that Providence has nothing for a guy in need of a nightcap. What's your floor?" The bellhop gestures toward the elevator control panel as Hap sheepishly steps in beside him.

"Seven," Hap says, causing the kid to snicker.

"Well, at least you didn't take the stairs." The kid scratches at the string holding his velvet bucket of a hat to his head.

Awkward silence oozes through the clamped elevator doors. Hap can imagine the bellhop judging him, probably internally calling him a "faggot."

"Hey, you go to JWU?" The bellhop pronounces it "Jay-woo." Before Hap can say he just graduated, the bellhop's smirking, snapping his fingers practically in Hap's face. "Film analysis, with the Goober." Soon as he says it, Hap recognizes him as the guy who always wore an obnoxious sweatshirt with golden Greek letters stitched across the front. "What, you can't wait to go back to school already?"

Hap doesn't know his name. The class was mostly a lecture with a charmingly eccentric old instructor who used to be a director. It was an easy four credits to cap out his Gen Eds.

"I'm actually, ah...." and Hap's excuses are sticking together before he comes up with a flimsy justification. "... switching apartments and, go figure, the water's leaking at the new place, so here I am." He shrugs and wishes he had been a communications major.

"That's rough. You workin' in the city this summer?"

Hap has a brief flash to the email he sent to the *Providence Journal*. "No, but I'm looking. Still waiting on a few things."

"Man, late start looking for gigs," the kid says. Of course, it's the end of June. Most kids have jobs by now. The elevator grates open.

"Tell me about it. See ya around." Hap smiles, his best bullshit smeared across his lips as he steps into the hallway. The bellhop refuses to leave, clamping his hands over the elevator doors to stop them from closing.

"You know, I could talk to somebody for you, to work here," the bellhop says.

"Yeah?"

The kid nods. "We're hiring here. They'd let you make your own schedule once school starts back up."

A bell starts ringing in the back of Hap's mind. What better way would there be to check out this place? "Um. Sure, that'd be cool." Hap tries to hide his grin.

The bellhop nods again. "Yeah, I know it's fuckin' late,

huh? Well, my name's Luke. Ask for me at the desk tomorrow. Lucky me, I've got seven hours of sleep before I'm back for the morning shift. But the pay's not bad, and the tips are solid. Have a good one, man." Luke waves halfheartedly as the impatient metal doors swallow him up.

Hap's next step has risen out of the muck. Work at the Miskatonic? That's a good idea until somebody realizes who he is and kicks him out. He's not even a student anymore, but Luke wouldn't have to know that. JWU offers plenty of master's degrees. The fucking Miskatonic. Hap debates riding the elevators back to the Garden Room, but what if he runs into Luke again? Or worse, what if it's not a pimple-headed frat boy waiting for him behind curtain number two? No, Hap has to be smart. As he curls up to sleep, he tells himself he's no longer that same hysterical, sniveling guy who got dragged out of a hotel lobby while sobbing his girlfriend's name

Somewhere, between heavy eyelids and flickering traces of dream gibberish, Hap imagines all manner of strange things wriggling through his room. At one point, he's fairly confident the door to the hall is standing wide open and that something is splashing around in the bathroom. He can nearly hear the lock to his door clicking on and off. There is even a moment when he feels a weight on his bed. He imagines the softness only a girl could ever provide, slipping between his arms and nuzzling against his neck.

In the faint blue midmorning light, Hap rips himself upright with a half yell, having imagined somebody standing by the side of his bed, peering over him. The shadows in the room are all but banished. The door is closed, locked like he left it, and all is right with the room and himself.

On top of the alarm clock is the ring he bought Tiff, its dark yellow diamond hungry for a glint of sunshine; it's been kept in its box for too long. He glances over the room, double checking along the sides of the bed before sprinting into the bathroom, crouched low. Nobody else is here. The ring was in its case, zipped up in his backpack; he was sure of it. Like the pictures of Tiff on his camera, he can't bear the idea of looking at it; he hasn't since she disappeared. Not until now.

"Hey!" Hap shouts, looking around the room, studying the ceiling as if an intruder could have crept down from some secret porthole. A whine escapes his gullet as he picks up the ring. Is it just his imagination that it's warm? "Tiff," Hap whimpers. He is an active sleeper; who knows what he got up to in the middle of the night? The hotel bed is comfortable. Somebody took that ring out. Tiff isn't dead; that is a stupid, silly little idea. Hap either took the ring out in some sort of delirium, or a living intruder did.

Sliding to the floor, he leans against the mattress and scrolls through his phone. The message he sent the *Journal* says it was read at eight thirty this morning. There is no reply. "Fuck," he mutters and prepares himself to call down to the front desk to see if Luke the bellhop is in. There's something here. He knows that now. Here's to the rabbit hole, Hap thinks, as the girl on the other end of the phone picks up.

CHAPTER 4
THE DRIPPING MANDIBLES OF DR. DREAM

Paul awakens to the sound of a record player emitting a slithering, jazzy rhythm that crescendos into a thump from somewhere beyond his bedroom. Warm things curl naked on either side of him. Before he can claim the surplus of loose flesh and ponder the idea that he doesn't actually own a record player, the lure of sleep pulls him away.

In a dream place, clearer than a picture, a saxophone plays while he settles back into his cushioned seat. He's sitting in a convention hall at the Miskatonic, full of fellow sleepers propped up on thick chairs of their own. Before them is a stage bearing a stone coffin of an altar. Something from the twenties intersects with the bits of jazz, echoing faintly through the domed ceiling of the hall.

A crimson curtain ripples softly behind the altar. A milky-eyed black goat emerges and climbs up onto the slab of stone. The animal's cry is that of a human infant, sending shudders along Paul's arms.

Clapping warbles out from behind the curtains, creating a cylindrical echo of applause. The sleepers idle silently, breathing in the sounds of unseen approval. The goat collapses, all four of its hooves sprawling out like they've been kicked. The crying becomes hysterical.

With a sudden spasm, the goat stiffens. Its back begins to ripple as if a slew of worms are festering beneath its fur, and

Paul feels his stomach acid begin to churn up bile. The outline of a humanoid head begins to press taut against goatskin that now stretches like elastic. A head is followed by the wiggling, curvy outline of a feminine being.

Like ripping Velcro, the ripples along the goat's spine pull apart in a pulpy spritz of blood. What emerges is a woman soaked in gore, wearing the goat's entrails over a faint purple cloth that glows like fading neon. The woman's head is thrust into the stump of the goat's skull as she extends her arms in a syrupy slouch of loose blood.

The shawl of purple is little more than a half-shrugged cloak, defiant of any intent to clothe. The woman spreads her arms wide as the clapping from behind the stage returns once more, alongside cheers and howls of fanatical appreciation. The vomit looming in Paul's throat is shocked forward by the stirring erection below his belt.

"Faith, a strong thing," the woman says, her voice a sea of tumbling sand that warps over the faint jazz riffs.

The curtain rises as if yanked up and tossed away by a massive hand from above. There on the stage behind the goat-woman, coated in dusty film, sits a shack, squat and rotting. Upon the shack's door is a backward crescent moon, dimly shining with celestial light. Hunched over things with painted white faces and crusty orange hair hop along the sides of the moon house, croaking, "Mooshuck." Clowns on stage congregate beside the structure. The stage fills with their multiplying, writhing forms, and the woman bows her black goat's head. The jazz record cuts to a jagged, screeching stop as the seats beside Paul slide back in unison. The rest of the crowd stands and turns their glowing faces to him. A thousand faces have become a thousand moons, hungry with a radiant light that wants nothing more than to swallow him.

Paul's stinging eyes blink back something already slipping from memory, and the softness of his bed has hardened to the point that the doors of sleep are now closed. His nostrils flare and burn as if a cigarette has been lit and blown across his face. There is flesh on either side of him, grazing and dampening his fingertips. Two strangers with ample breasts are draped around his bare arms like silken pillows. A full sized bottle of Johnnie Walker Blue stands empty on his dresser. Though his memory is aerodynamic and full of holes, the only mystery here is how he can be so spoiled.

What used to be a badge of victory and celebration for Paul is now a vague sense of déjà vu and loneliness. To whom could he brag about a threesome these days? Who would even want to hear about it? Even the college kids on Thayer would spit at him.

Later, he's alone and out of toast, orange juice, cash that amounts to more than reasonable cab fare and also, potentially, one of his watches. This is what happens when you let strangers into your home when your words are plastic promises, and you hunger for only contortions of the flesh and a buzz in your ears. There is no maturity with age; you only learn, as Paul has, to choose partners who know exactly who you are. He thinks about work, and so he thinks about the Miskatonic and its Candle Lighters and shrouded parties. He decides to skip a shower, figuring that the hotel deserves his stink to freshen it up.

You don't have your driver take you to get coffee if you want it made right. Before he leaves, Paul sticks his dad's revolver into the front of his pants and tucks his shirt over it. It gives him more power than a pen and a job title, that's for sure. According to Johan's hushed updates, there has been a second killing. A former bellhop who didn't speak much. It won't be much longer before it's in the papers "for our best interests," as Johan put it. The guy who was killed lost his eyes and had a half-moon sliced into his head. When Paul slips on his sports jacket, he's confident no one will notice the gun.

Like a true Providence native, Paul walks, minding the remnants of puke on the sidewalk, courtesy of the club across the street where Paul ends most nights. For a man twice divorced, there is nothing better than having an apartment a few skips and a hop away from a couple of the more lively joints in the city. Paul knows all of the owners. The only downfall is that this neighborhood makes it hard to sleep, with Paul's thirst and arousal in constant need of maintenance. There was a period, six years ago, when he thought his diminishing drive to do anything besides play golf and eat apple pie meant he was getting old. Now, his appetite could rival any college boy's in town.

Paul has to remember that working for assholes doesn't make you the bad guy. If he had been elected mayor in a different world, then he would have owed big favors to all sorts of awful men with deep wallets, and he would, in some ways, have had to tolerate them. Just like he now has to tolerate Johan, who will get him something more than mayor, if only Paul could properly imagine what that might be and if only Johan would tell him that he is anything more than a lucky candidate for a once in a lifetime opportunity. The motherfucker's tried to butter up Paul so much, it's a miracle he can still walk without slipping and cracking his skull.

Half promises, half words, and half ideas. It's going to be a cup of the icy black stuff for Paul today. No cream, no sugar, it'll be bitter and nasty enough to wipe his thoughts clean.

Paul spots a familiar bum on Waterman Avenue outside the Bean Machine Café, "Namaste Nicky." Paul bows to the Jesus-bearded homeless man wearing a Patriots-themed beanie. The same jacket he wears all winter is tied around his waist. It's surprising to see that Nick's arms are teaming with the promise of muscles.

"Poli Paul, what the fuck you doin' to this city!" Namaste gives Paul a high five, and Paul's comfortable with high fives; hell, he wishes they were the norm for all conduction of business. He's known Namaste for some five years now, having met the guy right when he was about to begin funding his siege for the Rhode

Island capitol. He doubts Namaste is the bum's real last name, but that kind of ambition, to reinvent yourself, it's something Paul can respect, at least as much as he can respect a man who slinks off to pump his veins full of melted morphine twice a day.

"Well, my friend, that's all because you weren't eligible to vote me in. I'm getting a coffee to wash the puke out of my mouth. Want one?"

Nicky's already folded the paper sign he holds at the intersection into his jeans. He hides it when Paul comes around. While Nick doesn't ask for money, he always seems to hang around just long enough for Paul to hand him a ten or twenty. He keeps meaning to buy a bottle of something nice and get drunk with Nick by the river. "How's work?" Paul asks, and Nick's green and yellowed grin tells him all he needs to know.

"Lot of people not showing up like they used to, which means more corners for me. Guess they walking down to Florida or something. Warwick, maybe."

"Fuck Warwick. Who chooses that place over the city? And why would the other guys go south in the summer?" Paul asks. Nick's talking about the other homeless men who occasionally come out of the woodwork. Half of them mix in so well with the visiting country bumpkins from twenty minutes out of town that people new to the city probably don't even realize Providence has bums.

"Hey, Warwick has a lot more bakeries. I'm lucky if they throw out pizza here."

As far as Paul knows, Nick's lived in Rhode Island his whole life, and, given that they're both pushing fifty, he often wonders how close their lives came to intersecting when they were growing up. Guy never went to school, but there's a lot to learn from him. You have to be street smart if you never have a roof over your head. There is no real difference between the toll that shooting heroin and running a city takes on you, except maybe the quality of your teeth.

Walking into the café, Paul can feel the eyes of the girls at the counter fluttering at the contrast between him and Nick. When Paul goes to pay, Nick squeezes a hand past him and deposits some coins in a tip jar, grinning at the girls like he's a dog with no bite.

Later, as a driver for the Miskatonic takes him to work, Paul tries to figure out what really fueled Nick's smile, hovering over the sugary caramel macchiato Paul bought him. What's Paul missing out on? When's the last time that guy even got laid?

What makes conducting an interview interesting is that, for the first time in a long while, Paul feels like he's the boss and he can control something. Also, he has only interviewed maybe half of the Miskatonic's new employees in the past five months. Johan hired the rest, discreetly. All the drivers, custodians, kitchen staff, and various strangers disguised in the royal velvet attire of the Miskatonic report directly to Johan, and so Paul hardly knows their names. He doesn't even get to pick the cook who makes his lunch.

Randal, the hotel's bartender, who has been there for years, says the last manager of the Miskatonic was the quitting type. Whatever that means.

"New boy is waiting for ya." Cassandra smiles at him while scanning a guest's credit card. The guy, an Indian kid with big eyes, is standing by his office door. He straightens up when he sees Paul, and that fucking handshake is coming, from somebody inferior, no less.

The interviewee doesn't have a sports jacket or tie, but hey, kids do it differently these days. They think they can impress you with what's inside their head. "Hap Malik," the kid says, and Paul takes that hand and squeezes it like a doorknob, applying more pressure than he should so that he feels less awkward. Kid's got shifty eyes, probably wishes he were at the beach. When's the last time Paul went to the beach? As he sits down at his desk, feeling the thrill of telling somebody to take a seat, Paul forgets he has his gun tucked into his pants until the everlasting moment when he has to reach over his shirt and adjust himself in plain view.

Paul will keep a steady face, but as far as he's concerned, unless this guy's a total lunatic, he has the job. Hap seems nervous, sweating lightly. Paul figures that, like any other college kid, Hap probably can't wait to be somewhere else with a cold beer and a pretty girl.

CHAPTER 5
THE EXTINCT GIANT SLOTH

The phone vibrates on the table, causing Hap's glass of sweating water to ripple as if something earth shaking were approaching. There is nothing outwardly evil about the restaurant on Broadway with the black star save for its chicken wings, which have too much fat on them. He prefers them fried and crispy so that they crackle between his teeth. There are two locked back rooms just near the bathroom across from the table for two where he sits alone. Hap wonders why there is a need for locks.

One of the doors has a seven-pointed star with a dash in its center; each of its points leads to a half spiral of seven more circles descending in order from biggest to smallest, forming a near psychedelic sphere. It would be more ominous if there weren't about a hundred other semi celestial shapes scattered around the restaurant's walls. The owners appear to be former Rhode Island School of Design students, and any association it has with the Miskatonic is probably nonsense.

Hap watches as the caller ID for "Mr. Jones — Boss" goes to the missed call notification screen, followed by a buzzing voicemail alert just as the waitress comes by and asks him if he's all set. "I think I have a job," he mutters. The waitress congratulates him hesitantly while his eyes remain fixed on his phone's screen.

Congratulations indeed. He's lucked out. He's kidding himself if he thinks he'll call Mr. Jones back, right? There is nothing worse than sounding awkward on a phone call; he's blown off

plenty of job offers in the past because of that alone. He's sure
he always aces the interviews, maintaining eye contact, offering
a firm handshake and displaying an aptitude for answering
bullshit questions, so that's still good enough for him and his
confidence. Almost deleting it, Hap raises his phone to his ear
and the voicemail dashes all hopes of peace. Mr. Jones wants him
to come in for training with Luke as soon as he can. Hap stares at
his water and his soggy wings, wishing he could take comfort in
the idea of getting drunk.

Instead, he pays his bill and wanders, retracing his
footsteps along his and Tiff's old street. He half wants to raise
a middle finger to his and Tiff's old apartment, especially to her
roommates, but there were too many decent memories there.

Hap's somewhat aimless wandering leads him to a place
he should have visited six weeks ago: the abandoned house just
before the busiest road on Federal Hill. With black windows
and scratched and faded white shingles, it occupies a desolate
lot between an apartment building and a valet parking lot for
an Italian restaurant. *The haunted house*, that's what Tiff and him
used to call it.

On Halloween, Hap and Tiff would always make a point
of admiring the swirling leaves that somehow added a wicked,
spiritual essence to the house. At that time of year, you could
count on finding at least a couple of jack o'lanterns carved, lit,
and scattered among the weeds in front of the house. It's as if the
concerned denizens of the city felt a need to guide the lost spirits
that inhabit the place. He and Tiff would always joke around,
walking by it, imagining what might be crawling around behind
those windows. About who, or what, might be watching them.

As weirded out by the place as she was, Tiff might as
well have said, "If I ever disappear, this is where they've taken
me." At the time, Hap would have asked her "who," and now
he will find out soon, somehow. He slips through a scraggly
gate, minding the glass from broken bottles sprinkled along the

walkway. Kids have definitely broken in here before. Probably partied and scared their girlfriends, like inferior versions of him and Tiff. Or maybe this place is some kind of hellhole. Maybe there's a witch inside, collecting young girls.

"Hey, buddy!"

Hap knows it's a cop yelling at him before he even turns around. Past the front gate, he's not even within five feet of the damn house. It's like cops train their voices to that same gruff alpha male tone. Hap turns sheepishly back to the fence. Like a shark that's silently snuck up on its prey from the deep, there's a white Providence police car pulled onto the curb. Hap's brother, Derek, told him about how these hick cops in their hometown pulled him over one time and asked him where he was hiding "the bombs." Derek got the shit kicked out of him, and their parents didn't know what to believe. Hap's dad pressed charges, but it never seemed to go anywhere. The lesson learned and repeated over and over by everyone else with dark skin was that *cops are not your friends.*

"I, uh, thought I saw a dog trapped in there, howling at the window." Hap is a concerned, confused citizen, jerking his thumb behind him as an attempted display of compassion.

"Oh boy, huh?" The cop in the driver's seat turns to his partner. Some kind of coded exchange plays out between them, or at least that's what it feels like. Whenever Hap thinks of cops, he always assumes they have everything planned out, but maybe they're just winging it like everybody else. The cops step out of their car in that slow, hesitant way that cops like to strut. "We'll check it out," the driver says, black sunglasses blocking out his face. Why couldn't they find Tiff?

"Cool." Hap steps aside as they walk past him. He then mumbles that he has to get to work. He's not going to stand around and give them any more of an idea about who he is and what infamous case he's related to. He shouldn't give the eyes of Providence any reason to linger upon him.

With the summer solstice having passed, the night is a herald for the looming, darkest days of the year. Hap realizes just how utterly alone he is while reading the news on his phone in an apartment without food and so much as a sheet for the bare mattress. He's hungry, but there's a clot separating the hole in his stomach and the impulse to grab something and shove it into his mouth. The wings and bagels will sit, for today, rotting in his belly like whatever's sitting undisturbed in that crumbling house. There's no way she's there, right? The cops would've reported it by now...surely somebody would text him if she were found.

Hap's new aptitude for waking up early is useless, as Paul tells him to come in around four o'clock the next day. The first thing Cassandra, the blonde at the front desk, does is tell him that since Luke recommended him, he gets to be Hap's mentor. Having a clueless kid show him around is only the most unproductive start he could imagine, but it'll be temporary. What's even worse is when Cassandra, with a smirk, tells him he has to go try on a uniform.

"You'll learn where all the AC vents are and stand in front of them when you're not busy. Trying not to sweat's the priority around here in the summer," Cassandra says, and Hap can't tell if she's being sarcastic. He notices a ventilation duct along the ceiling, directly above Cassandra's head; it's what adds the invisible wind effect, tickling through her movie star hair. Do they intentionally pick somebody with hair like hers to work the front desk? They choose pretty faces to represent themselves while they scurry around in their back offices. That guy Mr. Jones was straight ugly, with a nose like a tomato and a haircut like a *Goodfellas* spoof artist.

Employees have their own locker room tucked behind a thin metal door opposite a kitchen. Hap wonders how many hidden rooms a hotel can really have. The locker rooms are separated by a thin tiled wall, and that's about the only degree of organization to the place. Maid carts seem to be scattered at random; it's a storage closet, as well as a locker room, with stacks of toilet paper decorating one wall, mops and garbage bags cluttering up another. How anybody makes it through here without tripping is an Olympic feat.

Hap is in his underwear, trying on a pair of cotton pants from a shelf full of milk crates containing uniforms and even spare belts and shoes. That's one plus for this gig at least. He doesn't realize there are separate changing stalls next to a cluster of showers until a bubbly brown-skinned maid walks in on him pulling up his pants.

Hap finds that his bellhop pants don't have any pockets, which means no room for his cellphone and wallet. Hap thinks about asking Cassandra what he's supposed to do with his phone, but he's an employee now; he's not supposed to be on his phone. The wallet's another thing but screw it. He folds his regular clothes around his phone and wallet and stuffs them into an open locker. He'll have to buy a lock.

Hot and itchy with what feels like a ten-year-old's birthday party hat strapped across his head, Hap begins reconsidering the idea of burning down the Miskatonic the second he finds proof it has something to do with Tiff's disappearance. Unless they're keeping her hostage in a neglected room. There is no right decision to make. He's choking, drowning from each and every possibility.

"Hap, thanks for coming by." He nearly bumps into Mr. Jones, who's heading into his office with a covered silver platter of food. "I'm sure Luke will show you around, warm you up," he says, not even feinting interest in him before disappearing into his office. Could he really be responsible for something happening to Tiff? The guy seems exhausted as if he doesn't want to be here at the Miskatonic anymore than Hap does. Could there really be a monster hiding beneath his skin?

Hap doesn't make it to the center of the lobby before Luke's shouting his name, coming up to playfully punch him on the shoulder. "I'm gonna give you the quick look and see, man." Luke's mouth gets so wide every time he talks that Hap wonders if it's possible to see what's in his stomach. "We're like waiters who don't have to wait on the slow-ass kitchen staff. Faster we move bags, faster the guest is settled, faster we get our tip. When it comes to that, every man's gotta do his own thing, though. Nobody wants to see two bellhops helping one dude, 'less he's got a moving van out front; you feel me?"

Hap nods, wondering if Luke is showing off for Cassandra and the other desk girl. He's certainly talking loudly enough. Great, this guy's a typical college clown. Hap should have expected as much.

"Map by the elevator tells you where everything is. Except where the hookers are, but let me tell ya, you'll learn how to spot those disease-bags soon enough." Luke's nodding to a floor map between the two silver elevator doors adjacent to the great glass one. Hap didn't even notice it the night he spent getting lost within the hotel. A map? There's a fucking map of the hotel, and he didn't even look at it. He'd slap himself in the head for being so stupid, but then his hat would fall off.

"People are always gonna ask you about stuff that's labeled right on the map, but it's easy. They usually wanna' know about the ballroom, or the barbershop, or the bar around the corner or, occasionally, the Garden Room, but that's only for special events, and they put up signs for those." Of course, the map won't reveal anything criminal. Or haunted.

The grand tour gets no farther than the first floor, as Luke shows Hap the kitchen, introducing him to a gang of four men in white aprons and one heavyset woman who could pass for one of the guys. Unless you've got long blonde hair, uniforms steal your identity. They are the ultimate mask.

Next is the bar attached to the main lobby. The cryptic decorations go a step further in here; there's a painting behind the bar of what looks to be a peaceful seaside town with mountains ridging along its borders. Descending down over it is a vague, black orb that's nearly lost in the shadowy slopes of the mountains. Luke introduces Hap to the bartender, Randal, whom Hap hardly registers because he's so focused on the painting. Then he comes to and realizes the tall, dark-skinned man is standing right in front of him with an outstretched hand.

He's bald, and his forehead slants back so that his complete lack of hair is hardly noticeable. His face is smooth, shiny, as if it's unfamiliar with the idea of a beard. When his hands clasp Hap's, they are cold and void of any softness. "He's an Egyptian storyteller and half a fuckin' wizard," Luke explains, and Randal's laugh is deep but ends sharply as he enthusiastically shakes Hap's hand up and down, looking through him.

"Only with my drinks, I swear," Randal sports a wise grin that says he is a guy to trust. Hap wants to believe he's a master of mixology, and by working here, he's doing what he loves. This desire to believe is so strong that Hap finds himself speechless as Luke leads him away from the bartender in all black. Randal's the guy with the answers. For reasons he can't quite understand, Hap is sure of this.

A large woman with her hands clasped over her face is sobbing through the lobby as she heads toward the elevators, and a calm man in a Hawaiian shirt walks after her. "Oh, you see weird shit all the time here," Luke tells Hap. Finally, the cracks in the Miskatonic's veneer that he's been looking for.

"Yeah? What kind of shit we talking?" Hap asks. The crazier, the better.

Luke then proceeds to tell him a story about a really proper businessman who checked out, paying in cash, and when the maid went to his room, she discovered both the floor and walls smeared with shit. After Luke tells him this, Hap is pretty sure he read that same story on some website's "Top Ten Worst Jobs" listicle, but he doesn't mention that to Luke. Hap's fellow bellhop might just be a liar. He has that cocky "I know everything" undergraduate sort of swagger to him. Hap can't trust what he says, even if Luke outs the Miskatonic as a front for the mob.

"What about the ghosts? I keep hearing this place is haunted." Hap tries to turn it his way as they face the lobby doors and the incoming guests, the customers. He didn't need to get a job to ask a question like that, but it has to be a start, right?

"Man, those stories are just to give this place publicity. Scariest thing I ever saw was a weird doll one of the guests left in their room. I'm talking Chucky shit, dude, with black thread all over it like somebody was trying to practice giving stitches. But the ghost stories are, like, there's this fat ghost that rattles empty room service trays, and apparently people from when alcohol was illegal partied so hard here you can still hear them running around getting freaky late at night." Luke laughs like a goon. "You know, boring stuff like that. No women in black or hallways full of blood. All right, see this guy here? Help him for me." Luke is pushing Hap toward, what, work? Bag slinging? Hap needs more stories, more information…did he really sign up to be a freaking bellhop?

Thoughts of Tiff are pushed away for a mechanical onslaught of *Yes sir; no sir; of course, sir,* and, most importantly, *I've got that, sir.* After getting caught up in the constant whirlwind of greeting a guest, taking their bag, and hauling it up to their room, Hap's back starts hurting, and he keeps getting the wheels on the luggage cart mixed up, causing the thing to come grinding to a halt until he gets it realigned. In an hour, he goes back and forth down those elevators at least fifteen times. After that point, the number becomes murky, and the sheer scope of the Miskatonic Hotel dawns on him, especially when other bellhops keep running by him busy with their own guests.

Luke tells Hap that he usually tucks his tip money under his watch, given that their pants have no pockets, and he advises that Hap tuck his tips into his shoes. It's great advice until Hap starts getting blisters along his feet; he needs to invest in a watch.

When running back and forth up the elevator, Hap doesn't check to see if cash is leaking out of him with every step. He's not here to make money.

This place is eleven floors of business with a small town's worth of employees. He's not just looking for Tiff in some building. The scope is beyond that, more than a needle in a haystack, more than a diamond in the sewers. Riding that elevator up and down, he is travelling the arteries of something vast, old, and alive.

After dropping off his luggage, one hairy man in business attire and a pair of flip-flops asks Hap to get him a "highball" from the bar, and Hap doesn't even know what that is.

"Guy wants something called a highball?" Hap calls to Randal, relieved to find the bar mostly empty.

"Whiskey and ginger ale, for a man who thinks too highly of himself," Randal says, rapidly mixing the drink and placing the glass in front of Hap. "Just call me a reader of fortunes," Randal says, and is he kidding?

"Really?" Maybe Hap's face is too serious when he asks because Randal cracks into a grin. For all his smiling and laughing, there's no warmth to him. It's like he's older than he looks, playing a part. This is what it's like, working for tips. You play your role. You trick everybody until you get what's yours.

"That's what you have to tell everyone." Randal's small eyes dart past Hap to the open doors leading to the lobby. "Want something to commemorate your first day?" He shrugs toward the bottles. Hap doesn't know how to tell a professional bartender that he can only stomach hard ciders, lemonades, and small volumes of red wine.

"I'm all set, too much running." Hap holds his stomach, and call him a racist, but he feels like he's talking to one of the bartenders on one of his parents' Caribbean vacations. Randal is more than staff. He is *the* guy. "Hey, uh," Hap says, leaning in over the bar. "What do you know about this place being haunted?"

Randal's ensuing grin becomes something more than

delight. It puts something weird in Hap's mostly empty stomach that's already gnawing at itself. Is Randal ridiculing him? Is that a sneer? No….

"This place…." Randal looks up, his eyes turning near white as his pupils disappear to the ceiling. "…it's never empty, yet you can become lonesome rather quickly."

That's a riddle if Hap has ever heard one, but he nods like he gets it, like it makes sense.

"Every hotel has a ghost," Randal continues, peering at the corners of the ceiling as if he's seeing something Hap can't perceive. "Do you know why?"

"You have enough people come through somewhere, eventually one of them is going to die somehow?" Hap has heard of people dying at the mall, on campus, in the backs of ambulances wailing through the night.

"Yes, that's why people believe hotels are haunted but do you want to know the real reason?" When Randal lowers his eyes, they fall like weights that force Hap to stare at his glossy reflection in the polished wood of the counter.

Like slipping a key into an old, neglected lock, Hap swallows back his desperation and then says, "Yes."

"You walk on the fourth, the seventh floors, and you know the difference? Besides the numbers on the doors?" Randal asks, and Hap shakes his head. Randal is starting to seem like a dud of a scratch ticket with just one little corner left to scrape away. "Nothing. The modern American hotel is a maze. You're familiar with labyrinths? You know why there are patterns and spirals everywhere? Just because they look pretty? Spirits get lost easily because they aren't all the way here, and they aren't all the way there, like the last breath of a corpse. They become stuck, in circles, trapped in loops and shapes and hallways that look the same." Randal shrugs. "You won't see any ghosts here. When a place gets old enough, they must find their way out eventually, right?"

"Can't say that doesn't sort of make sense, except if you put it like that, I don't see why a ghost wouldn't just jump out a window, get out of the maze."

"Maybe they're afraid." Randal is smiling like he wants the joke, if there is one, to be funnier than it actually is.

"So you've never seen anything?" Hap asks.

"It's not about what you can see; it's what you know," Randal says.

"And what do you know?" Hap asks.

"Every hotel has a ghost." Randal gestures to a pair of guests strolling through the lobby, and the bartender is only as serious as Hap desperately wants him to be. This is just an old man joking around. Hap tells Randal he'll keep his ears open anyway and then goes to bring the asshole upstairs his drink.

He's so exhausted by the end of the day that the urge to pull open the Miskatonic's secrets is muddied. Between the ache in his knees and his own stink that's accumulating worse than the times he's gone hiking with Tiff at Furnace State Park, today was exhausting and pointless, but it was a genuine start. Maybe the most he can hope for is that someone sneaks up behind him, slips something over his eyes, and abducts him to where Tiff has gone. She doesn't deserve to be alone.

Before the end of the shift at around eight, Luke pulls Hap aside and shows him yet another unthinkable room through the kitchen: an employee lounge complete with a soda machine, a microwave, a fridge, and a glass-paneled freezer full of Hot Pockets and tacos. Moving around as much as he has in his stifling and bulky clothing has knocked down the membranous wall of Hap's appetite, and he's soon digging into piles of microwaveable meat.

Hours later, as midnight approaches, there's a frenzied urge to take a dump as Luke's telling him about how the front desk girls usually punch them in and out each shift. Hap's mind is instead occupied by whether or not the maids actually clean the employee restrooms. The pain in his stomach stabs into an unbearable cramp just as he slips into a stall. All of his public phobias about people hearing him shit from outside the locker room become fully realized, and he has never pitied himself more.

He nearly presses his weary head against the wall, not minding the hordes of likely fecal bacteria hungry for his cells. He sees an odd little poem. It's scratched along the stall. No, the words are too neat. Somebody must have used a knife.

the Moon Shack dreams.
lo, fire and corporeal doom.
lo, The Old Ones, Those Who Loom.
else?
what else?
Else?
what Else!?

Hap rereads it and then laughs, the remainder of his tears scattering over the tucked-up shirt of his stuffy uniform. The only thing he'll find here at the Miskatonic is delirium.

CHAPTER 6
THE FESTIVITIES

It's one of those big white mansions by the sea in Westerly. It's called The Palace of the Komodo, according to the card Paul found slipped under the hidden door to his office. The surrounding neighborhood is probably the wealthiest in the whole state, which isn't much when you think of all Connecticut has right next door. The house lies at the end of its own forest-clenched drive, overlooking a slight rise of dunes and an empty, secluded beach. Protruding from the far side of the beach is a dock. Paul isn't sure who owns the place. Johan, maybe. The Newport mansions may showcase the century-old colonial wealth and excess that began in Rhode Island, but Westerly is all about the modern-day millionaires.

The driver pulls out all the stops, opening Paul's door for him as he steps into the glow of an old antique streetlight. A gleaming, pebble-sprinkled path winds up to a manor with more windows than eyes on a fly. How many hurricanes have toppled this place? How can its wood still seem so old? The home's foundation lurches as if its roots are uneven. Paul's never understood the practicality of having a beach house, especially in New England. A storm could come along at any moment and swallow it all up.

Paul can hear a dull roar of voices from inside the mansion, but it doesn't sound like a party, not exactly. Are people singing? The clouds above are clotting out the stars alongside a nearly ripe full moon. Some kind of pipe drones around a disjointed, rather irritating melody and Paul feels as if he's slinking backward in time.

The driver, unfriendly as ever, disappears back into the car before Paul can so much as thank him. The men waiting by the pebble-and-seashell-lined walkway leading to a front porch framed by white columns aren't cut from the same cloth as the bouncers or doormen Paul would expect at a gathering of the elite. The men, one on either side of the walkway, are dressed colorfully and casually, in khakis and Hawaiian shirts? These two guys look like they spent all day working out and fixing cars. They would be better suited at some dive bar in Warwick, splitting pitchers of Pabst, playing pool, and courting cheap dates with thick, spray-painted tans.

"Paul Jones, right?" One of them waves a finger his way, and Paul feels awkward in his stuffy suit and sports jacket. In truth, all he did was toss on the jacket and polish his shoes without changing out of his work uniform. He's even still wearing the Miskatonic tie, but given that this is Johan's event, it seems appropriate.

"You know it," Paul smiles and, ah, a handshake. He goes for one of his trademark, potentially finger-crushing grips. With this kind of stranger, it seems more appropriate than any sort of hesitancy. Of all the banquets and fundraisers he's been to since he was a little, chubby boy in a suit waddling around at his father's side, he's never been this uneasy.

This is a cult; Paul is under no illusions. Johan thinks there's something special to Paul, and as much as Paul doesn't believe that, he won't argue. Who would? These people, this organization of Candle Lighters, are all freaks with a mile-high list of fetishes. They need someone to defend them, perhaps. They need a sane voice to even out their mad chattering, and Paul gets it, kind of. To their lunacy, he is a dose of reality, and beyond that, could he be a leader? He'd be Johan's puppet, all the same, but to the Candle Lighters? To the people of the world when they finally come out? Paul has always been one to smell an opportunity wherever it may lead him.

"So, what kind of party is this?" Paul says, trying not to imply that the Hawaiian shirts make the two men suspect.

"Oh, you'll see, man. Nights like this are when we come together like a family; you feel that? You get to be how you really want to be, no shame, no lying, no playing pretend." The man in an orange sun-splattered Hawaiian shirt talks like a hippie or somebody on vacation and his breath smells like pungent garlic. Despite the darkness, Paul can make out strange little scars scattered all over his face, as if he were gently dipped into a pool of glass.

"Well, I'm here to finally see what it's all about," Paul says, as they begin to walk the almost too cutesy seashell-lined path to the main house. The other, silent greeter with shadowy palm trees along his tropical shirt, spits out something against the walkway that makes an unexpected, metallic clink. He has a weasel face, congested with wet rashes. They aren't rich men dressing down, and Paul wouldn't be surprised if these guys were from a trailer park somewhere. He figures he should have left the sports jacket at home, but maybe there are women here who will appreciate his taste. Nothing justifies the strange like some strange. Beyond whiskey, it may be the only way Paul can wrap his head around any of this.

Incense-filled air creeps down Paul's lungs the moment he steps through the mansion's double doors. Down the gullet of the Komodo he goes, having the same feeling he gets when he wakes up from a dream he can't remember. The guy in the orange shirt brushes past him, and he told Paul his name, he literally just mentioned it, yet Paul's already forgotten. He's already failed the first lesson his dad ever taught him: show up in a crowded room, shake everybody's hand, and remember everybody's goddamn name, right down to the host's pimply son 'cause you never know, he could grow up to be a senator one day. Paul is slacking.

The front hallway is low ceilinged and formed by shadowy, cavernous plaster as it funnels out to a grand wide room full of light and people. It's grander than the Miskatonic's front lobby, as Paul makes out a second-floor balcony stemming from a great staircase. The living room or front hallway or whatever it would properly be called is more museum than a home. Every stretch of wall displays some strange artifact or oddity. There's an Egyptian coffin propped under the dual staircases that wrap around to the second floor. Adorning the walls are display cases featuring rusty medieval swords and wrinkled, leathery books that appear to have survived a fire or three. The walls are covered in portraits, yet, unlike any portrait Paul's seen, each face is grinning from ear to ear. He's suddenly aware that he's never before seen teeth in professional portraits.

The guests wave around everything from glasses of wine to fading cans of Narragansett beer. There are jeans and flowery dresses beside bathing suits and bikinis, tuxedos and the latest Gucci vests. Apparently, there is no wrong way to dress for these affairs.

A tall, young girl with jet-black hair wearing a slender, hip-hugging black dress approaches Paul and slips into his embrace. "Mr. Jones, you can call me Lacy. Mr. Weissebokf has assigned me to you tonight. I'm to answer your every question and keep you safe." She pulls away from Paul, and in his stirring mind, he's thinking for a moment that she's hospitable enough to be an escort. This wouldn't be the first time he's been sent a girl; after that day Johan showed him the hidden rooms of the Miskatonic, all manner of women have been coming up to him.

Lacy's smile doesn't seem as fake as Paul's gut tells him it has to be. She seems curious, and the way her hands are clasping behind her back is more than businesslike. The way she told Paul that she would protect him gives him the sense that her teeth are serrated and that she is ready to bite, over and over, at a moment's notice.

"I feel as though some people are a little overdressed," Paul whispers in Lacy's ear, trying to be polite.

"That's because this is the comfortable part, Mr. Jones," she replies. "Once we get into our gowns for the celebration, we take off our masks."

"What's your last name, dear?" Paul asks. Last names are important; they connect people. Plus, Paul may know a relative.

"Lacy is new; I thought it was pretty. I thought up a last name, too, something Japanese, but then I thought it went against the whole idea of pretending to be something that you aren't, so I dropped it. I'm thinking of a last name that has to do with the moon and the stars, but I'm not sure."

Okay, she's a hippy chick. Doable. "What happened to your old name?" Paul asks.

"It belonged to someone boring and predictable who was satisfied with simple things and silly boys." There's a flicker of sadness across Lacy's face that's only visible in the way her cheeks seem to droop for a moment, but then she laughs. She probably hates her old self. Paul can relate.

"Okay, maybe I'll come up with my own name for you. So, what's the actual celebration?" There's a fluttery feeling in Paul's chest, similar to heartburn. He knows what this is. These people worship some pagan Earth goddess or collect potions from roots and herbs in the woods; if anything, they stole from the Wiccans.

"A late-night swim if the moon overcomes the clouds. Either way, there will be a great fire and a burning," she muses.

A chubby man with curly hair and thick Clark Kent glasses yells a nasally "Finally!" as a door between a large vase and a display case containing leather bound books bursts open. A man in a suit holding a silver platter strolls into the room. The chubby man is accompanied by an elegantly dressed, mostly attractive woman as he drags her over to the platter. The woman, fancy as she looks, has wide eyes, and she doesn't look entirely comfortable. Just how open to the public is this little gathering?

"Our citizens below had an appetite tonight, up to three servings!" The man who looks like a butler holding that silver tray saunters over to the curly haired guy. The tray is a platter of squirming, pale worms with black, pointy things at both ends. The chubby guy in too much plaid pops one into his mouth and moans. "Hallelujah!" he shouts as Lacy squeezes Paul's arm. The woman the chubby man is with reluctantly selects her own worm, her face puckering up as if she's sipped cheap tequila.

"Trust me, baby. This is where it's at!" The curly-haired man is telling his date, and the girl is young; Paul wonders if she belongs to the group, or is she the man's plus one?

"We tend to call them lunar larva; I have no idea what their scientific name is. They're rare, active only during the full moon and bred in soil like plants. Before you become judgmental or squeamish, you should think for a minute about LSD, shrooms, and all the wonderful things people do to escape their reality. Toad licking? Gasoline sniffing?" Lacy smiles at him, and Paul's stomach is devoid of nausea. Hallucinogenic worms? Okay, that's not so bad. Like the one in a bottle of mescal, drink the worm and see the stars.

"They give you more control over where you wish to steer your imagination. They're very rare." Lacy is almost too anxious to defend what Paul just saw, and maybe that's what Johan intends her to be: a buffer.

"Where do you get them?" Paul finds himself asking as if the pulpy plate of dirt eaters he's looking at are an exotic blend of wine.

"Where do you think? Australia, the toxic kingdom. After Johan became the man to listen to, he went on something of a vision quest to the land down under. According to the older citizens, he made a bunch of great discoveries. The worms are as much a tradition as anything else, and I find it charmingly fitting, given how horrible their very existence is." Lacy's teeth flash as she grips Paul's arm, her fingernails digging ever so lightly into his skin. She's wearing a black bracelet with a faded design. Paul can make out the corners of what must be a star. "There's no better justice than breeding them and chewing them up." Her flash of anger (or is it insanity?) makes Paul want to move outside, where the air is fresh, and there are no squirming creepers in sight.

"Politician Paul!" Johan's voice makes Paul think of a kindly old relative who's thrilled to see him. What makes Johan anything but genuine? What's wrong with Paul where he can't consider a man who embraces him with open arms to be good, just because of his strange passions? "Lacy, you're not tempting him with sampling this hatching of larva, are you?" Johan asks.

Johan shakes Paul's hand, and there's an awkward moment before Johan gestures to the wing of the house Paul has yet to explore. "Let's gather everybody for dinner, right dear?" Johan points to Lacy and draws his finger toward the guests clogging the main hall before he gently grabs Paul by the arm. "Tonight, we're going to push the envelope just a little. If you feel uncomfortable at any moment, Lacy will take care of you. She's new; she'll understand. The dining table is scattered with whiskey. Scotch is at the center, and toward me, there will be Canadian imports, and running right down the table will be the more American stuff. Feel free to choose your seat according to your preference."

Johan abruptly turns and places a hand on Paul's chest right above his heart. He thinks the priest with something to hide is going to comment on his Miskatonic tie, but then his hand travels to Paul's belt. Some old awkward disdain for another man touching him below the belly button results in goosebumps along Paul's neck. "You don't have that gun on you, no? Good. Things may become rather intense, and if you shoot one of us, that would make you less special than we prefer you to be. For that matter, what you're about to see is consensual. Well, most of it...."

Following Johan along around the curve of the hallway, Paul gets a good look at the dining room table and the naked men and women shackled beside it. There is a long table cloaked in purple cloth, sprinkled with an uneven assortment of candles. Great heaving bowls of meat rest beside trays of vegetables in between royal bottles of booze. There are also cats scattered across the table, assorted in shades of color, scattered between the conventions of a dining table like china displays. Petrified and presumably the products of taxidermy, given how life-like they appear, the cats are in various walking positions. Some are resting and hunched over, while others are on their backs, peering out with lifeless black-marble eyes. Paul soon disregards them because of what else pervades the room.

There are thirteen men and women around the table, shackled to the floor, bound by their feet and hands. Toward the head of the table, there is a man and a woman with ball gags in their mouths. The unhappy pair kneels on either side of Johan's humble head chair. Hanging behind them, and taking up most of the back wall, is a large purple banner with a seven-pointed star and a number of spiraling circles from biggest to smallest. Johan reaches to pet the backs of each prisoner he walks past before finally ruffling his hands through the curly red hair of the woman by the head of the table. Paul could choke on his own tongue when he recognizes the woman as the mayor of Providence, who immediately rests her head submissively against Johan's knee.

These are politicians and rich folks, all stripped bare; they don't even seem distraught. There are no tears or struggling attempts for freedom. Some have their eyes closed, and their heads tilted up to the ceiling. Their pupils are glazed. Could it be the worms drugging them? The lunar larva that gives them the reins to their own mania? This is a hidden world indeed.

"I couldn't have you miss this one, Paul!" Johan says his name like Paul needs to be reminded of himself. Does he?

The other guests, some forty Candle Lighters, file into the

grand room. They pay the nude prisoners no attention as they scoot into their chairs. Some of the people who Paul guesses are guests of the actual Candle Lighters giggle, but perhaps because of whatever drugs they're on, they find nothing too strange here. One old man bumps his chair into the foot of a shackled nude man and even mutters a humble "excuse me." Paul takes a seat at the halfway point of the table, purely because the thought of sitting too close to Johan and the mayor is too much for him. An elbow nudges him, and Lacy's grinning as she takes her seat beside him.

"Remember, any questions…." Lacy lets the question mark hang like a hook as she shrugs toward the naked man behind her.

"Are they here because they want to be?" Paul whispers.

"Of course not! But it's part of their job. Who ever really enjoys their job? It's fine. These celebrations are only monthly," Lacy says.

"What happens if they say no?" It's fucking good seeing Franco over there, no doubt about it, especially after the things her campaign spewed about him. Good, but if anybody told Paul to strip naked and slip on a ball gag, even for all the respect, luxury, and pussy in the world, he'd give himself a heart attack attempting to beat the living hell out of them.

"They resign. You're telling me you never asked your friends growing up what kind of sick stuff they'd do for a million dollars?" Lacy has to only be in her mid-twenties, but she sounds older. Has Paul become so used to professional people that he's become disconnected? Lacy continues, "Imagine what they would do for something more important than money. They've seen what you'll see, eventually, and when that happens, you'll understand."

It's dawning on Paul that these people aren't the misunderstood weirdos he assumed they were. They're in control. They don't want to be understood or led into judgeless coexistence. What are they doing, and why is he here?

A whining bell strikes three times, followed by a silence that only Johan dares break. One of the petrified cats is staring Paul in the eye through the reflection on his plate. They don't all have marbles? He glances at the closest feline, and no, there is that same black emptiness. He must have imagined the yellow-pierced spark of color on his plate.

He refocuses on Johan's words, just as the priest gets done thanking everybody for making it out tonight. "We come together as citizens under new testament, in a time where our own friends and family are being taken from us. Early Wednesday morning marked the fifth killing of one of our own this summer cycle. There is a heretic, full of hypocrisy, with every life he takes. The public has been notified." Johan, with his hands clasped behind his back, casts a glance to the mayor by his knee. She appears as though she's almost purring. He runs a hand through the hair of the other man beside him. Recognizing the mole on his cheek, Paul realizes he's the mayor of Newport.

"We must remain extra vigilant," Johan continues. "Keep our pleasures behind closed doors, such as those of our own hungry Komodo. Keep your knives sharp and your guns loaded; keep your teeth filed and your masks ready. The outsider fears us, for we are civilized. We must also pity the outsider, for, in his confusion, he preys upon his own kind. Our place in the universe shifts with every passing day, and more than a single point in our two hundred and thirteen years, many an eye is upon us. Eat, be merry, and stomp your feet for the dirty ones below and let us celebrate!" Johan's curse rips through the room, followed by a loud procession of foot stomping in which even the chained, naked ones partake.

From beneath the floorboards comes a near-ghoulish chorus of laughter and whistling. Paul leans to Lacy, and she's already answering him. "The kids' table is in the basement, near the worm farms. Not everybody likes to be as prim and proper as us; some just like to sit alone in the dark and pant. I'll introduce you later."

"In one sentence, tell me what the Moon Shack is," Paul asks as the stomping dies out and the sound of plates clinking fills the room.

Lacy leans her lips to Paul's cheek, and her words are punctuated by the sticky smack of her gloss as she says, "Shelter from everything you might ever fear, as long as you have the ability to commit the undoable."

A man to Paul's left who was engaged with a conversation of his own abruptly leans toward Paul's ear, making him jump a little in his seat. "It's a celebration of humanity," says the man, an old guy with short, buzzed white hair and blue eyes wide and unblinking. Then he leans across Paul and addresses Lacy. "Date?" he asks with a click of his tongue over his teeth. Paul wants to push him away; he stinks like stagnant pond water, and the cologne he's using hardly acts as a mask. Regardless, sudden movements may not be wise at this table.

Lacy laughs coldly. "Date? This guy?" For a moment, Paul is insulted. Not that a woman who insults you is un-beddable. "He is the one Johan has chosen," she says with breathless adoration. The old man with eyes that seem to be too young pulls back from Paul, his mouth dropping open.

"Hi, Paul Jones." Paul puts up a half-hearted smile and offers his hand like it's a flimsy morsel waiting to be snatched away. It's clasped, gently, as Taylor McKinley introduces himself.

"Proud spawn of Charles McKinley." He cracks a grin, and his teeth are too clean and immaculate for a man who looks to be in his seventies.

Lacy leans against Paul's ear, filling in the blanks. "The son of my idol. He's one of the original prophets. I'm not sure if Johan intends for you to meet him." Paul's not sure if she's talking about Taylor or, impossibly, his relative, who would be somehow older than this guy....

Johan's attention-seeking bell rings. Paul can't get a good

look at the instrument over the Candle Lighters around him, but it's one of the saddest metallic sounds he's ever heard. Who knew a bell could have such depth? "My dear friends, the clouds have parted," Johan announces. Paul can literally hear his smile as there's a unanimous clatter of silverware dropping along the table. It's no surprise this isn't about everybody having a peaceful dinner.

Lacy pulls on Paul's arm. "Come with me while everybody gets changed." She's pushing her chair back, brushing an elbow against the shackled naked man behind them. Toward the head of the table, silver robes are being passed around and snatched up by eager hands. There is an excited murmur throughout the room.

"I'm going to introduce you to the kids at the kids' table," Lacy smirks, tugging him along, and he almost hates how well the shape of her body wriggles beneath her dress. If anything is clear, this shouldn't be a time of pleasure. Plus, she is way too young for Paul; she hardly seems to be twenty-eight.

Lacy leads Paul into the main hall, and then he's eyeing that basement door instead of her ass, and he doesn't want or need to meet anybody else. Why can't whoever is in the basement come up here? Why is Paul being led into the dark, cramped place? If they shackle up the actual government officials, then what would they do to a lowly hotel manager?

Paul's flinching nervousness causes him to eye an open book in the display case by the door. At first, he took the leather bound volumes to be collectibles or perhaps some assortment of pagan bibles. The open, yellowed pages are scrawled with what looks to be purple highlighter. Are those doodles in the margins? Paul makes out the word "fuck," and it reminds him of when he used to mess around with schoolbooks when he was a kid.

The basement steps are sleek and finished, reminding Paul once more that this is no mere house. The lighting is dim, and he recalls what Lacy said about some people preferring the dark. So, is this where the freaks live?

"After playtime, she would bring me a rag soaked in dirt, addin' to the blood and dust on my skin, telling me above my blood, I am of Earth. She covered me from head to toe," a big man's voice bellows. Paul's nostrils fill with the stench of tobacco and incense. The basement is stacked with wooden crates and scattered with not one but at least five circular tables pocketed with scraggly men and women. This really is where the monsters are kept.

The closest man to the stairs is a big bald guy who looks like a pale-skinned Buddha. He's turning in his flimsy fold-up chair, craning his rolling neck to peer at Paul.

"This is the virgin," Lacy says proudly, and Paul thinks she said "version" for a moment until the actual word hits.

"Hey!" He turns to her as her laugh is echoed throughout the closest table. Disinterested, scattered conversation rattles onward elsewhere in the dim of the subterranean floor.

"We mean that as in you're important. We're aware you're a man with prowess." Lacy's lips are no longer seductive, but Paul feels the stir anyway.

"She means you ain't popped no cherries." A man at the table laughs, and these are green felted pool tables they're sitting at. The assortment of men at the first table reminds Paul of a group you might find at some factory rec room. Hell, hanging with a bunch of dirty guys drinking whiskey and playing cards isn't such a bad way to spend an evening, but this bunch? The Buddha is shirtless, and the scars ribboning around his torso almost look like some kind of fungus.

One kid at the table is covered in what may be dried blood, and he stands up, walks around the table, and sticks a hand Paul's way. His hands are clean from his wrist to his fingertips, so Paul has no choice but to take it. "Derek Woodbury, sir. I recognize you from the hotel." He's polite, a young guy; if it weren't for the smears of red clinging to his wife beater, he'd almost seem respectable.

That summoning bell is ringing from upstairs. "So he's cool!" says one of the men who looks like a normal guy in his thirties, dressed as if he's going out bar hopping. He then swings out a mangled, bloody something, smacking it onto the table just as Paul realizes what some of the darker stains along the green felt are. The blood covering Derek is explained as the mutilated black cat's stomach flops open.

"I wanted to be presentable." The regular guy laughs, and it's then that Paul recognizes a sticky trail of dark fluid leading away from that first table toward the shadows clinging to the rest of the basement. Beside a stack of crates, just off in the darkness, is a heaping pile of dead cats.

The bell rings once more as Lacy clasps Paul's arm, waving to the men at the table. One of the women in the shadows hollers out Lacy's name in a craggy, smoke-throttled voice, and Lacy calls back, "We're going for the swim! Then the party!"

A number of the basement dwellers cheer at the mention of a party. Paul hears something stomping around off in the shadows by the crates. He catches a brief glimpse of a man lurking around there. Cat killing is a great many steps in the wrong direction for tonight, but is that really where Paul is going to draw the line?

"Why the animal killing?" Paul asks Lacy as she leads him up the steps.

"I've recently learned that cats, like other imposters, would like you to believe that just because they kill mice, they are somehow lesser vermin themselves. Cats are worshipped for all the wrong reasons, and I have since quit having any problem seeing them get what they deserve. Plus, I'm a dog person." Lacy's smiling his way, and there's a familiar sickness reemerging in Paul's stomach. Good thing he didn't have a bite of anything. Animal sacrifice wouldn't surprise him, but that pile of dead things in the basement is something else entirely. It's as if those mongoloids sitting at the pool tables enjoy the killing.

Emerging back into the main room, there's a crowd of silver-robed men and women marching toward the back deck. Some of the people in robes look bewildered, and Paul remembers what that Taylor guy with the young blue eyes said about "dates." The bewildered ones are mostly young girls, though there are a few confused looking guys being ushered along by grinning older women with large teeth. The robes are hoodless and appear more like gowns.

"Here you are, Lacy." Johan's creeping behind them with the books from the display case stacked under his arm, handing Lacy a silver robe. So they were bibles of some sort? Paul wonders if they sum up the Moon Shack any better than Lacy did. "Thank you for showing him around." Lacy's nodding, running a hand along Paul's shoulder. Before she runs off to join the rest of the silver crowd, she tells him to let her know if he needs anything.

Johan adjusts the books in his arms and catches Paul looking. "These are blasphemous texts, full of lies."

"So, nothing about the Moon Shack, then?" Paul doesn't mean to sound condescending, and he's immediately concerned for how Johan will interpret his words.

"No," Johan smiles, and of course, Paul can't read him. "There's only a poem by a man called Charles McKinley; he'd sing it to his special guests. I'll show it to you sometime, or maybe I'll recite it for you if you won't consider such a thing cheesy. There's only one copy."

"Listen...ah...," and Paul wants to mention the cats in the basement, but what kind of answer would he even want? "Do you live here?" he asks instead.

"Not here." Johan looks up and smiles, then points to an older man wearing black glasses that appears to be blind. "Elliot Sampson is the keeper of the komodo. I was just about to introduce you two. Come with me." They follow after the last of the robed Candle Lighters. Paul finds it funny that Lacy told him she'd answer all his questions. He still knows nothing.

"I move around a lot. Sometimes the Shack has me; other times, I reside with friends." Johan grins at Paul, reshuffling the books. "Don't worry. I won't ever ask to sleep on your couch." Except for in Paul's dreams, maybe. "Not a bad place, overlooking the bay."

The blind Elliot Sampson steps out onto the porch ahead of them; he takes off his black glasses in the moonlight, letting loose a throaty cheer. He must have been wearing them for some sort of stylish reason; he doesn't seem to be blind at all anymore.

"How come I don't get a robe?" Paul asks, not liking the idea of standing out more from everyone than he already does.

"I'll clear things up when I address everybody, but I'm going to have to ask something of you, Paul. After I formally introduce you, and this had to wait until now — you'll see why — but after I introduce you, these people will see you in a new light. You're our symbol of humanity, and in many ways, our virtue," Johan says.

"Lacy called me a virgin," Paul says.

Johan adjusts his glasses. "Figuratively, she meant. Because everyone else here has, ah, done what you haven't. It'll become clear in time; don't worry. There's no need to overwhelm you. I am going to have to ask that you watch us perform our ceremony when we go into the sea. Just stand by and watch, and so you know, this is new for everybody. You are the first person to have a position such as yours, so forgive me for how coarse and alienating this presentation may seem. There are other guests here, as you may have noticed. It's customary for a select few to join us in the ceremony you're about to witness." Johan's not waiting for Paul to respond as he leads him to the back porch.

Elliot Sampson is swaying and staring up at the moon. He's a trim and proper looking guy with neat hair and a clean face. He's probably the same age as Paul, which makes it slightly frustrating that he owns a place this nice. It's probably not even his main house. Johan introduces them, and when Elliot takes

Paul's hand, he nearly rips it off.

"He'll be nothing like that fuckup Harrelson, eh?" Elliot says to Johan in the midst of wrenching Paul's arm up and down before releasing his grip. "Oh, what a night." Elliot turns away from Paul and Johan as he makes his way down the porch steps, following the throng of silver men and women streaming along the beach in a gleaming line. Just before the water's edge, a bonfire cackles, throwing up dancing columns of flame that Paul could stare at for hours on end.

The citizens of the Moon Shack stand up to their waists in the gently rolling sea as if the moon can pacify the ocean. Johan tosses his armful of ancient books into the fire, and it immediately surges upwards with renewed strength. "Ladies and gentleman, may I just say, fuck all that comes from the night sky save for our mother moon." Johan raises his arms, his curse still sounding so strange in Paul's head. The clouds have been completely banished, as have the stars. The moonlight drowns everything.

"For those of you who do not know, this man...," Johan begins, thrusting a finger toward Paul as he steps toward the sea. The Candle Lighters spread out in the water as Johan comes to a stop with the heaving tide coming up just over his shoes. This feels like some sort of baptism. Are the politicians still shackled up in the dining room?

"He stands for what we will never lose! He is the decency we have not lost nor will ever lose! The Moon Shack is our haven, but Paul will lead us! Paul will stand clean from our sin! And so sin we shall!" There are sudden thrashes in the sea as the Candle Lighters seem to turn inwards on one another for a moment, and quickly, there's a thrashing of silver shapes in the water and faint, strangled screaming. Johan jogs, wading into the tide, joining the squirming fray, and Paul's unsure of what he's watching, as the books cackle and crisp into ash beside him.

The angle of the moonlight illuminates a man pulling back a woman's hair and biting her throat, nibbling down her neck. Are there people fucking? Men and women are shouting in thrilled unison. Something deeper, almost whale-like, seems to be crying out from the distant sea beyond the splashing crowd of partygoers, but Paul can't be sure. The smoke from the fire is making him dizzy, and just as he turns away, someone comes running out of the water.

It's Lacy. Her robe is gone, and her body, more boney than Paul imagined, is naked, dripping, and vaguely tinged red. Some kind of scar or tattoo is slashed above her hip. Emerging from the sea, she offers her arms as an embrace. "Don't be afraid; only the outsiders get hurt," she says. "You're not a guest like them. Don't worry. Don't worry about a thing." She's resting her head against his shoulder. Those drugged guests, tripping on the worms, oblivious, with those songs in their head, what's going on in the water looks like a ballet. It hardly seems violent. People are swinging and splashing, dancing.

Someone else is running out of the water as Lacy slips out of Paul's arms. A naked old man is the next to hug him. "You are so good. Don't be afraid. We won't hurt you, you are no lamb." Paul doesn't know who the man is, as his clothes are becoming soaked and someone else is hugging him as the man moves away. One by one, the Candle Lighters slink from the sea to squeeze him.

"We will be your knife," a man whispers in Paul's ear after he's squeezed so hard he's afraid a rib will burst.

A woman slips into his arms and grabs his crotch, and says, "We can make our apathy burn."

Paul wants to cry out when Johan replaces the woman's embrace. He would keel over if it weren't for the endless parade of hugs.

"You have nothing to worry about. Our appetites are stayed." Johan's leaning against Paul, and there is much worse than hugging a naked man. "You'll never have to watch again." Paul's aware of things, or maybe people, left behind, floating in the water. The fire beside him begins to die, having gorged itself to death on unknowable tomes. Dripping from the sea, he is left shivering in the moonlight before the Candle Lighters usher him back to the big house, the Palace of the Komodo.

CHAPTER 7
THE MID-SUMMER RITUAL

There is a killer in Providence, and there are no such things as coincidences. Hap is going to need a scrub brush to get all the blood out of his fingernails.

A car in the city means all sorts of bullshit, from the two-hundred-dollar-a-year overnight parking pass to the nightmarish one-way, back-and-forth streets. Since moving to the city with his car, key scratches appeared along the sides of Hap's doors, presumably from jealous, nocturnal homeless men. Now, accompanying those scratches are splotches of blood and tufts of hair. The deer came *for* him, dipping out from beside a crumbling stoop and charging toward the right side of his Ford. His windshield shattered, his airbag gave him a solid punch, and Hap now wears a fine badge of scratches across his face.

Hap is on autopilot when he engages the parking brake and howls into the night, wiping blood from his eyes and picking glass from his body. The upper half of the deer's head is practically in his lap, its antlers tearing into the fabric of the passenger seat. If that thing had come in from the right instead of the left, he would be in pieces. What the hell's a deer even doing out of the country? Providence is surrounded by strip malls and suburbs. It's a long walk from the woods.

Somebody driving past calls the cops. At least that's what Hap figures when the blue flashing lights break through the orange streetlight-slashed shadows behind him. There forms a small gathering of humanity's finest good Samaritans, alongside its most perverse auditors, who surround the wreckage. When Hap emerges in one piece, there is a collective gasp of relief and also a quieter sigh of disappointment, as if some wanted the crash to be as dramatic and deadly as possible. Hap wanders over to sit on a stoop, which is the same cracked set of stairs from which the deer leapt. The approaching sirens make the city seem as though it is alive and squealing in anticipation of wrapping its lips around him. Casting his eyes down, he notes long, syrupy lines of blood on the pavement. From him? He's not bleeding that profusely.

Mosquitos pick at Hap's raw flesh as the golden sky of dusk becomes rotten with shadow. Some of the people remaining on the street utter meaningless questions at him, while others eye his wreckage and their flashing, clicking phones remind him of insects rubbing their mandibles and chirping away. Hap feels a nostalgic ache for his own camera and that peaceful sense of completion just as he lines up a shot.

The post-accident headache throbs onward. Once the ambulance attendees get tired of Hap reaffirming that he is fine and doesn't need to go to the hospital, they take off. The cluster of citizens along the sidewalk disperses, leaving only a cop, a tow truck driver, and an animal control officer whose job it is to mop up the mess. What looks like a couple of news guys in a white van show up, but the one officer on the scene jogs over to them, and they are almost immediately nodding with grave frowns before driving off with hardly a glance Hap's way. In order to get Hap's car back, there will be another bill for his parents to cover. He almost lets the tow truck take the car before he remembers the prize in his trunk.

A cop approaches him, asking if it's okay to get Hap's statement, but Hap has to raise a finger for him to wait as Hap frantically clicks his keys at the trunk of his Ford before running to the open hatch to peer at his treasure. During his lunch break, hours earlier, Hap had seen that someone on Craigslist was selling a telescope reminiscent of the one Tiff had. Hap immediately told the guy, who lived over the bridge in East Providence, that he'd pick it up after his shift. Taking the mercifully undented telescope from his trunk, Hap approaches the patiently waiting cop with it cradled in his arms, trying to act as though it doesn't weigh nearly sixty pounds.

"Least you didn't buckle that up front with you, yeah?" The cop is friendly and confident; he's taking control of the situation, which helps break away the shock of the accident a little. The cop looks at Hap knowingly, and Hap feels his heart skip a beat. "Hey, aren't you the kid that said a dog was trapped in that house on America Street? I bet you saw a rat instead." Hap had forgotten just how small Providence is.

Hap notes "Dylan" on the cop's little golden nametag. *Cops are not your friends,* Hap vows to try and remember.

Officer Dylan takes Hap's information and then keeps waving around the clipboard containing Hap's information like it's a fan as he eyes the wreckage of the Ford and watches Animal Control haul the deer carcass out of Hap's windshield. "Ya hear about coyotes on rooftops in Manhattan, so I guess this is believable, huh? Least you didn't run into that fucking lunatic who's running around."

Hap flinches. All day long he has been thinking about the actual, reality-stopping serial killer who's allegedly roaming the streets. Providence has its first serial killer in as long as anyone can remember, and Hap doesn't even want to consider what that might have to do with Tiffany. There is a thing about coincidences.

"If only this could've happened on my way to work instead," Hap says, halfheartedly trying to make the cop laugh as they stand side by side watching a rough-looking tow truck driver in a Boston Red Sox hat begin hooking chains around the front of the Ford. This guy's not a racist, at least. There's something satisfying about the idea of making a stern-looking cop or grumpy professor laugh. Hell, for Hap's own assurance, it's worth the effort.

"Maybe you'll get lucky tomorrow. Where you work?" Officer Dylan tucks his clipboard into his glove box and crosses his arms. Is it because Hap has watched too many movies, or is there really something to how penetrating a cop's eyes are? Standing in front of Officer Dylan suddenly feels worse than giving a presentation to a room full of snobby philosophy students.

Officer Dylan's eyes flash with recognition when Hap tells him about the Miskatonic. "The haunted one, huh?" he says with a grin, and Hap eyes the handle of the man's gun for a moment. It seems like it's such a part of his uniform that it isn't capable of detaching.

In the brief silence that follows, Hap decides to do something that may just make this all worth it. Shuffling the telescope so that it leans against his knee on the sidewalk, he tries to take advantage of having a Providence cop's ear. "My girlfriend, Tiffany Lorice, disappeared while attending a party there a little over a month and a half ago." Hap doesn't know what he expects the cop to tell him.

"Well, shit," Officer Dylan says, and Hap shrugs off a guilty tingle over making the guy feel awkward. He's a cop; awkward is probably in the job description. "Some stretch of luck you're having, huh? I heard about her...." He nods, and maybe he remembers hearing about Hap being given a break by that one cop outside the Miskatonic, who gave him a ride to the bus station instead of arresting him. That day didn't happen. His girlfriend disappeared, and now he's undercover, searching for her. There is nothing sloppy about this.

Hap accepts a ride home, only a three-minute drive to the other side of the hill. Officer Dylan tells him about his wife while Hap eyes the strange controls along the cruiser's dashboard. Dylan mentions how he and his wife have been together since high school before he joined the service and went overseas. Dylan's somber for a moment. "I don't know what I'd do if something happened to her."

Hap nods in agreement. He still doesn't know how he himself will inevitably act now that Tiff is gone. "Nobody's doing anything about Tiff. Nobody's told me anything." The ensuing shrug Officer Dylan gives him is at least honest. There is only so much that can be done. When Hap sees discomfort on a cop's face, instead of that mask of authority, well, nothing could make him feel less safe.

"You know, missing girl just over a month ago…I'll see what's going on for you. And hey…." The squad car pulls up to Hap's, and his chance to pitch his case to somebody in charge is over. Officer Dylan smacks a business card with his contact information into Hap's palm. "Now, don't fall asleep for a few hours, in case you have a concussion, you know?"

And Hap does sort of know. He's planning something, and sleep has got nothing to do with it.

In his apartment, Hap secures the telescope, splashes some water on his face, and decides he is going to get very drunk. Thumbing through the fresh bills in his wallet, he realizes he's been using that damn credit card so much he's forgotten what cash from a recently deposited paycheck even feels like. It's been nearly two weeks, which seems hard for him to believe. Two full months since Tiff disappeared. Hah, money, how useless. Could he really sit at a bar right now, full of people his own age, laughing and smiling with their friends?

He knows how people in real life get drunk via a bottle of whiskey or something similar and then, obliteration. But with Tiff, even after hitting twenty-one, he only ever had a couple of Bud Lights when they went out. Even then, he was never really comfortable with the resulting buzz. Something about losing control didn't jibe with him. He only ever got drunk on his twenty-first, primarily because of the shots Tiff's roommates kept pouring into him. If he closes his eyes, he can still smell the resulting puke.

The main strip of restaurants and bars on Federal Hill, Atwells Avenue, is not the place, with all that noise and local kids going wild on a Saturday. Hap crosses the far side of Broadway, conscious of how bad his fresh wounds must look. He will look like a fighter, a troublemaker. The funny thing is, the ache across his face almost feels good. It's something to concentrate on, as opposed to the meandering explorations of the Miskatonic. Tangible things are better than ethereal. Something to touch is better than a memory or an idea.

Today has been full of ideas that didn't go anywhere. Hap finally explored the Miskatonic's Garden Room, and big surprise, there were a lot of plants. He learned that its walls are stacked with potted green things, some of which have the faintest exotic flare to them, while others are no more spectacular than the weeds sprouting up from the cracked ends of the sidewalk. In the Garden Room, there is something of a sunroof, though the ceiling seems to mostly be covered in a mirror that reflects into the plants. In the center of the room, there's a large boardroom-style table where the hipsters of the business world presumably meet. If they really want to be clever, then they'd call it the Oxygen Room.

The one exception to the Garden Room is that there is a half-moon carved along the top of a wall facing from the east. The Miskatonic is built by the occult; that's obvious to anybody, even Luke, who says the place was built in the golden age of gypsies, Aleister Crowley, and tarot cards. Notably, this morning, Hap asked Randal, the bartender, if he knew of anybody going missing in the hotel. The response he received was some new-age philosophy about how buildings are more alive than suspected, how places can swallow you up, especially when they seem comfortable.

Just as cities have personalities, certain buildings have

"appetites," as Randal put it. Color him a superstitious foreigner, but he's the only person who almost says something Hap wants to hear. There is something he said that stuck with Hap after he helped a guest to her room and walked by himself down the lonesome corridor to the elevator. There's a theory that hotels' mazes can trap ghosts. For some reason, when Hap thinks of ghosts, it's always graveyards, spider webs, pumpkins, and pale wispy things in the dark. Graveyards are mazelike if they are big enough because most of the tombstones look the same. Spider webs, too, could play a part in trapping spirits as orchestrated patterns spun from the back end of a creeping thing. Maybe they trap ghosts; maybe ghosts lurk in every lonely place full of cobwebs. Maybe there is a big old spider that lives within the Miskatonic, spinning its spirit-trapping pattern over and over. What would a giant spider want with a person like Tiff? A meal? What would a ghost want with her? Company?

Blowing his cover as an indifferent clock puncher after a few weeks of dry leads, Hap asked Randal what he knew about what was really going on in the Miskatonic.

Randal's bemused response, lacking the playful ideology that set Hap's imagination briefly spinning during their first encounter, was that he never goes farther than the first floor. He then added, "Believe half of what you see but nothing that you hear. You don't need to set foot in here. You stand outside in the park, and you look at this building compared to the ones beside it; this place pulls you in. You can feel this place. It comes from your head. Then it comes for your head." Luke then appeared beside Hap, mentioning how he couldn't wait to finally receive his stupid paycheck. It seemed like Randal was going to continue and give Hap more of the slivers of ideas he had been craving, but Luke ushered him away. Randal had finished packing up for the night, and Hap couldn't find him after his own shift ended a few minutes later.

There's what looks to be a dark bar with no sign on the

corner of a square. Hap has never noticed. It's right off Broadway, and he's surprised he hasn't discovered it before. Cities and their hidden fucking corners. There's a street called John Parkington Lane; Hap doesn't know who that is, but the guy's probably another politician or doctor or civil rights activist. Why aren't things named after the people who go missing? Why isn't more done to try and remember them? To find them?

Something about the shadows of the bar seems appealing, as Hap glides in without being greeted. He's met by soft jazzy rifts on a low radio. Shadowy men and women wear their achievements in their wrinkleless collars, and elaborate skirts kick back on plush velvet chairs. Hap is debating turning around and walking right back out, but the bartender, a tall woman with hair so black it seems like a dancing shadow stuck to her head, greets him in a take-it-or-leave-it tone and he is here for a reason. He takes a seat at the bar and stares at a drink menu.

The bottles on the shelf are all rare brands Hap hasn't seen before. There are tequilas with strange, robotic owl logos and whiskey bottles warped and crooked, circular and spiraling. A mug bearing the logo of locally brewed Foolproof beer is labeled with the symbol of a leering and devilish jester's face. Hap would think it was a hipster place, being a nameless bar and all if it weren't for the upper-class people around him. This is where maybe a mobster would go, or whoever made this place wants to give it that sort of playful vibe. Perhaps "elite" is the more appropriate term. The walls offer carved wooden designs, outlining buildings that faintly resemble downtown Providence. On the fringes of the buildings are winding tree branches and naked, dancing women, some with antlers, some with what look like birds flying from their heads. The shadows cling to just the right places, and Hap can only get a vague notion of the mural wrapping around the bar. There are triangles and vaguely Egyptian trapezoids embroidered both above and to the side of the front door.

What isn't occult? What doesn't pay attention to the strange and the perverse? Coincidences, as far as Hap is concerned when it comes to Tiff, are coming back into play. The killer in Providence is another story. There have been three bodies found now, all with their eyes carved out, which is unique enough to be getting national attention. It makes sense that, instead of some grand conspiracy, Tiff was just killed by a murdering lunatic. This eye doctor, is there any way Hap could find him? He also can't let the Miskatonic off that easily, what with coincidences and all.

A drink on the menu has cucumber vodka and banana liqueur. It's probably light and dorky, so Hap orders it. It's called a Lost Alice, and its name brings to mind a wonderland of delirium and missing girls.

With his head down, the shadows are almost like closing his eyes. When he's halfway through the drink, he feels the faintest tug of disassociation. He remembers Tiffany's ring, the box opened, the ring on the Miskatonic nightstand. Was it him in his sleep? People black out when they're drunk. What else scatters memory and turns life and light into fog and dream?

Alice is lost down Hap's throat. He thinks he recognizes Tiff's old landlord, that douchebag called Cort, sitting in a corner of the room with an old woman. At first, it seems like Cort is having a polite drink with an elderly family member, but he's rubbing the woman's arm slowly, starting at a dark elbow and reaching, sliding his fingers toward the woman's face. Cort's lips quiver with excitement, causing Hap to feel a little sick. What would somebody else do? Walk over to the guy and shout, "Thanks for kicking me out of my fucking bedroom!" and then splash him in the face with banana liqueur? Maybe he could crack the glass across his face, drag him outside, and stomp his heel into his face. Violent people are alien. Hap can't picture ever crossing that line between fantasy and action. It's not possible. The bartender is peering at him, asking if he wants another, and, yes, Hap hardly remembers what Alice tasted like.

A third drink becomes overkill. Upon standing, Hap feels as though he's stuck in the sensation of leaning slightly backwards. Free from the nameless bar, it occurs to him that an additional twenty bucks after buying just three drinks is too large a tip. One move, and you can't get something back. He forgot to call out Cort for being a prick and a perv, that granny-fucking king rat.

Hap's skin is thick as he prods at his fresh bruises from the accident and stumbles down the street. Did he really run into a deer? He's never killed anything with blood running through its veins before. Where would it have gone if he hadn't struck it off its course? He's pretty sure he remembers the blood already around its neck, in that split second flash of the deer thumping against the hood of the car and floating up the windshield; its neck twisted, and he saw its black eyes before his windshield shattered. Where had it been? Hap begins making his way back to the hill. Who, or what, gouged its neck open, and why? There are places to explore, things to investigate.

The sky is alight overhead in fluttering, snaking yellow, via a sudden crackling burst as the stars are brought to Providence, and burning green tendrils slowly creep down over Broadway. Fireworks, from the weekly water fire festival downtown. In a city this small, there are no concerns about the rockets hitting a stray office building. They just angle the bombs over the flatland slums of East Providence and rest their worries. What weekend is this? The Fourth? It's already the Fourth, yes; there are too many American flags and people saying congratulations to each other, so they don't forget to be happy. Where did June go?

Just as he's wondering why he hasn't been invited to any cookouts, Hap remembers both the missed calls and voicemails from his mom and his brother Derrick. *Fuck the Fourth.* That was his motto, wasn't it? Another rocket splits the sky, erupting into more multi-limbed magnesium tentacles that grip the city in its celebration.

There's a liquor store nearby, and he lets the headlights on either side of him rely on their driver's reflexes as he strolls along a crosswalk, staring straight ahead. He selects a cheap six-pack of blueberry-flavored Newport Storm bottles because he got a sample of it one time at a festival in that aforementioned seaport town with Tiff. The cashier asks Hap for his ID and then a second form of ID. Hap drops his wallet, fumbling for his now-expired school one.

A second clerk appears; they're both Pakistani, so of course, there's no kinship with Hap. One of them mentions that Pennsylvania fake IDs are the most popular because they're the easiest to make, which is funny because Tiff had a fake ID from Pennsylvania under a fake name when Hap first met her, which made their relationship seem even more like destiny. At last, the clerks take Hap's money, and before he's even fully out the door, he pops the cap off one of the beers and starts guzzling.

He wanders over to the abandoned Federal Hill house. The six-pack is too much, so he places it by one of the fence posts. The firework show's grand finale is erupting behind him, so he casts one obligatory glance over his shoulder at the pretty orgy of lights before refocusing on the den of pure fucking evil before him. He tilts his bottle back for a good long sip, studying the peeling paint and unshuttered glass windows that reveal only blackness. The thin porch is cracked in as if somebody hacked away at it with a bat; this is the building farthest in from the sidewalk around here. The porch of every other house practically dumps on the road, yet this one has an actual front yard if you call broken glass and weeds a yard. The front door is locked, so Hap picks up a chunk of the crumbling cement walkway and throws it through a first-floor window. Knock-Knock.

The breaking of the glass seems to mesh well with the fading echo of the fireworks show, as Hap finds another slab of cement and uses it to chip away the sharper edges of the remaining glass that's sunk into the waterlogged gums of the window frame. There's a chill to the air in the house that causes Hap to shiver after he scrambles inside before the bloated warmth of alcohol once more seeps over him.

The walls must be full of dead, rotting things. Entire generations of mice and squirrels have been swallowed by the house. Hap finishes his blueberry beer and throws the bottle at a silent husk of a refrigerator, but it doesn't shatter like he expects; it just clinks and rolls off into a dark corner of the dingy kitchen. Dust, spider webs, and rot, all spectacular and terrifying if this exact scene wasn't replicated in the laundry room of both his new and former apartment building basements.

"Is anybody home?" Hap yells, after a cursory check of the barren room abutting the kitchen. He crouches and listens, holding his breath. There is a faint, clicking scurry, but it's something small. He burps, and his throat burns while he glances over a bathroom that seems to be made of black mold. He takes to kicking at walls, trying to see if any are hollow, but he isn't exactly sure what sound he hopes to hear, as his shoes leave black marks along the faded white walls. Hap finds stairs leading to the second floor just as he discovers the basement door. Where would they keep a prisoner?

He doesn't ask himself who "they" are before ripping open the basement door and yelling, "Hey, Tiff?" His voice cracks, and he's silent, pausing to listen for a response before bounding down the wooden steps. His alcohol-wobbled legs cause him to repeatedly bump against the walls. The basement is nothing but a burial ground for green and blue molded boxes, a child's rusted tricycle, and an old bathtub with a coat hanger emerging from it. The hidden things, they won't be obvious. It's not enough to glance over. Hap has to actually search. He kicks over the boxes and shines his light into the tub. He goes over every inch of the walls, remembering the intricate woodcarvings of the bar he just left.

He finds a fire axe with rust that looks like blood. On

top of a couple of dozen volumes of *Reader's Digest*, there's a Halloween costume magazine from 2004 for a locally famous store in Warwick that has a giant inflatable pumpkin on its roof every year. A bloody bunny mask occupies one corner of the magazine's cover, and a George Bush mask another. He finds Easter Bunny decorations with the famous white rodent's smile having faded to a sinister grin. Hap picks up a book with the picture of some great serpent embroidered across its cover, along with words that read in an eerie font, *Solomon Kane*. Believing it to be a spell book of some sort, his hands shake with anticipation as he illuminates the first page and drops it to the floor. It's just some pulp fantasy novel; these are all pieces of nothing.

In a second floor bedroom, it takes Hap's alcohol-fogged mind a moment to correlate the symbol formed by black tape along a closet door—a seven-pointed star with seven circles descending in size from each point. Not quite a satanic pendant, but something celestial. Through the uproar in Hap's skull, he believes it to be one of the same symbols he saw at the black star restaurant on Broadway.

Hap chucks himself forward and pulls open the dual closet doors, scattering the tape and destroying the symbol. He's ready to kick at whatever lies within, but a snarling, hissing black thing darts at his feet. As he stumbles back, falling onto his ass, he knows he is going to die alone, drunk, and confused. It's not until the creature moves into the hallway and meows crankily that he realizes it's just a stray cat. It didn't even scratch him.

He sighs and pushes himself up, his hand closing over a rubber band. With drunken amusement, Hap prepares to fire it across the black-dusted room right before realizing it's not a rubber band but a hair tie. A familiar hair tie, decorated with little psychedelic suns, stars, and moons. Tiff had a whole collection of them she bought at some shop downtown. Hap drops it to the floor and begins to laugh. He'll wake up every goddamn mouse and bat in this place. There could be hundreds of girls in Providence who bought those things, and it probably means nothing in an abandoned house that has empty beer bottles and used condoms kicked into every corner.

Hap howls out his exasperation and kicks through the symbol over the closet door, enjoying the crack of fragile wood. There's an empty jar in the corner of the room that he grabs and smashes against the bedroom window. He finds an old metal part of a pipe frame and decides to beat the truth out of this place, and he begins to smash everything in sight.

Later, having puked from all the physical excitement, Hap remembers, dearly, his remaining five beers. Of course, when he wanders out of the house, he discovers that they're gone, plucked up by some eagle-eyed passerby. His wrists hurt from swinging that pipe around and breaking some of the windows and every spare dish in the house. His ankle wants him to limp as he hops over the fence and heads toward another liquor store.

Drinking a tallboy of Twisted Tea out of a paper bag, Hap's drunk legs deliver him to the weekly summer water fire festival. One of the first unique things about Providence that he discovered his freshman year were these literal water fires, erected on blocks of wood in the middle of a canal that runs through downtown and tended to by volunteers in gondolas. As some sort of artist's statement that may be in conjunction with the RISD, there are all sorts of food vendors and tents where actual artists sell their work. Along the waterway, a speaker system pumps out eerie, ambient sounds and opera-like wailing.

He and Tiff paid for a private gondola ride once. While they were coasting along the canal, somebody up on a bridge threw them a rose that Hap still prides himself for catching against all of his athletic inhibitions. Now, the overcrowded walkways and police conducted street corners and crossways leave Hap nothing but agitated as he sips and seethes. At one point, he bumps into a dirty, bearded guy in a Patriots beanie, sipping a frozen Del's lemonade that he spills all over Hap's white, dust-stained T-shirt before being swept up by the crowd.

Overlooking the water, Hap realizes that a series of ten fires form a massive circle in the middle of the largest portion of the river, overshadowed by the Providence Place Mall and a cluster of fancy restaurants. The eerie music loses its beautiful touch as Hap takes note of the water fire volunteers, dressed from head to toe in black and silently paddling around the waterway on gondolas of their own, adding logs to the fires. This is a ritual of some pagan sort if Hap has ever seen one. Is the whole city haunted? Who really started the water fire tradition, and what does it mean?

Hap, whisking himself away amongst the crowd, feels like jumping into the black and grimy river, but washing himself in Providence water would be the opposite of a cleansing. He sees Tiff's old roommate, Erin, and tries to avoid her, but the pushing of the crowds causes them to cross paths. She's dressed up with a group of unfamiliar girls who reek of the present college fashion of brown boots, matching jeans, and white blouses. Hap smells their perfume from ten feet away; it's strong enough to overcome the smoky musk that clouds the water fire celebrations.

Pushing through the crowds, Hap tries to evade Erin, who notices him and begins calling out his name, repeating herself with, "How are you doing? Are you okay?" In his drunken attempt to escape, the next thing Hap's slowing mind comprehends is a cop screaming at him as he picks his way through a streaming line of cars stuck in traffic, having ignored the cop's hand signals to not cross. Hap drops his Twisted Tea onto the sidewalk and breaks into an all-out sprint. By the time he realizes no knights of authority are chasing him, he's climbing up a steep street next to a fire station. He is only dimly aware of where he is.

Prospect Park, where he was supposed to propose to Tiff. Hap's heartbeat begins to rest as he notes the emptiness of the park. The statue of Providence's founder, Roger Williams, overlooks the city with an extended hand, palm down as if he's urging the tiny metropolis to be calm. Directly above Roger Williams's stone head is the edge of the waxing gibbous moon that shines just under a week away from being full. The statue lines up with the moon. Could this mean something? The way the city aligns with the stars, Roger Williams, and the moon?

Hap finds a soft bench beside a massive, strange rock in the middle of the grass, which looks like it once had a sign on it. In a plaque on the bench are the words: *All that sleep shall awaken. All that are lost will rise.* The city is speaking to Hap, over and over, yet its riddles are only decipherable to the insane. Maybe Hap will get there one day. The stars lull him to sleep.

In the morning, Hap's wounds from the accident bring him back to life, aided both by the roughness of the bench and the leering cop standing over him. The unfamiliar black officer threatens to give him a ticket as he asks for Hap's ID. "Keep it in the dorms next time," the cop tells him. Fighting back vomit, Hap doesn't have the heart to correct him.

CHAPTER 8
THE LAST GULP (OF FRESH AIR)

Within Paul's dreams, he entered his office to find a collection of clowns. One of them was perched on his desk. They were not the fun kind of clown; somewhere within Paul's inner consciousness, he knew the moment he saw them that they, somehow, were *real* clowns and not people in makeup. Hunched over like monkeys, at least a dozen of them filled the increasingly confined room. They wore white onesies with black buttons, sporting an assortment of curly orange hair, orange beards, black-rimmed eyes, and pale faces that complemented their crimson lips. They smiled and showed off the perfect holes in their teeth. A circle was taken out of every crooked, yellow tooth, large enough that Paul wondered how the lower half didn't just break away. "Mooshuck," the clowns croaked, froglike. No, they were saying something real. Moon shark? No, not quite. "Moon Shack," the clowns croaked again. The one on his desk was cocking its head, studying him, trying to gauge if he was a threat.

"Well, what do we have here?" an old man muttered from behind Paul just as his office door slammed shut and the walls melted black. The clowns were banished, replaced with an old man who glowed with a faint, silver aura that complemented his mostly white hair and black beard. In one hand, he held a telescope. The other, he extended Paul's way. A handshake, he couldn't do a handshake. Paul was paralyzed as the old man, old Charles McKinley himself turned and pointed the telescope at the blackness in front of them. Stars began to sprinkle in, one by one, as if tumbling through a clogged saltshaker. Other planets appeared as colorful orbs as the galaxy made itself known.

The Milky Way spun into a spiral, and the sun thinned into a pentagramno, a seven-pointed star — as the planets in the solar system spun faster and faster, joined by other galaxies and hidden worlds. A vortex began to form. The flashing crescendo of blurring lights from outer space became the connected tendrils of a living thing. The word *chaos* popped into Paul's mind.

"The cosmos is going to swallow us up unless we make ourselves superior." McKinley jabbed the telescope through the swirling mess that was beginning to radiate strange warmth over Paul. Screams began to fill his ears, and an image of the earth hovered over him, zooming in to reveal the flesh of billions boiling and popping. He saw incomprehensible flying things with dripping tentacles and too many teeth ripping men and women apart, nuclear warheads combusting before they could leave the launching pad, something rising free from the oceans and towering *through* the atmosphere as it raised its humanoid arms and uncurled a black pair of leathery wings. The telescope slashed through the image of the earth as McKinley grunted, screamed in fury, and stabbed his silver scope once more until the images faded.

McKinley, glowing, alone, stood toe to toe with Paul. "We cannot comprehend them," he said. He raised the telescope in the air like a freshly thrust spear, ready to strike again. "What they will do to our minds is worse. We need *your* help to stop them. We need *you* to give us courage, Paul, for we must plunge into wickedness with only your devotion as a harness." McKinley clapped a hand on Paul's shoulder and whispered into his ear, "We have allies, though they are few. Always trust your closest clown." He breached off into high-pitched laughter that dug into Paul's ears, sending him screaming awake in a bed filled with women and men still basking in the afterglow of untold pleasures.

Paul is not doing okay as he walks all the way from the waterfront district to Federal Hill. The heat soaks through his sweats and T-shirt. He feels as though his skin is stretching, becoming something else. The Candle Lighters, they are not wrong, though they do awful, awful things.

Where has his friend Nicky gone? Are the bums the first to be sucked away?

He has friends on the Hill. More accurately, his father's friends. The genuine Italians, the old school kings of the city. The idea of the mob is fictitious. There are only those who make agreements, compromises that go on the other side of the law, depending on who is in office. More than one mayor of Providence has paid his respects to the old men who dwell in the shadows of myth and reality along Federal Hill. *The Godfather* need not apply to modern times, but there are those who make backroom deals and give desperate women and men a chance, only to punish them if they step out of line. These are the people who really own everything, from the strip clubs to the cigar lounges to the new, hip clubs that only cater to college kids. There are many secret organizations in the world. They just don't always give themselves a goofy name and follow mandated traditions and pointless ceremonies.

Mike Santalio is a good man whom Paul called "uncle" when he was a boy. He was younger than Paul's father by almost ten years, but they were close. They shared experiences ranging from dark and desperate to delightful and successful. One of them solidified his career as a politician. The other became what every good politician needs: a man of the people, and solely for the people, who gives the people what they are too ashamed to personally fight the government for. In the time of Prohibition, Santalio's kind supplied the alcohol. In these modern times, they cover every other illicit desire.

Uncle Santalio owns a bakery. Paul's been joking with him about being a baker ever since Santalio bought the place when

Paul was sixteen. To this day, Santalio still makes Paul pay for his own bagels.

As usual, Mike's in the back room. Paul knocks, shouts, "Open up, you old fuck."

He cracks a genuine smile when Mike replies, "Pauly boy, get the fuck in here. What are you doin' knocking?"

Paul takes a deep breath. He can almost remember what his life was like a month ago. Narrow misses, humble pleasures, good friends, and the idea that he would somehow defy the odds, defeat his enemies, and succeed. He promises himself he won't break down in front of one of the few people he respects. Then again, the way his thoughts have been jerking him around since that night at the mansion in Westerly, there's still a chance he might grab Mike's gun and end this horror show before it begins.

Mike used to be fat enough to dress up as Santa Claus during the family holiday gathering that Paul always receives an invitation to. Now he's bald, his gut's gone, and he's somewhat fit for a man in his sixties.

"Where the hell'd you pop outta, huh?" Mike embraces him, gesturing to a greasy brown bag on his desk. "You want some clam cakes? Fresh from Narragansett. This nephew of mine wakes up every morning at the ass crack of dawn to surf. Then he brings me back a heart attack."

Clam cakes: a fistful of dough and clam fried into a red ball of delight. While Paul's memory swells, his stomach does flip-flops.

"Jesus. Look at you. You need coffee first."

Mike claps Paul on the shoulder and shakes his head, his glasses partially sliding down his round nose. Paul wonders how bad he looks. It takes a lot to burst Mike's bubble, even when he's mad enough to bend a guy's neck with a pipe.

Paul begins to refuse the offer for mind-altering caffeine, but the air inside the bakery is near freezing. Back in the old days, the oven would've nearly boiled the place over, but now bakeries have no affiliation with warmth. The heat of the day is a memory that clings wet to Paul's skin. Save for the two employees behind the counter, the shop's mostly empty. For once, the smell of baked goods does nothing for Paul.

"Here, get that into ya. Those people...," Mike mutters, shuts the door, and gestures for Paul to sit on the leather couch in his office. "They've brought you all the way in now, haven't they?" Mike says, crossing his arms and leaning against his desk. Behind him and stretching from one corner of the wall to the other is a framed picture of Fenway Park, fortress of the Red Sox.

Mike's the one who encouraged Paul to go for the position at the Miskatonic. Mike, who knows Johan by name, had called him "just one of the guys in charge." Paul knew the Miskatonic was vaguely associated with Mike's organization, which spreads from Providence to Bar Harbor, Maine, with a concentration, of course, in Boston and fragments in New York. Paul was never entirely surprised by the Miskatonic's hidden walls. Given its Prohibition history, Mike's ties to the building itself make more sense than anything else in this damn city.

"What?" Paul asks, realizing he spaced out.

"You don't have to tell me what they're like. I've got an idea. They're not hurting you, though, right? No threats? If you want out, you tell me. Only people who get to push you around are those bozos in city hall, and only the ones in that specific cocksuckin' office."

Paul smiles, vaguely remembering the government officials he saw naked and chained at the Westerly mansion. "They treat me well...." He can still feel the warm bodies that have been pleasuring him nightly.

"Then why you look like shit? You...." Mike's seen it all. He jumps to the next logical conclusion, and Paul can't blame him. "What kind of drugs are they into? Coke? The tar? Opiates? Something new? I've been wondering. I asked, but you know by now how they are when it comes to answering your questions."

Mike's had business with the other hotels in the city. Special kinds of business involving girls, mind-altering consumables, and meetings with important people with important connections from different corners of the country.

"There's no drugs." Paul remembers the worms from the party. They weren't part of a dream. "I'm hung over, man. That's all. Wanted to see ya; it's been a while. How's Carol?" Paul doesn't mention how much he craved a friendly face far removed from the hotel. He was willing to shuffle all the way here like a zombie.

"She's good, great. Doesn't ease up on me any, her age." Mike's arms loosen as he leans against the desk. Paul shouldn't have come here. The gears in Mike's brilliant mind are spinning. "You know, they asked me to tell you about the position, but they had their eye on you for longer. Hell, your dad had dealings with them. Aside from banging the maids at that hotel."

Paul didn't know that, but his dad was private, only told his son the sort of things that would interest him. Burning his tongue, but liking the pain, the way it washes the bad taste out of his mouth, Paul attempts to get a solid sip down before replying, "What do you mean, dealings?"

"You know. Miskatonic plays ball with powerful people from all over. People a bit classier than my kinda guys. Scientists, inventors, weird geniuses you read about in the *Journal*'s interest pieces. That was back when your dad was thinking of the governor's seat. Till he backed down."

Paul remembers his dad one time drunkenly ranting about how he wouldn't give money to people who didn't appreciate him anymore. Maybe that had something to do with it. For Paul, it's never been about money. Paul Jones Sr.'s last will and testament pretty much saw to that. But the other day, Paul glanced at his bank account, and it was not as he left it. With the last paycheck he received, you'd think the Miskatonic was a Four Seasons. Of course, Johan and his people own much more than just a hotel.

"You ever hear about the Moon Shack?" Mike asks Paul, who flashes back to his dreams. He remembers the smell of people burning. How can he remember a smell from a dream? Those abominations, in the sky, the sea, there was nothing silly about them. They carried a feeling, a weight to what they were and what they signified. Paul's hand spasms, and a splash of coffee lands on the couch.

"Whoa, hey, what the fuck!" Being a typical neat-freak Italian, Mike pulls a rag practically out of thin air and tosses it to Paul.

"Sorry, sorry, I just—" Paul tries to defend himself.

"Hey, hey, it's okay," Mike says. It's embarrassing how concerned Mike is for him. "You look bent out, kid. Jeez. Your back okay? Businessmen like us sit down too much. If you need a good chiropractor, I know of a guy right on Broadway—"

"Nah, nah, I'm okay. And I've been there." The doctor's another Italian who grew up on the hill; Paul used to go drinking with interesting people like that. Mike originally taught Paul that knowing useful people leads to a simpler life. He gives all of his friends gift baskets loaded with wine and cigars come the holidays. Doctors, cops, lawyers, strippers, and, of course, politicians. You never know what you might need.

"I should go, actually," Paul says. "I have work in an hour, believe it or not." It's bullshit, and Paul's kidding himself if Mike doesn't detect that. Paul's not sure when his next shift is. He's not sure if anybody at the Miskatonic, except for his immediate staff, even cares.

"Yeah, yeah, you sure as hell need a shower, all right, but we gotta get dinner soon, okay?"

Paul sets the coffee on Mike's desk and gives the guy a handshake that turns into a shoulder hug.

"Remember, you're working with them *for you*. They got their...belief in that place, and it's okay to play along with it, but remember, you are in this for yourself. Not them. You hear?

Remember, religion's just a philosophy, and every man should live by one of his own making." Mike bought himself a gold filling a year ago that catches in the light of the office.

Paul clasps Mike on the arm before leaving. "I hear ya on that," he says, lying through his teeth.

CHAPTER 9
THE CONSTELLATIONS, PAINTED

Hap realizes his feelings are becoming dulled when he shuffles the two fat, pink duffle bags off the luggage cart and, not for the first time, wonders if he's really just transporting bags of clothing. There are no metal detectors; there could be anything in these shoddily zipped containers. It seems possible that some of the larger, square suitcases could have a body stuffed in them. Hap makes himself sick thinking about a pretty girl being tossed away into something he himself lugged through the elevator and out into a car waiting on the roundabout.

The night before, Hap was hunched over his new four-hundred-dollar silver tube on a tripod, looking through it with one eye shut. He scanned the moon's pale craters contrasted by shadow, looking for any signs that Tiff got swept up there. As if the moon's somehow a magnet for special people.

His camera, the damn thing that Tiff used to criticize him for living his whole life through, has been banished to the top of his dresser like a museum artifact on display. The pictures of Tiffany on its hard drive are voiceless ghosts. All Hap would have to do is give it life, and he could see her. He wouldn't be able to look away; the resulting bedsores would bubble his skin into mush.

What originally turned Hap on to photography was how to properly take a picture of the moon and capture some of its fool's magic. That's when his artist's fever started. If there was one reason Tiff fell in love with him, it's because he could take the moon from the sky, exactly how she saw it, and give it to her as an image she could admire over and over again. The moon is meaningless. It glows because of the sun, a big ball of cosmic radiation. It's a stuck asteroid, a balled up glob of chalk. That's the worst thing about the moon: it reminds you that something so damned beautiful can mean absolutely nothing. One of Tiff's glow-in-the-dark stars from her old bedroom wound up in Hap's luggage. Even though it has lost its ability to stick to a wall, it matters more to him than *everything* in the night sky.

He's been working so much that whenever he dreams, he is helping guests unload their luggage at the hotel in a hellish form of payless overtime. He's been aiming for as many late shifts at the Miskatonic as he can get. No clues, or ghosts, will appear in the mornings. The nights when his shift ends at six are a defeat, as he's sent home to scrounge up a couple of boxes of leftover Chinese takeout. At first, the most exciting thing Hap would do with his free nights was walk down from Broadway to Onleyville, where there's a famous New York System wiener joint where a bunch of too-happy cooks makes the best greasy food Hap's ever had. He tried coffee milk for the first time there with Tiff, and now, whenever he eats there, he fixates on her memory while the cooks joke around him, a silent sap chewing his food. As of late, Hap has been brought to more drastic means to discard his free time.

A week after his accident, Hap found that the Spanish-speaking chefs in the Miskatonic's kitchens were serving venison as a room service special. He almost puked, mainly because the Miskatonic seems to mock him at every turn. One of the chefs had a bandage smudged against his nose, and Hap wondered if the chef had been kicked by a stubborn pair of hind legs.

Now there's a presence behind the peephole for Room 353. There's a slightly muffled moan as the door swings open to reveal a woman with artificially wavy brown hair. She arches back, flaunting a heaving chest tightly wrapped up in a yellow silk robe. This is a diva hurled into the form of a busty woman in her thirties with pouting lips that stretch back into a pair of wild eyes. Starkly put together as she is, it takes Hap a moment to recognize she's beautiful while he hauls her bags into her room.

There are plain white candlesticks scattered around the suite, flickering like a galley of spectators, which definitely doesn't adhere to local fire codes. The door to the second bedroom that's a part of the suite is cracked open; the glow of more candles paints shadows from within. Hap sets the bags down, trying not to intrude any further. Going into the guests' rooms is always awkward; how often do you stand with a stranger beside the bed they sleep in? The eccentric looking woman who held the door open for Hap asks him for his name before swinging the door shut. His personal space is tossed aside as the woman thrusts her face in front of his.

The candles, combined with the stench of incense, mix with the shadows of both the room and the strangeness of the woman in the robe, who Hap swears was dressed plainly and unspectacularly down in the lobby only minutes ago. She asks in a sexy purr how old he is, if he has a girlfriend, and her smile is one that labels her intentions as much as they can be communicated. Beyond the artificial familiarity of a teenage boy's fantasy, there is something wrong here.

Hap recently had one weird guest asking for flowers, as the wormy guy who spoke too softly gave him some kind of specific list of plants. When Hap asked Paul what he should do about it, Paul said he'd take care of it himself. He took the list away before Hap could Google any of the names.

Someone is moving in the other room. Some of the candles are black. There is something in a wooden box on the nightstand behind the bed. Is Hap in danger? How many stories are there about horny boys being devoured by sexual temptation? There is no stir beneath Hap's itchy, suffocating bellhop pants. The woman smiles as she plucks his silly hat off his head, tossing it to the floor. "We have a thing for strangers. You want to play? You don't look too busy, and I promise to leave a nice tip," the woman whispers into Hap's ear. She's trying too hard; she's been taking notes while watching too much cheesy porn. This is the Miskatonic, and it's finally showing him something. He has no choice but to play along.

Hap is remembering that long before the soul comes into play, human beings are animals first. He's the one who hasn't been watching enough porn. His shirt's suddenly being whisked off by the woman in yellow. He has to remember that she's practiced that purr in her voice. He has to try to figure out what's actually going on in her head as he's stripped to his underwear and her heavy hand smacks his ass. A finger pokes hard against his chest, pushing him toward the adjoining room of shadows.

"There is one thing you have to do." She walks around the bed to the nightstand, gracefully leaning over to pick up something out of the wooden crate. The candles bring to life what looks like a buffalo's head. When she holds it out to him, he realizes it's a mask. "You put that on. Then you can take those off." She gestures to his underwear as she leans beside him and places the mask in his hands.

The woman grabs Hap's arm and leads him to the half-open portal to the next room. There are fewer candles within. "Put it on," she commands as she takes it from his hands and forcefully slips the mask over his head. It's scratchier than a face full of his bellhop hat. It has a heavy, chemical odor to it, and its weight seems to throw off his balance.

In the next room, there is a girl—white, slender, and naked—lying face down with her skinny bare ass arched into the air. Her arms are stretched, and her wrists and ankles are shackled by black tendrils of rope on either side of her that extend from each post of the bed. Her mask is that of a white goat, expressionless with its marble eyes unblinking. Hap's eyes linger over her hairless exposure of flesh.

"The masks stay on. Everything else is fair game," the woman in yellow whispers into Hap's ear, pushing him toward the bed. The hunched-over girl is moaning pleasantly. Above her, on the wall, scribbled along five conjoined pages of Miskatonic notebook paper, is the familiar symbol of a seven-pointed star with seven descending circles spiraling from each point. The symbol clicks within Hap's memories, tearing all of his doubts away. There was that abandoned house on the hill and now the Miskatonic itself. His insanity hasn't been lying after all. The pale, potentially drugged girl on the bed is tall, and her blonde hair pushes back from the nape of the black goat's head. Oh god, Tiff....

Hap is casting his mask aside as he rushes to Tiffany's bedside, cracking to his knees as he tears off her mask. An unfamiliar, snarling face is suddenly spitting and hissing at him, calling him a "cheater." A hand on Hap's shoulder hauls him back as he drops the mask, his back forced against the bathroom doorknob as the woman in yellow is all over him with flailing nails and bared teeth. "You couldn't follow one simple instruction!" The purr is gone as a hand slaps across his face. Hap's grabbed by his hair, and the next thing he knows, the blinding light of the hallway is searing his eyes. He whirls around, catching a glimpse of a flapping yellow robe before the door slams shut, and he's left lying in the middle of the hallway in his underwear.

He debates pounding on the door, but that wasn't Tiff. He's okay, for now. If he knocks on that door, his cover might be blown. If he causes a scene, if he acts like anything other than a dweeb who's afraid of the kinky stuff, then he'll only know as much as he does now.

He runs to the stairwell with more hop in his step than there should be, given he's half-naked. That sign! That symbol! There is something real! There is something real! Who was that woman? He can't go downstairs. He.... Fuck, he's onto something, and if some guest sees him in his freaking underwear, then he's fired or worse. Hap scatters down the stairs to the second floor, peering in through the window of the steel door that sections off the stairway that overlooks the right wing of the corridor. There's no way he can walk through the lobby; it's only five-thirty. His phone is downstairs, and, not that it matters, his tip money is still tucked under his watch.

Running back up the stairs, Hap checks every floor's window, going all the way up to the sixth before heading back down. He finally spots Luke wheeling luggage through an empty hallway, but there's a couple in front of him. Hap pokes just his head from the stairwell door and hisses for Luke's attention. The couple looks at Hap strangely while Luke goes about his business settling their bags in their room before heading Hap's way with a confused grin.

Ten long minutes later, a giddy Luke has brought him a spare uniform. He's also demanding, for the second time, that Hap explain what happened (while calling him a lucky bastard the whole while). Luke doesn't matter anymore. Hap should call out sick for the rest of the day; he has too much to think about. Plus, he should lie low, right?

Luke, understandably, won't leave Hap alone once they reach the lobby. "I wouldn't worry. I mean, do you know who that was?"

"Who was she?" Hap asks. The woman upstairs is the most important puzzle piece he now has.

"Augustine Sanfresco. She's kinda hot in her own way, but she's big in the fashion industry, which means she's real big on models and crazy-hot girls. Man, I can't believe you just got pulled into that. She's been coming here for a while, too. Man, how has this never happened to me? I can't believe they just kicked you out...your balls must be blue as fuck, man." Hap all but tells Luke to leave him alone, as he lies to Cassandra at the front desk about how he has some type of food poisoning and needs to go home.

"I know exactly what you're going to do when you get home, you bastard!" Luke calls after him as Hap hurries into the street. His lie might not be so far-fetched. The idea of puking from his excitement seems like a real possibility.

When Hap gets home, he delicately picks up his camera and attaches it to an umbilical wall plug as a sliver of red light indicates its approaching life. Augustine Sanfresco? Hopefully, the NSA isn't still monitoring phones because he is going to Google that name until he knows enough to write her unofficial biography. The star symbol, too...sex acts with animal masks, everything. He is going to start a file, and he is going to email it to his parents, maybe his brother, for safekeeping. He is going to build something nobody can take away from him.

It's not until the next morning that he remembers the uniform he left in Augustine Sanfresco's hotel room had his nametag plastered over it.

The next day, as soon as Hap checks in at the front desk for his four to twelve shift, Cassandra tells him Paul wants to talk to him. A lump begins to form in his throat as he realizes Luke is off hauling bags and he is on his own. "Make sure to knock. Who knows what he's doing back there?" she says, and there's a pause before she giggles as she thinks of something. What's the worst that could happen; Hap gets fired?

There's no answer after the standard knock, so Hap opens Paul's door partially. Paul lifts his head from his desk, his face red and compressed as if he were taking a nap. "Ah, you're in uniform." He burps twice in a row and gestures for Hap to come in. "I saw what happened...." Paul waves at Hap, who remains standing. The office is bathed in shadows as if the lights are about to blink out. "...and I don't care." At Paul's words, Hap's heart rises, and this is nothing, only a reprimand. "Can't say I'd have done differently in your situation. Hey, take a seat." Paul burps again, gesturing toward a chair. Hap has no choice. Even in the dim light, he can see the redness in Paul's eyes. "I didn't want to see the security video, but, uh, it was brought to my attention. Try and be a little less accommodating next time, yeah? Even if they offer you a tip." Paul waves his hand, and it seems like he's trying to make a joke, but his heart isn't in it. "You're not in trouble, but, ah, why didn't you go through with it?" Paul asks, and Hap isn't sure if he's serious. "What? You have a girlfriend or something?"

"No," Hap says, maybe a little too quickly. Has Paul figured out who he is?

"Well, get one. This place, dealing with people like this, can get messy. There's a whole lot of temptation. All sorts of stuff is going on behind closed doors, and you've gotta know not to go knocking."

Hap doesn't correct his boss by mentioning that he was pulled into that room. He also doesn't mention the overbearing stench of alcohol wafting over from Paul. The guy has tears at the rims of his eyes, shining in the glow creeping under the door from the lobby

"Anyway, was curious is all. You surprised me, kid. Now off you go," Paul gestures, and Hap has to do everything he can to stop himself from running out of the room.

CHAPTER 10
THE EYE EXAM

When the cop car pulls halfway into the valet lot, stopping just before the pickup zone, Hap wants to throw his hat on the ground and stomp on it because he's pretty sure he missed something. It's probably just a random fight between drunken tourists, but with the hotel being as big as it is, there could be a mass murderer having a field day on the seventh floor, and he wouldn't even hear about it until it was over. There's a cold breeze that replaced the setting sun a few hours ago, and another New England summer is beginning to fade.

Hap doesn't recognize Officer Dylan until the cop is standing right in front of him and asks, "Hap, right?" There's a natural, panicked moment of disorientation as one of the uniformed guys with a gun, whom Hap has trained himself to avoid eye contact with, breaks the fourth wall and enters his reality. Officer Dylan ushers him away from the two unfriendly valet guys and Luke, whose hands are clasped behind his back as he raises his eyebrows at Hap, mouthing out the word, "Shit."

When they're out of earshot of the others, Officer Dylan says, "I'm glad to see your bruises look better. Your car getting fixed?"

"Nah. Still waiting to get a call back." In truth, Hap hasn't even checked his phone for missed calls. His parents have definitely tried calling. If only they had what it takes to be a part of this.

"I've gotta tell ya, I spent the whole rest of that night thinking about your story. You see a guy with his eyes uh…gone, and then you go home and eat leftovers. But your story. It's been occurring to me, though, as I drive by here, about your girlfriend, and it hit me. You working here, it took me a while to realize it… you're trying to figure out what happened to her, aren't you?" Officer Dylan grins, but it doesn't make Hap feel as stupid or crazy as he thinks he sometimes is. Guy's less than a decade older than him, but Hap gets the impression he's being looked at as a little kid. "Well, you find anything?" Officer Dylan asks.

"I'm just…keeping my ears open." No, wait — doesn't the expression go keeping your eyes open? Hap immediately feels like an idiot.

Officer Dylan leans in, and Hap isn't sure if he should take a step back or not. "I've been having a hard time swallowing all of this, but I think there is something weird going on with the investigation, something I'm trying to figure out. I think you should come with me."

Hap feels a twinge of low-grade panic flow through his insides.

"I'm going to show you something, so we're on the same page, and I…. I wouldn't ask you to keep doing this, but since you are, maybe you can help me since you're kind of like a man on the inside?"

Hap's no expert in gauging the concern in someone's eyes, but for a cop, Dylan seems genuinely troubled. It's in his eyes, and it's backed by power, by an assurance. Officer Dylan might turn out to be Hap's savior.

"All right. Um, I'm working till one. Maybe tomorrow or if that's not too late…." Hap glances at Luke, who is still staring at him with his arms crossed, trying to figure out what's going on. The two valet boys, near identical with their buzzed black hair and broad shoulders, are staring off at the street like the silent, miserable bastards they are.

"You could come now. Your boss is Paul Jones, right? Leaving three hours early ain't bad on a Tuesday. He'll let you go if you ask him; mention your accident and how you have to follow up with me about your insurance information. I'll come in with you, if I have to, but...." Officer Dylan leans in once more, releasing a gust of coffee breath. "I'd rather leave my name out of this, so we should get going. Depending on what we're dealing with here, keeping our heads down would be smart, right?"

Hap agrees, trying not to sound too nervous or excited. What's the first thing he tells him? Maybe he'll leave the part about breaking into the Federal Hill home out of it, but the stuff with Augustine Sanfresco? That seven-pointed star spiral? Hap isn't going to have much to say, but maybe the cop can fill in these two blazing clues. Right now, Hap knows as much as Wikipedia, and the only search result he got for the star spiral was a crop circle from a UFO news story that looked exactly like it. Aliens, yeah, right.

"While you check out," Officer Dylan chuckles at his own pun, "I'm going to grab a coffee and park around the other side of the building. You want one?" Officer Dylan's turning toward his car, and Hap shakes his head. Coffee? He doesn't need the energy; he's amped up as it is.

Hap gets a "figured" out of Luke when he tells him his conversation with the cop is only about hitting the deer. Luke asks an additional question, but the sliding glass doors are already separating them.

Hap feels weird, suddenly being back in his clothes, his shorts, and a shirt featuring the band Sublime's sun logo that Tiff bought him. Hap already gave in to a night of work and misery, and now he has a partner. More than that, he might have a lead on Tiff. Shit, this changes everything. Hap slings a new Nike string bag over his back, loaded mainly with just his camera that he's wishing he used for more than just the Federal Hill house; if only it wouldn't raise suspicion if he took pictures while working.

A cop who might as well get his detective's badge is going to guide him right to her. They are going to find out what happened. There will be pictures, a front-page picture, and then somebody will learn about Hap's picture-taking skills, and he'll have a job. Tiff will be famous, and she'll write a memoir about the experience, and then they'll both be rich and living in Westerly, spending the rest of their lives staring out at the sea from a king-sized bed with silk sheets and a stash of secret chicken wing recipes. Tiffany has been missing for two months. Lifelong PTSD can occur from an event as short as fifteen minutes. Pretty dreams tell the ugliest lies.

Cassandra, eyeing Hap from the reception desk, asks if he's sick again. He tells her it's something much worse: he has to go refile a report at the police station because his car did damage to a building when it hit the deer, and he has to go prevent himself from getting sued. In fact, just as he's walking by her, he realizes he probably doesn't even have to face an awkward confrontation with the bleary-eyed Paul. Cassandra can just tell him, can't she? Hap asks the favor and walks away without waiting for much of a confirmation. He figures he's all set until he walks into Paul coming out of the coffee shop that's adjoined to the hotel with a large ice coffee clenched in his hand.

Hap skirts past Paul, seeing Officer Dylan's car through the shop's windows.

"Quitting on me?" Paul musters a smile. He really must be sick; his hair is growing long and turning grey. He seems thinner, too, particularly around his stubble-tattered cheekbones. A few days ago, Hap saw Paul come stumbling out of one of the guest rooms, looking as if he had ducked in to take a nap. His fly was down, and he greeted Hap with an awkward mutter that was half choked out by a burp while they both avoided eye contact and went their separate ways.

"I'm just, uh…," Hap explains himself.

Paul seems to wince for a second before crossing his arms

and shrugging. "Day off is a day off then, huh? Good luck." Paul, avoiding eye contact, takes a deep sigh, and his mouth seems to tremble for a moment as he brushes past Hap. That guy must be dying or getting a divorce or something.

Hap blanks out for a second when he gets to Dylan's car, wondering whether he should get into the back seat or not, but Dylan laughs, jerking a thumb over to his passenger seat. "No shit from the boss?" Dylan asks, turning down the local rock station. Hap shakes his head, adjusting his bag by his feet. He rejects another offer for coffee, giving a polite smile when Officer Dylan jokes about how, with this weather, you could easily go for both iced or hot coffee. When they pull away from the coffee shop and the night-swallowed shadow of the Miskatonic, Hap is not sure how to begin talking without asking too many questions.

"So what'd you find that's so weird?" Hap kills whatever comfortable pretense Dylan's trying to establish. He isn't a kid. He gets to the point and shows how serious he is.

"Better yet, what didn't I find, from the way the investigation was filed to the way it was recorded? It went straight to the papers like a vandalism job that nobody is going to bother following up on. The main guy assigned to the case had three other unrelated assignments lined up before and after your girlfriend went missing. It's like, uh, what's it called? I saw a *Twilight Zone* episode once where everybody keeps forgetting about this guy the second they turn their heads away from him; that's sort of like what has been going on. I'm showing you a house the investigator marked in his notes. It doesn't make any sense. I couldn't get ahold of him, but you'll see for yourself when we get there. You tell me if it makes any sense."

"I don't know anything. The Miskatonic is weird. It's connected. There's this symbol, this —"

Officer Dylan cuts him off. "It's good you're working there," Officer Dylan says as they pull onto the worst strip of highway in Providence, where four lanes merge onto one, making

Hap thankful he's not the one driving. Dylan's in control; it's buddy cop movie time. "That place is ground zero, right? Yeah, you'll be my inside man. You keep working there. This could all work out."

The orange glow of Providence's streetlights is taking over the sun's job once the hills of the horizon eat it up.

"One thing I'm thinking, though, is that these murders — you've heard about the murders, right? These start up right around the time she's gone. Four of 'em. That's about as much as Jack the Ripper now, isn't it? Your girlfriend disappears before the biggest, ugliest thing to hit Rhode Island since them hurricanes and the frigging Prohibition and King Philip's War."

"There's stuff; there's shit that just plain stinks of coincidence around here, like everything about the Miskatonic." Hap unintentionally gets Dylan to laugh, and Hap's face is going red. He can't go telling a cop the Miskatonic is his chief suspect because it's allegedly haunted. It being where Tiff was seen last should be good enough.

"Hate to tell you, but my theory is that maybe our guy works there. See, this lunatic's only taken out men so far, or at least we've only found the bodies of men. He's taking their eyes, see, maybe in some kind of perverted way. I don't want this to be true, I don't, but wouldn't it fit if this nut has something to do with women too? You're right about the coincidence, though. We're going to figure this out."

Dylan, who must not be on active duty, rubs a finger over his GPS monitor, turning the screen off as they take an exit into North Providence, a more residential area than the rest of the city. It still has its share of fun restaurants and a big craft beer store called Nicki's that all the hipster kids are always gushing about.

"Wait till you see what's in this place. Then we play ball, come up with a plan, okay?"

Officer Dylan's driving them through a dizzying nexus

of neighborhoods. The streets are full of potholes like there's a meteor shower that has been eating away at the foundations of society. Hap's sense of direction soon becomes scrambled. He catches the sloppy graffiti word "purity" in white on a stop sign, and its meaning could be infinite.

There's a fence around the crumbling brick building Officer Dylan brings him to. The place is claimed by a forest of weeds. The closest streetlight is the block over, only serving to soak the ruins in more shadow. Officer Dylan gets to use a cool and sleek, high-powered flashlight. He gives Hap a dorky, battery-operated lantern. Dylan puts his hand on his belt, sliding his palm over his holster as he casts a look Hap's way. "Stay behind me. Hopefully, nobody's in here that we have to worry about."

"Are these the projects?" Hap asks.

"You're a country kid, huh? Projects are government housing, usually big buildings that look like crappy apartments, which they basically are. People care about the projects, believe it or not. Nobody cares about this place. Junkies aren't known for their sentiment, though."

There's graffiti scattered over the ruins. There are no seven-pointed spiraling stars, just the typical, random squiggles. The front door has a sprawling mess of yellow rippling across it like a welcome sign for decrepitude.

There's a squeal of tires somewhere in the distance as Officer Dylan cautiously pushes inside the abandoned home, or whatever it once was. A heavy silence clings to the ruined street. Would even a homeless person stay somewhere like this? How does a place on the edge of the city get this empty?

"So, what's in here?" Hap follows Dylan into a stuffy hallway. This was some kind of business. Something smells horrible, like piss and maybe sour milk. It's always hard to place a smell. Hap holds his lantern by his side just so he doesn't step on anything foul. Dylan's light is good enough to peel back the majority of shadows in their way. There's some kind of waiting room with a cluster of metal chairs hugging the walls. A random poster of a family of four playing with a dog in the grass probably means it was some kind of veterinary clinic.

"Take a look at this, and you tell me."

Dylan pulls on a door that's slightly stuck, and the sudden eruption of sound it makes gets Hap's heart pumping. If Dylan weren't here with a gun and a uniform—well, how did Hap manage to explore that empty house on the hill at night alone? That primitive childhood fear of the dark and leering closets and hallway corners is reborn here. Alcohol and anger are more useful than Hap ever imagined.

Hap follows where Dylan's pointing his flashlight; it's some kind of wide, open room with tiled walls, scattered tables, and what looks like a refrigerator tucked into a corner. Front and center is a hole in the cement floor—a private root cellar, from before this place was a vet clinic. Or does it lead to some kind of tunnel?

Hap leers over the open, square hole. It's only a couple of feet deep, but there is a thick stink coming from within. Heavy and wet, almost like low tide, but more particular. Is this what rot smells like? There's dirt below, framing a white something. A piece of paper, a picture. He kneels down, tilting his head and the lantern over the hole. The picture becomes clear. Tiffany's face, a selfie from her Facebook profile. Somebody printed it out on a printer running out of ink, and…the skin on the back of Hap's neck prickles as he becomes aware of Officer Dylan standing over him.

Hap glances to his left, and in the shadow of the flashlight, there is a stick, an arm—no, a gun, pointing at him while he kneels. Hap can't stop himself from trembling.

"What are you...?" If Hap turns around now, he'll look down the barrel of a gun, and then there will be a flash. Maybe the sensation of the bullet entering his head will only be a distant throb. Hap raises his hands in the air and turns his head slightly, just so he can see Officer Dylan's shoes and the stance he's in, with both hands forming over the weapon now. There is a gun, a *gun,* pointed at him. The tears run rampant down Hap's cheeks, dripping into the hole in the ground.

"It's all right. You see her down there? She's as good as dead. Them, uh, them people? You're their first mistake, ever. I've never had to do this before. They're so in control. It's always so neat, and this is fucking me up. They're supposed to be neat; they've always been so neat. What if they kill my wife? I want you to know...." Officer Dylan's getting choked up. He won't do it...he can't.

"Please...please, look. We're on the same side. We...." Hap is finding it difficult to talk. His mouth is trembling too much, and he might just bite off his own tongue.

"You're saving her. You're saving a woman, my woman. Think of it like that, like it makes up for your girl, yeah?" Officer Dylan says. Hap somehow tunes into it: the electricity that he never knew percolated in the air before a murder.

Something metallic skitters along a wall, followed by the solid clop of a shoe striking concrete. Hap turns, mirroring Officer Dylan, who's turning to look over his own shoulder, his gun clenched in one hand. Before Hap can even comprehend the gun that was just aimed at him, he realizes there is someone else in the room. There's a flash of a thick beard and crazed eyes before the tall and skinny intruder collides with Officer Dylan. In the twirling artificial light, the two men begin to fumble for control of the gun.

A stray foot from the writhing mess of colliding men strikes Hap in the ribs, and he's falling, tumbling into the hatch as his lantern rolls away on the floor above. Falling head first, the side of Hap's face scrunches into the dirt. Amidst thrashing on the floor and the grunts of wild animals with their existence at stake, Hap twists and rights himself out of the hole. His foot strikes against something plastic and soft. There's a black bag and the rough impression of a motionless somebody inside. The corpse is heavyset — it's not Tiff. The lights being kicked from above reveal a couple of other bagged bodies in the shadow. Plunged back into the dark, Hap stretches to free himself from the crawl space.

A rolling flashlight and the kicked over lamp give life to a tall man climbing on top of Officer Dylan. There's a gleaming knife in the intruder's hands. The gun's nowhere in sight as Hap pulls himself from the crawlspace in time to see the knife's blade sink down into Officer Dylan's chest. What follows is a spastic frenzy, as that dark knife is thrust in and out of the wailing cop's stomach before his cries gurgle off. There is only one way out of here, and Hap ignores his throbbing ankle as he rushes toward the open doorway. A hand latches around that same ankle, and he falls, cracking his chin against the cement as pain and blood flood his mouth.

Hap's rolled onto his back; the tall man crawls over him, straddling Hap's waist with a gleaming sharp something clenched in a fist. A hand grabs Hap's throbbing jaw. He whines and tries to thrash out with his hands, but the gaunt and bearded face is thrust into his as the man leans over him. His beard is patchy and uneven in spots. He jabs fingers into Hap's face and pulls his eyelids open, one after another before he twists Hap's head left and right, looking him over before lightly smacking the side of his face with the broad side of the sticky, warm knife. The killer makes a sucking sound with his teeth. "You run along now, my little mad Arab. I'll catch up. His friends will be coming." The broad side of the knife smacks against Hap's cheek once more, and a drop of blood stings his eye. The tall man clambers off him and hunches back over Officer Dylan's corpse. Hap's clawing at his cheeks, trying to clear his face of Dylan's blood, wondering about that body in a bag at the bottom of that crawlspace. Was that going to be him? Tiff wasn't down there.

In the hallway, Hap trips over another corpse. The killer was disturbed while hiding another body. From the vague outline,

Hap can tell that it's a woman, and through the pale glow of the streetlights outside, he can see that while roughly as tall as Tiff, the dead woman has black hair and is skinnier, more bone than flesh; in this moment where he really should be running, that's good enough for Hap. *Not her.* He checks the corpse off his list without a second thought.

Outside he passes by the familiar stop sign with *purity* painted over its command, and he's picking a direction and running, despite the burning in his lungs. He can just barely see the downtown lights from here.

He's made it. Nobody's chasing him. Does he call the cops? Yes, that's what they tell you, right? Hap pulls out his cell phone, perking his ears up at distant sirens from the direction he just left. Hap remembers the brief squawk of Officer Dylan's walkie-talkie. He was showing Hap bodies and a picture. He was showing him something any other sane cop would have reported to a hundred other people before showing some college kid. Hap really was going to get shot in the back of the head in that empty clinic on that lonely street.

He runs through a more residential neighborhood. Though the houses are still in various states of disarray, there is still a sense of life here. TVs flicker beyond curtainless front windows, and porch lights illuminate children's bikes and beat-up family cars. Hap probably still has blood all over his face. The sound of an approaching car doesn't quite register in Hap's head before he turns around and sees that it has no headlights on. An old Cadillac, piloted by the tall man.

Long-limbed, his face is even more ghoulish under the streetlight, and his hair is short, despite his beard. In spite of his visage, there is a semblance of upkeep to him, even with his unbuttoned shirt exposing his bare, tattoo-scrawled chest. Hap barely registers a "No, wait, hey," before he's grabbed and hauled away from the closest home with a familiar glowing TV shimmering in a living room. Faces are pressing up against the glass of the house, children's faces, with eyes growing wide, as the boogey man drags Hap kicking and screaming to his car. Hap's phone slips from his hands as he's thrown against an unforgiving metal door, and the mad murderer stomps his foot down, extinguishing the glow of his Apple product with a simplistic popping as plastic and glass meet the heel of a boot.

Hap is knocked to the asphalt by the swinging passenger door. Before he can catch his bearings, his hands are clicking together behind his back. Did the tall man steal Officer Dylan's cuffs? Hap is rolled over onto his back, and that same knife, wiped clean this time and smelling of rubbing alcohol, is under Hap's chin. On the tall man's wrist, there is the strangest tattoo of a black vertical line with three slashes across the top and two across the bottom, almost resembling a tree branch or the stems of a leaf.

"I cut you open, will stars pour outta you?" The killer asks. It sounds like an honest question.

"No, no," Hap shakes his head, playing along with the madness as the tall man picks him up by the front of his Sublime shirt, and he's thin but strong, aided by his height and weight. He's so strong that he tosses Hap effortlessly into the front seat of his car. It's a Cadillac; Hap recognizes the logo on the dash. Miraculously, that knife hasn't entered his throat.

"Poor boy in blue." The tall man climbs into his seat and immediately grabs Hap by the neck and pulls him toward his lap, holding his head by the gearshift. The knife is against his throat, lightly, as the man's grip loosens and the car rumbles to life as they pull away, and the Caddie's opening up, doubling the speed limit. "Stay still now, 'til I know whether to open you up or not."

"Please, I—" Hap begins.

"Police won't be a bother. They're going to help me figure you. If they look for a mad Arab, I'll know what they think of you. Moon Shack has so few children, but you're old enough. You call it home, the Moon Shack?" The tall man's voice is cracking as if he doesn't talk much. Is this the killer, The Eye Doctor? Is he going to take Hap's eyes?

"No, I don't. I don't understand what you mean." Hap's legs are cramping, pressing against the passenger door, and he can't kick or cause a scene. He could try and lash out and hit the gearshift, but how would that save his neck?

"No, no, they all say. No Moon Shack. No faith, no home, no Else. No, just them, just they hobbies, they own private killins'. So I ask, why so many? Why so many of them here, but no Moon Shack? That's when they cryin', if they can, and I see what they see, and then they see no more. Cop got a gun to you. I think, very odd that they hurt they own, but I can't be sure about you."

"Look, I.... Look...." Hap realizes that he's babbling and on the brink of spouting more of it. There is only one fact that sums him up. "They took my girlfriend," he says clearly. "From the Miskatonic." Is there a "they" that eye doctor is not a part of? The tall man starts chuckling, which soon swells into deep, goon-like laughter. Then there's silence, and to keep talking probably isn't best.

Officer Dylan mentioned he had a wife. Did she know what he was? Is she even real? Oh god, Dylan had a gun to his head...now Hap is with the man who put a knife through that cop's throat.

The moans of passing cars tell Hap they are still on the highway, leaving Providence. Abruptly, the blade is swept from Hap's throat. There's a strange moment when he keeps his head pressed against the center console, near the man's stinking legs. After several minutes, Hap cautiously sits up just as the tall man takes an exit that leads to the small suburbia of Johnston. The man's sunken eyes are unblinking against the road.

"They took my mother." The killer reemerges from his sunken thoughts to snarl as his Cadillac blows through a street loaded with gas stations and fast food joints. They are heading toward the woods.

CHAPTER 11
THE DAMNED ONE

Paul stretches his arms along the back of the bench as he looks up at the statue of Roger Williams. From where he's sitting, a waning moon is perfectly aligned with the top of Williams's head, where he stands on his perch overlooking his city. The moment he wonders if such an alignment is a coincidence, the sleek blade of a knife presses to his throat. The Eye Doctor has found him.

A numbness forms in Paul's chest as the tip of the blade prods his Adam's apple. He wonders if he'll get any last words in before his throat is opened up over the nice collared shirt Johan asked him to wear. It was the first time Johan had ever asked him to dress nice, and go figure, Paul was curious as hell as to why that was.

The knife is whisked away, and someone, the slender skull of a woman, tucks her chin against his shoulder, her mouth hovering near his neck. "My teeth are just as deadly as the knife," Lacy whispers. Paul pops into nervous laughter that she immediately mimics, swinging around the bench to sit beside him.

"Johan sent you to spy on me?" Paul asks as Lacy snuggles in a little bit closer.

"No, I'm not the one following you tonight," she says in such a way that Paul turns to glance for anybody lurking along the shadowy street behind the park, but if Candle Lighters exist there, they are well hidden.

"Don't see why he asked me to meet him here," Paul says, and Lacy shrugs, putting her head on his shoulder.

"Beats me. All I know is I wasn't invited. I heard things have been tough lately at the hotel. With the killings. S'what inspired me," Lacy says, her jeans are tight around her long legs. She doesn't look like she has a knife hidden on her. Paul pities the mugger that sets upon her on a night like this.

"What if I had a gun?" Paul asks, and Lacy laughs, staring longingly at the moon above Roger's head.

"You wouldn't. They chose you because you're not the type. Which is funny. Never thought I was the type," Lacy says.

He's seen her half a dozen times since that night at the Palace of the Komodo in Westerly, and always, she seems more like some silly young girl than a member of the cult. Johan said it was her job to make him comfortable. If he was right about that, then maybe he was right about Paul being somebody important. There had to be truth to that, right?

"You ever worry that you're being used?" Paul asks.

"It's not something worth worrying about. You went to law school. Was that your dad's idea before it was yours? I guess, like his suggestion?"

"Yeah, he made it clear. It was all his idea," Paul says, though he never minded it. He liked his dad telling him how successful he was going to be. Come to think of it, Johan was the first person since his dad to make him feel like he could accomplish anything. And to be honest, Paul doesn't feel any of that same warm fuzziness for Johan that he felt for his dad, so that really is saying something.

"We're all used a little bit. Some people want us to be something because of how it makes them feel. A politician, a doctor, a wife. Everybody you ever meet winds up wanting to make a plan for you."

"And what's your plan for me?" Paul asks, on the verge

of flirting but feeling no pressure to cross that line. It seems unthinkable, but Lacy is more of a friend than any woman he's ever known, even if he still can't keep his eyes off her humble curves.

"To make you comfortable," Lacy says, Johan's words coming out of her mouth. "I heard about…." She blanks out, trying to remember something. "That bellhop," she finally adds. That was exactly what Paul didn't want to think about. He still has no idea what Hap really did. Was he really a threat all along, right under Paul's nose? Is Johan pissed at Paul now? Maybe he had him wearing a nice shirt because he's going to some kind of candle lighter trial.

"From what Johan told me, this kid seems to have had issues letting go, the poor thing. He was working for…you know." Lacy runs her finger across her throat.

"He didn't seem like the type to be…well, anything. Johan told me this kid's girlfriend was missing." That's what he called Hap: "the kid," as if he wasn't anything else. And maybe he wasn't.

"She probably didn't know how to break up with him if he was that clingy. There's a very fine reason why you won't ever catch me dating anyone," Lacy places her hand on Paul's arm, and before he can say something cutesy back to her, a car rolls to a stop right behind them. *Johan.*

A door clicks open, and nobody has to call to him. Paul knows. Lacy pecks him on the cheek, and he leaves her sitting alone in Prospect Terrace, watching the moon and the stars. She'll be fine, he reasons to himself. She's likely one of the most dangerous people in this city.

***

"Augustine Francesco," Johan says a few minutes later as their drive brings them through Westminster street downtown. He lifts a fried octopus roll of sushi to his lips with a pair of chopsticks, and the meat crunches between his teeth as a tentacle dangles over his lips before he sucks it back in. Paul doesn't question him eating sushi off a china plate. He wouldn't be surprised if the limo previously stopped at the Japanese place on the hill, and a chef ran out to personally hand the meal to Johan on their finest dining plate. That kind of thing seems to happen to Johan a lot around Providence.

When Paul first started working at the Miskatonic, he met a woman seemingly obsessed with the color purple right down to her bra and panties. She called the front desk asking for him personally to come to her room, and while the front desk girls were too new at the time to joke with him about what was going to happen, they would've been right to. Augustine Franceso bent the world to her whim, and she chewed Paul up like he was a five-dollar piece of ass looking for a fix. It's no wonder then that during the limo ride from Paul's apartment Johan casually mentions that the reason they're going to an exclusive art gallery at one in the morning is to meet a single woman in particular.

"She was your final test," Johan said, and as with the sushi, Paul wasn't surprised to find that she was in on everything. He'd suspected it after she tempted the boy, Hap. He shuts his eyes and tries to ignore the sudden guilt that threatens to crawl up through his chest. Poor kid should've gotten laid when he had the chance.

The limo swishes them down a wordless curve of familiar streets. Paul can't keep track of all the hidden rooms and buildings Johan has shown him. There is a city between the city, just as there is a voice in everyone's head.

The gallery is in the attic in one of the historical preservation buildings on Broadway. A moldering back staircase, seemingly unfit for Paul's new status, brings them up to a moth-eaten studio of cruel artificial light that gives energy to a collection of strange masks on the walls.

There are masks of skulls, demons, and otherwise deformed things in between; the shrouding face templates are carved in everything from wood to obsidian. Masks are as big as doors and as small and eerie as doll faces. Before every mask is a lit candle atop a stool; throughout the gallery, the sound of an eerie violin continues to play. It seems to cling to every face on the wall, vaguely reminiscent of the haunting moans from the downtown water fire festivals.

Johan's immediately embracing a man in a tuxedo Paul doesn't quite recognize. It takes him a moment to realize that the little over a dozen people who are perusing the gallery are all Candle Lighters.

Paul recognizes an old man with buzzed hair as Taylor McKinley from the feast at the Komodo. Taylor's rubbing a hand over an expressionless mass of golden sparkles that carries a Middle-Eastern vibe. Paul turns to admire an old mask, more artifact than presentation; maybe that's its charm, something new that looks old. It's a grinning faceplate of yellowed cloth with miscellaneous cracks teetering from its eyeholes.

"My son, William, was the theatrical sort. He never could control himself, you see. Family ought to stick together; I regret leaving; consider your father." Paul turns to face the man he thought was blind, Elliot Sampson, who is still wearing his black shutter glasses, though Paul swears he took them off in the moonlight before joining the ceremony at the beach. When Paul embraced the soaking man after he rose from the sea, Elliot looked him in his eyes and smiled. Perhaps he only has an aversion to the light. Now, Elliot's being guided. He's holding onto the arm of another familiar candle lighter, the blood-drenched-boy from the basement whose name Paul can't remember.

"Mr. Jones?"

The boy, with a faint Southern accent, immediately moves away from Elliot. There's a hierarchy that comes with whom Paul will allow himself to forget first, and if he's drunk, everybody's an exception save the pope, but it feels like there's a hole growing in his brain. Paul can't put a label on the kid, and this isn't the first time he's forgotten somebody recently; the few skills he has are fading.

"Derrick Woodbury, sir," the boy says with the humble conviction that he hasn't introduced himself before. So Paul goes along with it, shaking his hand and telling Derrick that he remembers him.

Elliot, that rich Rhode Islander Paul still can't believe he's never heard of, smiles in Paul's direction, and perhaps the reason why the blind wear glasses is so that others feel their stare like it's a hungry thing sniffing out recognition.

"Which one is your favorite?" Derrick asks Paul about the masks. He sounds giddy as if each mask is a miniature carnival of hidden delights and wonders.

Paul shrugs. "I could hardly pick." He smiles, and he doesn't have to try and be likable, does he? He doesn't have to bullshit. He doesn't have to play any games. He has what these people respect, if only he knew exactly what that was.

Paul had recently given a motivational speech at the University of Rhode Island. He didn't write it or know he was attending until the day before when Johan and Lacy invited themselves into his apartment and laid out an agenda. There was no mention of the Moon Shack or the killer carving out eyeballs, and the next thing Paul knew, a Miskatonic limo delivered him to where he gave a speech to a few thousand kids. He gave a rousing monologue about unity, becoming a part of your community, and not standing alone, not trying to do it all on your own. The whole event was a callback to his rally days, and later that night, Johan asked Paul to give that very same speech to a different crowd gathered in the Miskatonic's ballroom. Who starts the applause?

"Well, which one would you want to wear? Me, I like the one sorta like a mirror: that one," Derrick says. Paul follows Derrick's pointed finger to a circular, plate-like mask of diamond. "If that caught in the midday sun, it'd be blinding, like my head was a star. Imagine seeing that run at you!" Derrick shudders with a grin that's too wide. When somebody tugs on Paul's shoulder, he's all too happy to turn away from the overeager cat killer.

The face of a cow, some kind of horned buffalo with brown fur, presses against Paul, its maw meeting his lips as he tries to jump back. Wicked laughter shrieks from the beast's throat as a slender pair of arms surrounds his neck. Augustine slinks off the mask, the red of her dress catching the light of the many candles consuming the room. "I couldn't resist," she says to the applause of Derrick's laughter. Elliot taps Derrick's shoulder, and the boy quiets and nods at Paul before helping the old man continue on with the exhibit. Paul focuses on Augustine's lips and the way such simple things can take on a different identity in different shades of light.

She hails from Los Angeles, but she runs fashion events all over the country. They met once before after she hosted an event at the Miskatonic. Paul imagines Augustine has men like him in every major city. She reels in whatever New England celebrities happen to be around, and while they don't stay at the Miskatonic, they still set the staff aflutter with excitement.

Augustine's hand reaches up to trace across Paul's face. "Silly little boy, you are the only one I know who doesn't need a mask," she says with such awkward passion as if Paul doesn't really know that the only reason an honest woman is interested in him is because of his words and promises. Augustine is scattered and strange. The last (and first) time they spoke, they avoided talk of fashion, models, and her business, unlike every other entrepreneur Paul has met. She is amorphous to the point of being unidentifiable. Yet just one purr from her throat, and he feels as though he's connected to the threads between everything she tells him. He tries to ignore the idea of her seducing Hap. The poor bastard. Now he's likely a corpse somewhere who didn't so much as get to dip his wick one last time.

"Johan's too polite to ask you something." Augustine's holding the side of Paul's face with slender, pale fingers. Her skin is smooth, unlike the other women of the Moon Shack, with their coarse and calloused hands. "I'm moving to Providence. He wants there to be a new power couple, as in you and me." The void returns, so Paul steps outside of himself, outside of the moment and the nonsense he's being told. "Nothing has to change, aside from us doing the rounds and letting people see us together. You can still keep your apartment and any bed warmers I'm sure you have." Her fingers trail along the side of his face. He'll say "yes" no matter how crazy the proposition, and it wouldn't be for her but for the others, for the people who are looking at him in a way he's never been looked at before. He and Augustine, what, married? Well, maybe that's the right kind of politics.

"So you want me to buy you a ring?" Not for the first time, Paul, mostly sober, feels as though he's completely drunk.

Augustine chuckles. "I'll buy myself one. You don't know what power the right stone can bring." It still feels like a sudden joke, a wedding ruse with a woman he doesn't know.

"Augustine." Johan's breaking the dizzying aura of obedience clouding Paul's judgment. "I brought Paul here to admire D'angelo's cosmetic work. You were supposed to save your little announcement for later." The man in the tuxedo has what looks like a snake or serpent tattooed on his cheek, seeming to drip from an eye. He's helping the old Taylor McKinley try on a mouthless mask of bamboo with eerie eyeholes no more than slits.

"Look at him; he's happy to go along with it." Augustine's hand on Paul's chest gives him the sudden realization that, if this actually happens, then she'll technically be wife number three.

A startling yet simple ringing noise blares from Johan, and it is the twenty-first century; of course, he has a cellphone, but still, Paul has a hard time picturing Johan owning one. The priest of the Moon Shack lifts the thing to his ear, and his eyes seem to bulge. Johan, while speaking into his little plastic box, seems to lose the carefully practiced composure he must constantly force himself to display to Paul and the others. His face seems to grow wider; his shoulders bristle; for a moment, he seems younger, as energetic as Derrick.

Johan mutters, turning his head away as Augustine's hand rubs along Paul's arm. "Whoever thought people like you and me could be so important?" She's smiling up at him.

Johan claps the phone shut and then folds his hands behind his back, looking first to Britt and then casting a single eye over Paul as his face settles back into that of the warm old priest. He stares ahead at a woodcarving. "I knew you would fall in love with each other."

Something starts skipping erratically in Paul's chest, but Augustine doesn't flinch as she leans against him. Paul feels dizzy, but both Augustine and Johan place their hands to him, keeping him on his feet. The silent gallery curator brings him a glass of wine. Before he can realize what's happening, everybody tears away from the mask they're admiring and joins together in a toast to Paul. There are too many smiles, but Paul joins them anyway. The room spins and spins; the masks are really faces and the faces, masks.

CHAPTER 12
THE ALPHABET CHART

When Hap asks if the handcuffs can come off, the man who can only be the serial killer the Providence Journal dubbed the "Eye Doctor" shakes his head. "Not without trust and the right angle of force," the doctor snorts to himself. A bump in the dirt road nearly sends Hap's head into the dashboard. "No key, anyhow," the man says, followed by what could be either a chuckle or a moan.

Streetlights become scarce as they drive further into the woods. With the knife removed from his throat, Hap becomes bold enough to ask the man who he is.

"I have a doctorate, you believe the news. Hah." The Eye Doctor speaks slowly as if English is his second language. The faint glow from the headlights causes his crooked teeth to form shadows that drip into fangs. "Mad Arab," The Eye Doctor, who may very well be a racist, muses to himself. A streetlight finally beams in the distance, but its glow is severed as the car turns, bumping down another dirt road where only blackness awaits.

Moments ago, they drove through a small, dead town called Scituate that Hap wants to say is familiar, though he can't quite recall if he ever passed through it with Tiff. Perhaps for a Memorial Day festival? The little post office, church, gas station, and fire station were consumed by small-town charm. Hap almost felt safe till he acknowledged the handcuffs shackling his wrists. The New England stone walls, lining property lines from the 1800s, are the biggest difference between here and the sticks of Pennsylvania. This whole woodsy countryside was once flat farmland.

The car twists once more before the tall man pulls into the short gravel driveway of a single-story home with peeling paint and black windows that remind Hap of the haunted house on Federal Hill. Oddly, there's a candy cane Christmas decoration glowing in the front window.

The Eye Doctor kills the ignition and leaps out of the car, crunch-crunching on the gravel over to Hap's side. He's hauled out of his seat and tossed onto the gravel as The Eye Doctor pats his handcuffed wrists behind his back. Hap looks up, trying to avoid gravel going up his nose. The stars out here, funneling along the Milky Way, would be breathtaking under different circumstances. The Eye Doctor trots toward the house, creaking up a front stoop. Immediately, a lamp beside the front door comes to life, and the tall man claps giddily before dragging Hap into his lair.

The house stinks worse than piss, and it's dusty, but it's a home — small, but arguably livelier than Hap's current apartment. Christmas lights hang dead along the walls. In the corner of a living room inhabited by a couch full of wool blankets and a coffee table stacked with junk, there stands an artificial Christmas tree with a toy train track encircling it. More than junk, the coffee table is cluttered with books, scraps of paper, and what look like stacks of loose-leaf filled with crude handwriting and drawings, all of which is weighed down by several knives and a hammer. The Eye Doctor ushers Hap toward the couch.

"Tell me about your girl." The Eye Doctor has his knife out as Hap takes a seat. There are knives on the coffee table. These potentially deadly weapons are closer to him than to the tall man, but considering how shit Hap's luck has been, it's useless to make a move for them.

The Eye Doctor's eyes are more sunken than Hap could

make out in the night's shadows, and his beard is even more mismatched than it first appeared. The killer reaches up to his face and tugs at his beard, explaining the patches along his jaw. This neurotic tic seems to confirm Hap's worst fears about this guy's sanity.

"My girlfriend," Hap says, "Tiffany, she disappeared at the Miskatonic hotel where she was working. Nobody's done anything."

"Was she cleaning? A maid?" The Eye Doctor asks. There's a small kitchen table near a stove and a sink just behind the living room. The Eye Doctor pulls over a chair, sits in it backwards, and rests his beard on his arms. His pupils are massive in the light; is he doped up on something?

"No, just working an event," Hap says.

"School girl?" Otis asks.

"Yeah, we were about to grad—"

The tall man flings the chair into the coffee table, scattering papers and tools. He points his knife directly at Hap.

"I'm stupid? American school girl? Nah, not them. They're not stupid, and I'm not stupid. They chose you wrong, little lyin' killer." The Eye Doctor pulls Hap up by his hair, exposing his throat to the awaiting blade.

"They took her, and she's gone!" Hap pleads. "Where is she?" he yells, as the killer begins to dig the knife into his throat.

"In your lies!" The Eye Doctor screams into Hap's ear loud enough to leave behind a faint ringing.

"Did you kill her? You fucking animal, you piece of shit murderer!" Hap's throat stings. He'd do anything to make this man hurt and cry and moan and beg. He's tossed back against the couch, his hands immediately rising to his throat, feeling for a massive slit that turns out to only be a scratch. The Eye Doctor tilts his head and screams into the ceiling, kicking a knife on the floor across the room and into the Christmas tree.

"The Moon Shack is for man. I can't trust man. I can't

trust you!" The Eye Doctor points the knife at Hap, causing him to cower into the couch. The Eye Doctor lowers his weapon, pressing the blade to his lips as his sunken eyes narrow.

"What is the Moon Shack?" Hap sobs.

"Harbor." The Eye Doctor rushes to Hap's side and leans over him, the knife arced down, ready to stab. "For killers who slaughter out of desire."

"Like you?" Hap doesn't understand. Didn't this guy just confess to being The Eye Doctor killer in the car? The tall man howls and throws his knife against a wall, grabs Hap by the ankle, and pulls him across the couch, bashing a fist against his eye, once, twice; Hap can't stop sobbing in chest-tightening gasps. This lunatic is going to kill him.

"It calls to me when I shut my eyes. I don't sleep without the dream. The door's opening for me as I walk without wantin' to walk. One day, I will wake and find it to be real. One day I may stop running, the dream shack. I'll turn around and head inside. You don't know about the Moon Shack? Your hands are spotless, bloodless. You want to know what's inside?" Hap doesn't respond. His tears make the throbbing spots along his cheekbone and forehead worse. "It's full of burning stars, and they talk and tell you about the moon and how bright she is, how she lets the dark in, like a door. The dream speaks for it. Other men, with my knife to their head, they tell me elsewise. They tell me inside is one big party for blood spillers. Well, the party's gonna end soon. I'm gonna burn it down." The Eye Doctor's voice grows distant. He's back on his feet, moving toward the kitchen. Hap wipes his face along the couch before sitting up. His eyes feel like they're swelling shut. He's starting to get used to maneuvering with handcuffs behind his back.

The killer pulls open the fridge, taking out a slice of cake on a plate and an unlabeled bottle of what appears to be Dirty Look brand whiskey with the label scraped off. Above the refrigerator door, a black ceramic cat sits perched, watching over the kitchen.

The Eye Doctor returns to Hap and places the food and drink on the opposite corner of the couch before righting the coffee table, kicking at some papers scattered across the floor. "I can't trust no one. You no killer, though. They have some who are clean from blood-spill, but not treachery. You a boy; how old?"

"Twenty-two," Hap says with hesitation. His face had only just started feeling better after the incident with the deer a couple of days ago.

"Young, not a puppeteer. Just a mad Arab. Eat. You have seen nothing worth taking. You live."

Does that mean the interrogation is over? The Eye Doctor gestures toward the paltry meal. The cake looks new, store bought. Even if his hands weren't still bound behind his back, Hap doesn't think he could stomach anything.

The Eye Doctor looks away for a moment before turning back to Hap. He tugs at his beard and says, "My name is Otis Lusk."

"My hands are still cuffed," Hap shrugs. Immediately, Otis runs out of the house, leaving the front door open behind him. Hap hears a garage door being heaved open with a metallic whine, and a second later, Otis returns with a pair of bolt cutters. Hap tells Otis his name before the clippers dig under the bracelet around his wrist.

Otis pauses, lifting his stinking beard to Hap's face. "Hap? Shit happens? Are you a joke?" The serial killer who takes people's eyes laughs and snips Hap's other handcuff off. "Call ya self Shit Happens, the mad Arab."

"I'm actually Indian." Hap instantly regrets his mocking tone, but for Christ's sake, the kind of racist, kind of joking around kids at his old high school weren't half as bad. Otis pays no mind as he repositions the kitchen chair, heads past the massive 90s-style television opposite the Christmas tree, and rights the coffee table. Then he kicks his boots off, scattering more scrawled papers across the floor as he reveals horribly rancid feet with overgrown toenails.

"When did you last see the girl?"

"Almost two months ago." Hap doesn't mention that it's been exactly fifty-four days because he's been trying to forget the exact number every morning he wakes up. Otis pushes the liquor bottle Hap's way, and Hap shakes his head.

"It's raw then. When they've taken from you, that's when you start hearing things. The old things, whispering. Telling you what the world is really about. You from India?" Otis asks.

"I'm from Pennsylvania," Hap says.

Otis snorts. "No goddess Kali of death? Hah. No vengeance for girl? You're playing Miskatonic boy, snooping around. You know anything?"

It's hard to follow the way Otis talks, but Hap is getting the gist of it. He mentioned his mother and Hap shouldn't bring that up if only to avoid getting beaten again. How did she disappear? How long ago? He needs to be careful. "The cops are in on it?" Hap asks.

"Everybody they need is theirs. Providence is infested worse than most cities, and I have been to many: Athens, Cairo, Orleans; nothing on Providence. Boy in blue tonight? They make him do anything long as he has people he loving, whether he wants to or not. Sooner or later, Moon Shack will call and if he answers? Stops a heartbeat? They grow."

"The Moon Shack." Hap tries the name out loud. It doesn't sound that threatening. Whatever Otis has been through has fucked him up in the head. Nothing he says is clear. "What's it have to do with the Miskatonic? Is the Shack the Miskatonic, like a code?"

Otis's first reply is a snort.

"Hotel is a temple for a handmade god, out with the old, in with the new. Citizens Under New Testament, they like sayin' they is. Cunts, I reply." Otis's laughter is rich and full, pouring from the center of his belly, and this goes on until he unscrews the bottle sloppily with his palm, ushering in a silence save for his gulps. When he's finished, he holds the bottle Hap's way, and Hap again refuses. The booze is one thing, but where would a man like this get a chocolate cake? It looks good but, no, now is not the time for food. Otis could still slit his throat at any moment.

"You live here alone?" Hap asks.

"Me and mother's footsteps you hear go creek-creek time to time when her spirit remembers me." Otis leans forward, plopping the bottle onto the counter as his eyes grow wide, filling the sunken depths of his skull. He's looking beyond Hap, his eyes flickering to the corners of the room. "Her voice echoes from right here time to time when I lie in bed. I smell her cookings, too." He's losing it again; the knives are still too close to his reach on the floor. What's the right question to snap Otis out of it?

"Never too early for Christmas, huh?" Hap says, and Otis chuckles; score. Making a cop laugh is easy, however crooked that poor rotten bastard turned out to be, but this lunatic? How can Hap get Otis to like him enough not to murder him? Otis's laugh becomes a lonesome wail as he tilts his head to the ceiling and howls.

Hand shaking as he tugs at his beard, Otis says, "Was supposed to take them down together, after New Year's." He's getting more emotional, more dangerous. "I'm told she wasn't there, making beds that night. She called out sick, they say. But I say, where her uniform? Why she take her uniform? All I had was talk of spirits in my memory and one little clue." Otis shrugs and bends over to pick up something. Hap is shrinking back into the couch, eyeing the door. Can he make it? Can he outrun this fuck?

Otis has his fists full of the scrawled up notebook paper, and he's dropping to a knee, frantically scooping up the scraps from the ground. "I was more boy than you when they locked me up the Butler." Otis giggles. Butler is a mental hospital in Providence that Tiffany told him one of her high school friends had visited while battling an eating disorder. "Uncle eventually helped. All he ever did." Otis looks up from his paper gathering and bites his lip, staring out the window. From elsewhere in the summer night, a motorcycle rumbles down a lonely back road. "I go everywhere, and I study. Everywhere. Hot, cold, boggy, I learn their words on other continents, forget our own." Otis giggles and stacks his mess of papers up on the coffee table, pushing them toward Hap. "Still hard to remember words, know too many. Some things I think in Arabic, others Greek. Latin, always in my ears. English speaking not meant for things unknown."

The papers are snatched away from Hap before he can make out the scribbles, which are at least orderly enough to stay in between the lines. Why would Otis rip these out of an organized notebook? Otis thumbs through his "notes" and then smacks down something too familiar for Hap to digest. A drawing of the seven-pointed star and its spiral of descending celestial circles. Beneath, mostly legible is the word *crops*, followed by little arrows to *Wiltshire, Eng. Donabree, Braz. California* and an assortment of other names of what must be places. Crops as in corn?

"I've seen that three times now. All over Providence." Hap sneers at the symbol, looking up to Otis. The Eye Doctor's functional. He's been doing this for a long time, if his mom really was taken when he was a boy. What else has he been doing all of these years?

"First I saw, it was cut into farmers' crops. Aliens, people want to believe." Otis shakes his head, walking over to the fake Christmas tree where an ornament has fallen. "A way of communicating. Flag raised. Aliens — no, just man." Otis chuckles again, re-hanging what looks to be a little toy firetruck on a plastic branch. "Not an old symbol. Not in any book."

"So they kill people for fun, or like sacrifices? They...." Hap realizes what he's just said. Information opens doors, but there's a flood of water behind them; he's got to stick his head up; he's got to breathe. A woman like Otis's mother doesn't just go missing for decades; she is dead.

Tiffany, dead. That's all but confirmed. Killers and a cult, and her. What are the odds they hurt her? What are the odds they didn't? "Do you hear them?" Otis's face is nearly pressing against his. "Do they whisper to you too?" Hap's arms are writhing snakes, shoving out on their own accord, pushing Otis away as he's leaping from the couch. His throat is cracked and stinging, and his armpits are flooding.

"Do you think they…? What do you think…?" Does Hap want to know? "What did they do to Tiff?" he asks. His face collapses. The tears come, encased in the hysteria that stretches down his lungs and rattles his stomach like a coiling spool of barbed wire.

"Have you not been paying attention? Tell me, detective, what you think they did to her?" Otis says.

"Fuck you!" Does Hap run outside? Where would he go? The woods are dark and the roads winding, but it's summer; it's still warm. He doesn't need to be here; if only Otis would let him go.…

The madman's bending over, picking up one of the knives—a little shank without a handle. Otis lifts his worn and sweat-stained sweater, and his skin is a map, carved from ink and scars. He trails his knife along an overdose of ominous symbols, each one a token of pain from (probably unwashed) needles. There are skulls, flying worms with bat wings and eyes, clusters of eyeballs looking out through faded ink. The scars do not coexist with the drawings; they are invaders with no purpose, a testament to the strength of Otis's victims. There's a fresh, oozing scratch across his chest, and Hap imagines a young girl with long nails doing the damage. "You follow the clues. You get raw; you heal, become more; you repeat. I have had friends, lovers, full of wisdom. The Moon Shack is young compared to the great old ones. I have nothing now. I come back home. I am the great worm Ouroboros; I will eat myself, soon. The Moon

Shack will be empty, abandoned, boarded up, burned." Otis's eyes are separate from his body; they're living, squirming things entrapped in those craters below his eyebrows.

Hap walks out the front door because his shivering has become unbearable. He keeps waiting for the cold knife to dig into his back, but it doesn't come, as the still air seems to press him further into a plastic bag. Hap stops at the edge of the front door's light, just beyond the strip of dirt serving as a driveway. He tries to focus on the song of the crickets and mosquitoes. Out of Hap's imagination, he sees Tiffany, crying, choking, whimpering, and then going still, while some leering lunatic wearing an animal's face thrusts himself inside her and throws a peace sign to the moon, the two moons that have gone by now while Hap has patiently waited for her to turn up. This is what always happens. There is always a skinny blonde girl filled with all the love in the world, and she is likely raped, choked, and killed in the dark. Any other outcome is a fucking fairy tale.

Hap is on his knees, and things are creeping along the crackling underbrush of the forest. The thought of being swallowed up seems cozy. He'll be a part of something, he.... Hap looks up at the stars, and those are eyes looking down on him, begging him to give them a show. They deserve to be torn to the earth and stomped until their glow bursts into chunks of glass.

"If you're leavin', let me follow. After they kill you, I'll follow the killers. I'll get more of them. Then I'll see what they see," Otis says, sitting on the porch, carving something into the wooden paneling on the side of his house; it's the symbol of that five-limbed stick.

"Why don't you just burn that fucking place down?" Hap looks over his shoulder, realizing he's kneeling in the dirt. He wants a dark room, a bed. He wants to cry harder. Maybe he can get everything out of him. What the hell was Tiff anyway? A bed partner? Somebody to fill the passenger seat of his car? A mother to his future children? What is that warmth, that ache? The idea of a life partner is ludicrous.

"I've started many fires. They rebuild and repopulate. You cannot take the killer out of man, but you can make him homeless, alone. Sum of one, never superior to the many." If Otis is seeking revenge, he seems restrained, even for the knife-wielding, voices-hearing murderer Hap knows him to be. He's smarter than he sounds, he's careful, and he thinks out every big move he makes.

Hap finds his way to his feet, swaying as if he's drunk. The shakes still have him. "They took your mom when you were a kid? How's it taken you this long?"

This time, Otis doesn't show any reaction to the mention of his mother. "All alone," he says. "Minus me, you know nothing. You'd be dead. Takes time to learn. You get to cheat cause I'll tell ya all I know, save you time." Otis gestures at him. "Ya youth, ya get." He chuckles, holding the tip of his blade to his teeth. "No reflexes, though. Arms limp, four miles an hour, tops, your legs…useless," Otis says, as if Hap really needs to know how weak he is.

"How do you know Tiff is dead? Have you ever seen what they do to the people they take?"

"Time to time, I seen the after-party mess. If she not dead, then she lookin' forward to it." Otis traces the dull side of his knife over the tattoo along his wrist. It's not the same blade he used earlier. That one's still lying on the kitchen floor like a dog's chew toy. That knife he used to stab Officer Dylan how many times in the chest before mutilating his eyes? Doing something like that to somebody goes beyond insanity.

"Why not walk into that building and…and shoot everyone you see?" Hap asks. He can picture that standard rifle in all his first-person shooters. Left bumper, right bumper of the controller and then activate rage mode, god mode, annihilate every enemy on the screen. Then Hap remembers the horrible shootings he's seen reported on the news; he starts to feel sick all over again.

Otis is laughing at him. Yeah, yeah, that's what you have to do. Laugh. Hap matches his guttural barks with a rolling chuckle of his own. You have to laugh! Because if you don't realize how ridiculous this is, then you go crazy and stupid and rabid all at the same time, and that's how they get ya. You've got to laugh, stay mad, and stay smart.

"A gun means only one chance for you go down. No cowboys living no more for a true reason." Otis admires his knife, taps it below his eye. "Call a blade a key to knowledge, yeah?" He flicks his eyelid. "Opens good doors."

Hap shudders, remembering the whole eye-stealing thing, and that is a message and a half. Could he really get behind doing that to somebody? To somebody that would hurt Tiff...a mother...a woman or a child — not even fucking Scarface crosses that line.

"Maybe...maybe she is alive." Otis changes his tune, and the tightness across Hap's chest goes to his stomach, ready to evacuate his tossing and turning body.

"What do you mean?"

"Maybe she's alive. They nuts! All possibilities with them. You with me, extra sight." He taps his eyes. "Two of our bellies can fit more of them. We work our way up 'cause they planning something big. Homeless, orphans, lost boys and girls. Now American college girls with boy lovers, all getting swallowed up and disappeared fast like they no care who's looking now. No covering up, no secrets, big things coming. They ain't about waiting for the stars. Maybe they're saving an' storing. Mind won't be good on the girl. She'll be wanting to know death, but alive? Yes, she may be, maybe." Otis bites down on his knife, clenching it between his teeth like a pirate. "Ya can't go home," he says with his mouth full. "What else?"

"What else...?" Hap repeats. He won't kill anybody, and he won't watch or help Otis hurt anybody, either. The cops and other seemingly unbendable forces have gone crooked. He probably can't go home. Would they go so far as to hurt his parents? "Why do you take their eyes? What's the real reason?" he asks at last.

"To see." Judging by Otis's frown, the way his eyes are starting to tighten and glare, he thinks Hap is insinuating he's demented.

"Can't we get them any other way? If we can't arrest them, and let's say we don't kill anybody, how can we hurt them? How can we see if...how could we find Tiffany?"

Otis's smirk drips out the sarcasm before he even makes a sound. "Suppose we ask and let them go, ta kill again. We have other ways, other moves, in a meantime." He points to Hap, then to himself. "Two man jobs — we wait for 'em; we cut another one of 'em, plenty to do in between." Otis points the knife at Hap and then says, "You and me." Revolving the knife back to himself, he steps into his home and looks over his shoulder.

Something cries out in the forest, a small thing that's not fast enough to escape the coyotes, fisher cats, and owls that rule the dark. The cry cuts off, and the crickets resume their song. What other move could there be? Tiff is still missing; there is an answer somewhere. If Otis should happen to cut the throat of some cult killer after they reveal exactly what happened to Tiff, then — well, how could that be such a bad thing? Hap follows Otis, wiping the tears from his eyes with the edge of his thumbs until his skin stings raw.

CHAPTER 13
THE RIPPER'S HEIR

There is a fear so powerful it becomes something real. If Hap were to paraphrase Otis's weird way of talking, then the guy is telling him that in the grand scheme of the earth and all her ancient scars, the Moon Shack is new. It is a product of the last three hundred years, where the dread and malice of man have become unbearable for the laws of the cosmos. As with all newcomers, it is the older things that fear it most. Now that the cruelty of man has become a living thing, all the old evils are lesser. Fuck if Hap knows what any of that means, but he keeps asking questions, and Otis keeps telling him nonsense.

Otis has become somewhat gentle since Hap dug into the cake and poured himself a tea mug of water. "What do they want, besides to hurt people?" Hap asks.

"To exist, free." Otis says the Moon Shackers are on the margins of humanity, but Otis portrays them as not without feelings. He speaks of loneliness, fear, and the desire for a family, of sorts. The Moon Shack has a first family. Otis's words would be better portrayed by a live fire in the cobweb-ridden, black-scorched fireplace behind him. The hum of the fridge and the cry of the forest's nocturnal things are, rightfully, all the emphasis his fairy tales are given.

"There is an Else," Otis begins, tilting his head to the ceiling, prying back the jittery recesses of his blackening mind. "A thing they call Else. It's not man or woman. Seventeen-eighty-

three, Martland, Arkansas, Eighth County." Otis's reminiscence
of place and date is rattled off like the token of information is a
sliver of computer code. "Entire town, hundred or so, clawed their
eyes out. All of 'em folk, in wintertime. Some moms and children
found frozen ta death in the woods, trying to escape. Explained
by bout of fever, tuberculosis, affectin' the head, driving 'em all
mad. We know what truth is hiding. Else is first killer, first one
from the long ago, so it's old, perhaps the oldest man, living in
tombs and cave holes till the Shack, cozy and warm, came along.
It's the first one, first inhabitant of the Shack. A sight so horrible
you become blinded. Have to burn 'em, one day, with all the rest.
Lookin' forward to stabbing with me eyes shut."

All Hap can decipher from Otis's talk of the Else is a town
of dead people. Given that some old cult can bend the integrity
of the police and maybe politicians, it's not hard to believe they'd
cover up the butchering of an entire town. Do they get off on
it? Hap can't think of what a real serial killer could be. It has to
be sexual, in some way, like child predators and other monsters,
an uncontrollable urge that makes them as miserable as they are
evil—a broken brain. There is a poem, that poem in the employee
bathroom that Hap snapped a picture of. He snatches his camera
off the couch and shows it to Otis.

"Oh how the Moon Shack dreams.
lo, fire and corporeal doom.
lo, The Old Ones, Those Who Loom.
Come, shelter from the cost
Come, all who live lost
The weak bleed from our need
The weak need us to lead
else?
what else?
Else?
what Else!?"

"Silly things they make it out to be." Otis smiles, shrinking away from the camera's glow. "A child's war chant, their spite for the sacred books of skin. McKinley, Charles McKinley, southern necromancing fool, he write it."

"The astronomer?" The only McKinley Hap knows is the guy Tiffany was into, the star of the Astronomer's Ball. Hap figured there was no connection between the event and Tiff, not with a haunted hotel and a man carving out eyeballs in the mix of things. McKinley, the author of a poem, scrawled in marker on a bathroom wall. The Astronomer's Ball. A Moon Shack. Could it all be connected, like some kind of constellation gone perverted?

"And Rhode Island native, according ta bull's shit. He was born in Louisiana, this I know, seventeen-sixty-three." Which doesn't add up — it's more of Otis's delusions. McKinley's theories came out shortly before his death in the early nineteen hundreds. Hap was always more interested in Edison and Tesla, as far as innovators from that period go. Otis continues, "Had a plantation once upon a time. The granddaddy of it all, host to the Else, father of a Purple Witch. They brought all they citizens in before they set they eyes to Little Rhody."

Hap is afraid to ask any more questions because, between fact and myth, he wishes Otis had some actual blank notebook paper so he could write everything down and organize it. From an Else to the secret life of an astronomical wizard — how the fuck does this help anything? If Hap didn't know any better, the cult and its Miskatonic would be one big joke, right up there with Scientology.

"Feelin' sleepiness," Otis says, pointing to the couch Hap's been sitting and sweating in. "Morning time, we do errands you'll want to see. After that, you in, with me." Otis points to his wrist, the branch tattoo. "We get you one these. No worries, I got steady hands."

"What is that?" Hap says, instead of asking why he should get some stupid tattoo that's probably more pagan nonsense.

"Elder sign. Might as well be a holy cross to them citizens, like they vampires. Sign on our arm makes them nervous, 'fraid of us. We hurt them enough, do enough non-killing things to them like you want, we'll get all they secrets. Who's alive and who's not. Like McKinley, girls…." Otis pauses for a moment as if he's discovering an old idea. "…mothers."

Hap's not going to say out loud that getting a tattoo to scare your superstitious enemies and forever scar yourself is a stupid idea, mostly because Otis has already gone and branded himself. Also, it looks like Otis is going to bed; he won't kill Hap tonight, which means he's sort of trustworthy, sort of a friend. Hap wouldn't want to go and ruin this merciful development. Otis says nothing as he passes through the kitchen, and to Hap's numbed amusement, enters a bedroom with an old Spiderman poster taped to the door.

With Otis in his little boy's room neglected by a long-absent mother, Hap sets about thumbing through the stacks of notes. The handwriting is scattered, like Otis's brain. It's more of a journal, out of order; even if it were organized, it'd still be illegible. The word "kill" appears an awful lot, always written so that the letters ls melt together; Hap spots things like "shit" and "fuck" repeating one after another for a whole line. Mention of McKinley pops up, while Otis usually mentions the moon and the Shack separately. Wood devils, groundskeepers, clowns, lizards, and words that are in no way actually real mix with other words that are all vowels. There are also impossible spelling combinations that seem like names and places written in such a messy way that it appears as if Otis were literally spitting and coughing through his pen.

Hap tries to focus on the drawings and symbols, but aside from the seven-pointed star with its orbit of circles, they're illegible, unfamiliar, and useless. Taking his camera, Hap makes himself comfortable on the couch before he flicks through the pictures he's taken of the Miskatonic. Soon the throb in his head outweighs his shaking stomach, alongside the buzzing nerves still dancing through him. He shuts off the lights and attempts to find sleep. He ignores the idea of how Tiffany would feel, spooned and cuddled against him. He closes his eyes and kisses the ugly lips of his dreams.

He doesn't wake up screaming, but he keeps rolling over, feverish from his anxiety, repeatedly making eye contact with the black ceramic cat atop the refrigerator. At times he experiences a reoccurring dream. In it, the ceramic beast purrs louder than the humming refrigerator, nuzzles his hands, and crawls along his chest. There's also the briefest touch of nervousness when Hap opens his eyes in the middle of the night to stare at the front door. In his fluttering half-dreams, a stranger keeps knocking on it and the handle twists and pushes inwards, and he keeps jumping up, rustling the scratchy blanket off his legs.

Come morning, an orange and brown tabby cat curiously prods its face against Hap's nose; Otis really does have a cat. The meaning of Hap's dreams instantly becomes nonsense of a different sort. He cranes his neck, still keeping the rather adorable cat on his chest. He can see that the black ceramic feline on the fridge hasn't shed its ceramic casing and come to life. The front door blasts open, and in bounces a raging madman with a scraggly beard and sunken eyes. It's Otis, waving around some kind of drill instead of a knife.

Was Hap that deep into his dreams that he didn't hear Otis walk by him? He wonders if Otis watched him sleep, hovering over him with a knife in hand. That's what Hap gets for — what? Trusting a guy who tears out eyeballs? A second cat follows Otis inside, a skinny Siamese with an especially lengthy tail, which begins playing with the dangling power cord hanging from Otis's drill.

"Given ya her morning blessings, is she?" Otis sounds like a different man, a separate force from the bloody, raving thing Hap barely survived the night before.

"What's her name?" Hap asks.

"Dunno, she don't talk much." Otis chuckles, slamming the drill down onto the coffee table and rattling a plate full of cake crumbs. "Ever ink ya self before?" Otis holds out his wrist and, what did he call it? The Elder sign, that five armed twig. He's still going on about fucking tattoos?

"I think I'm all set," Hap says.

"Ya? When somethin's chewing on your neck, crawling up yar ass, and laying babies in your insides? Better than a rabbit's foot, luck."

Did Hap promise Otis he'd get the tattoo last night? He didn't come close to agreeing, did he? "Let's hold off on that, for now. I don't know. Maybe that's a couple steps away." Tiffany had a tattoo of a shooting star just above her hip. She was complaining about it itching when she first met Hap; he remembers being turned on by it when she stripped for him that first time. Otis plops a container of ink on the table and crosses his arms, immediately breaking form to pull at his beard with both hands.

"It's on me, but they see nothing worth fearin' in you, and I'm left with just a boy, and my teeth are sharp, but my fangs ain't as big. Think this is the role I play for any other reason? We need a wear a mask worse than theirs." Otis disappears into his bedroom, leaving Hap to watch the two dancing cats as they saunter over to the faux Christmas tree to play beneath its branches. Jingling keys and sporting a dank, crumpled-up Boston Red Sox hat, Otis tells Hap it's time to go. Somehow, the coziness of sleep still clings to the couch, and it takes Hap an ounce of extra willpower to lift himself up.

Hunger pains rip across his stomach as he walks to the Caddie. In the daytime, the car's tan coat of paint loses out to the encroaching rust. The heat from the morning sun promises a stifling day void of wind and comfort. Despite the notion of sleep, he's hardly as rested as he believed himself to be; his back hurts from being thrown around by Otis at the abandoned vet's, and bruises from Otis's fists feel like they're scattered all over his face. Power lines weave through the trees. They're not as in the middle of the woods as the night led Hap to believe. There's the edge of a yellow house about half a mile down the road, and there are other homes only lightly shrouded by flat lands of foliage. It's not that there's a lack of light; it's just facing in the other direction.

Sitting beside Otis, Hap again wonders how a man so obviously a derelict like him can go out in public and not get thrown into some kind of kennel. A baseball cap tucked over his eyes only adds to his alienation. Otis changed his clothes, but they're still weathered, potentially unwashed, and smelling of stale sweat, as if he keeps them in a clothes hamper and pretends his mom washes them. Just what has he been doing since he was a boy? Mentioning a few foreign countries doesn't exactly cover enough decades to make Otis appear to be in his mid to late thirties.

Maybe it was the fresh murder Hap witnessed or the knife that may have been hungry for his pupils, but he didn't notice how viciously absurd a driver Otis was until the guy nearly jack-knifed the great boat of a Cadillac onto what should be a reassuringly paved road. They pass a church, a spikey, domed blur. How close is Coventry to Scituate? Tiffany's parents' house must be no more than fifteen to twenty minutes away, as the general distance between most towns in Rhode Island seems to be.

Otis slows the Caddie to a crawl when they come to a massive stretch of water, familiar yet refreshingly beautiful. A rippling reservoir that mirrors the trees and the sky and the idea of the morning sun, emulating the world as if to say, "I can do it better." Old ruins, the foundation of a submerged house, poke through one corner of the reservoir by the shore.

"Beautiful, no?"

Otis's sarcasm is out of place. Hap has driven through here before, with Tiff last summer. There's a parking spot the length of two cars up ahead where they pulled over to marvel at the water. Hap had joked about hopping the barbed wire fence to go skinny-dipping, and then that led to revealing whether they had gone skinny-dipping before. Hap said "no" and Tiff said "yes." She wouldn't tell him the details, and it drove him a little mad, picturing her swimming naked with some other guy.

"Used to ride bicycle by here, every nice day I saw. I would look here and think and think. Better than White Mountains of New Hampshire, I'd say. Right outside my house, even." Otis shakes his head. "Scituate," he says, pronouncing it like *shit-you-ate*. "The place was something so much more than was taken away by the demands of the people runnin' Providence. For they water supply, they needed a source. All that water ya drink in ya city, boy? Cursed. Providence water sharks is what them pushers and half a mobsters were called in the old, golden days when the wood of the Moon Shack was fresher. Water sharks came with they offers and notices, lookin' as men of the government. Scituate was once South Scituate, too, and there was Richmond, Ashville, towns all condemned; people kicked out, compensated with nothing but estimated costs for they homes. People were killin' themselves, goin' straight to the poor house while great Providence flooded their land and drank from it. Looks pretty now, uh?"

The Caddie picks up speed as Hap notices those barbed wire fences entangled by the water. He spots Providence Water Supply, Do Not Trespass signs faded and yellowed, stuck across the fence and accompanying tree trunks.

"Now I only see the ugliness they made it beneath that fucking glass surface." Otis takes something away from Hap; the town suddenly seems smaller, severed, as they drive through three blocks of life.

They pass a neon-ridden diner across from a McDonald's and a soccer field. Cindy's Diner flickers in old yellow atop a blue building, and it's the kind of place he and Tiff would've swerved off the road to get breakfast.

Pulling down a side road next to what looks to be an actual, bona fide video store next to a pizza shop, Otis again pushes his RPMs, and the abrupt curves of the road give more warning than a twenty-five-miles-per-hour sign. Hap flashes back to when his brother first got his driver's license and how he would try to terrify Hap and his sister on the way to and from school. At one point, Otis glances at Hap for too long a moment with his eyes off the road, and Hap isn't sure if he yelps out loud or if his terror stays in his head, but the old lunatic cackles anyhow.

It's not quite a house they pull up to, with the small paved parking lot stemming from its front walkway. A cutesy yellow picket fence distinguishes it as a place that's meant to draw attention. It's in the same sort of scattered neighborhood of country houses Otis lives on the fringe of. A sign stabbed into the ground and embroidered with fancy lettering announces Cidalia's Breakfast Inn. Nobody else is here.

"No veggie-tarian, are ya?" Otis tears his cap off and tosses it across his dashboard.

"No," Hap says.

"Good, have ta kill ya." It's almost as if Otis is trying to joke with him. Hap's stomach still shrivels up.

Hap flinches as Otis reaches across his lap to open the glove box, pushing away a pack of playing cards; no, those gypsy things, tarot cards, before settling his fingers over a yellow pack of Mavericks. "Like prison, good currency," Otis says. He taps the box in Hap's face before springing out of the car, running a hand through his knotted hair and pulling his pants up.

The old woman who greets them at the front door and immediately embraces Otis is a sudden source of comfort to which Hap wishes he could cling. When the woman smiles and says how it's nice Otis is bringing a work friend along with him, Hap wants to hug her too. She takes the Mavericks Otis offers, stuffing them into a front pocket of her lace shirt. He wants this woman to be one of many who will fix things, who will tell him that Otis is a good but strange man, that Hap and he are going to tidy everything up, that the real, warm, and sane people of the world are rooting for them to bring down the cult of the Moon Shack. It's when Cidalia puts a hand on Otis's arm and follows him back into her inn that Hap realizes she's blind.

"Dear, is your shower working? Both you Parks Department boys are sure stinky, huh? But I suppose it is summertime; you can't help but sweat out there."

She leads them to a wide room with just three circular dining tables. Each table has a pair of black and white salt and pepper shakers shaped like cats, which causes Hap to dip partially back into last night's dreams. They are alone, and the other dining tables are so close to theirs that this seems less like an inn and more like a house a blind woman desperately wants to be an inn. Almost immediately, there's a sizzling sound from a room or two over, as if Cidalia already had a pan heating on the stove before they arrived.

"Used to sit me when I was a boy, with Mom and Uncle workin'." Otis plays with the salt shakers, rubbing a greasy finger with a long nail over one of the cats' heads. "There's family we don't know, family we make. As a Lusk, I am descended from rippers, I come to find. Who my father was, maybe the Moon Shack knows. Coincidence?" He shakes his head. "Don't think Mom or I are privy to it."

"What do you mean, descended from rippers?" Hap asks. Otis is a code to crack.

"Follow my family tree, according to wise folk I met over the sea, there a famous killer in my blood. I figure, you look back long enough, somebody in all our families have gone and killed somebody, some point, war or otherwise. We all alive; we all come from blood at some point. Makes me wonder 'bout you, Mr. Shit-Hap. You really lost boy looking for lost girl?"

The more Hap thinks about what he doesn't want to think

about, the less likely it seems he'll just be able to go back to his apartment. Surely other people than Officer Dylan know of him and what was going to happen to him. They probably can't trace his credit cards or his phone, if he still had it, but to return home? If the cult is what Otis paints them to be, then they will be watching, and they will come at some point. What about his family?

"So, they are looking for me and you?"

"'Cept they know your name." Otis grips both sides of the table, and his eyes seem like they used to be browner, but as if he's been staring at the sun for too long, they've been bleached hazel. "They gone have evidence, a knife you never touched, a message fulla words you never said. With whatever it is they planning, building up for, I can't know 'em. They may do nothing. They see you, though. They do something interesting, for sure. Maybe they got cops 'tween Connecticut and Mass, little peepers next to the buses and planes. Square state like this, got ye boxed in; maybe there's something even lookin' from the water they got in they employ."

"But my family in Pennsylvania, are they safe?" Hap asks.

Otis smiles, and the reason why Hap can't trust him is because of that right there: that fucking half-smile. Anything that Otis could say in response to a question like the one Hap just asked shouldn't come with a smile.

"People disappear, all sorts of reasons. They smart is why they usually leave children, American children, alone. You have big family?" Otis asks, and Hap nods. "They can be fine, but they gonna wanna know what you know. They'll ask 'em. If only we could see who's askin', do us some good." Hap remembers what Otis said about him running back into Providence and how, after Hap is killed, he would follow the killers and do his eye thing with them. That doesn't actually make any sense unless Otis is simple and brain damaged, which does still seem possible.

"Why don't you wait outside the Miskatonic and track the

weirdos that come in and out? There are back doors everywhere. If it's really like a temple, then you should have no problem picking them off. Hell, isn't there, like, surveillance equipment anybody can buy off Amazon? Could get on a building across the street and snap pictures." Another hotel called the Omni and connected to the Providence Place Mall would be perfect. Why didn't Hap think of this?

"Everywhere is what everywhere means. Downtown is a cage full of 'em. They see me. They put it together. Moon Shack knows my dreams. All I know, there's much I don't. I get too close, Moon Shack knows my face, and they get me."

Cidalia returns with two heaping plates of bacon, scrambled eggs, and thick stacks of syrupy pancakes.

"So, where you from? Don't have much of the famous accent, far as these ears can tell, and they're sharp as a knife, let me tell you." Cidalia smiles, her pale eyes staring beyond Hap.

"Oh, Belfast, Pennsylvania, closer to Pittsburgh than Philly." The salty crispiness of the bacon throws a delicious veil over the traumatic memory of Otis stabbing into Officer Dylan. Like the warmth of his dreams, the faucet of saliva in Hap's mouth and the ensuing satisfaction across his tongue free him.

"Well, you won't be here forever, I imagine. Otis left home for how long? Over fifteen years? Should have seen me back then; I didn't need my cane." Cidalia's eyes have the faintest touch of color to them—she's not completely blind after all. "What's that thing, like a Frisbee?" Cidalia asks.

"A boomerang?" Hap offers.

"That's right." She grins; her teeth, those dentures, are white and straight; if Hap didn't have grandparents himself, he'd believe them to be real. "Throw you away, and you'll come right back. Hopefully, before you start saying *pahk the cah* like a real New Englander." Cidalia makes a little fist and swings her arm before grabbing a few scraggly tendrils of Otis's beard. "You're never going to meet a nice, pretty woman, you don't relearn how to talk straight and shave that thing."

"Silliness, I know you. 'Sides, there work to be done," Otis says.

"Oh you." She pokes him under the table with her cane. "Hap, take this hermit out of his shell. Why, he tells me some of the postcards he sent from, where was it, Nepal? Had pictures of him and his girlfriend. He knows I can't see it, and I'm still convinced he was trying to fool me. Can you believe it?"

Otis studies Hap with his sunken eyes while he finishes his meal. The food's not settling well in Hap's stomach. After clearing his plate, Cidalia's sad to see them go, and Hap wishes she could see him and how much he needs to be her adopted grandson and stay here in the woods and rest and cry and eat and never have to fear for his life again. Instead, he thanks her for the food before following Otis back into his murder-mobile.

Near the center of town, Otis pulls up to a small white church no bigger than Otis's house; there's a cemetery behind it, bordering the reservoir. From the trunk, Otis retrieves a tin box with fancy cookies on the cover. No way there's treats in there.

There's always a familiar last name in a graveyard, breaching the reality of death. Making a beeline off a loosely graveled path, Otis heads toward the woods at the edge of the cemetery. Beyond a prickly-wired fence is a shimmering portion of the reservoir. Otis falls to his hands and knees before a grave marker bearing the last name Sterling, which features a large circular stone covering a square cement block along the ground. Actually, it's not a grave; it looks more like a sewer cap. Otis runs his hands along its sides, and he's moving it, moaning—no, singing to himself, softly.

"What are you doing?" Hap asks.

"Nobody 'round, right?"

Otis is looking up, pushing aside the stone with ease. There is something glowing below. Hap scans the rows of slowly eroding tombstones and the graveyard entrance that's overshadowed by the church with an empty parking lot. It's a Sunday, isn't it? There was a bigger church they passed just before Cindy's Diner. Maybe that's where the heaves of backwoods religious folks could be. This is an empty town.

"'Magine my surprise when I learned of graveyard scribes an' found un in my own backyard, ah?" Otis rolls onto the ground and sticks his feet through the hole that's just a few inches wider than his waist. There must be some sort of ladder within. Hap wonders what the hell a scribe is.

"I'm not going down there," Hap says.

"Stay. You don't follow, you don't see, stay. Try an' do something with nothing, hah."

All Hap can see is the Red Sox logo on Otis's hat before he takes a step from the bottom rung of the ladder and disappears from sight. There is no stench, so maybe there is nothing dead in there. Follow the leader it is.

The fresh earth brings a cool air that resurrects October. Once down in the little tunnel, Hap whispers for Otis to stop, but he's a dozen feet ahead, hunched over and shuffling toward a wider room.

"Mr. Lusk, Mr. Lusk, what do you bring us?" A man's voice a few octaves too high echoes through the tunnel, and it's immediately blotted out by Otis's bark.

"Hap, cover the hole! Move a stone, quick!"

Hap can't move for a moment due to the snarl rolling off Otis's tongue. With jelly legs, he rushes back to the entrance, clambering partly up the dirt-clogged wooden stepladder. He prods at the edge of the circular stone with his fingers, and with one hand, he manages to drag the dead weight of the stone back over the entrance, sealing him in the darkness haunted by the glow of an inhabitant. The scribe?

Not having to crouch as much as Otis, Hap follows the madman into a circular room that is, indeed, a tomb after all. Silver coffins form a pentagon, stacked and gleaming in each corner of the room. A chandelier swings above a dancing man who's nearly all bones, covered in grey powder and wearing nothing but his underwear. The chandelier's powered by some source of electricity, almost like this is a real place. There is a solitary chair in the center of the room; Hap can imagine this skinny man, with all his ribs ready for counting, just sitting in that old thing, among the six coffins. Or maybe he just dances down here in the dim light.

The dancing man has the tin cookie box from Otis's trunk clasped in both hands. "A boy? What's inside?" The dancing one shrieks; he's clearly crazier than Otis.

"Maybe good intentions," Otis replies, his hands hanging limply by his sides. This dancing freak must be cool, but didn't Otis say he has no friends?

"What is this?" Hap asks.

"Appeasement for an appetite we will never dream of!" the dancing one says, rattling the cookie tin above his head. Something seems to clunk around inside.

"This is good for you; lucky a lord's day it is, much better than his office, this his real office," Otis mutters, his eyes never leaving the half-naked man...no, that tin. Otis's eyes never leave the tin. Hap isn't going to ask what's in there. It's not cookies, that's for sure.

"Why are we here?" Hap asks.

"Offering. The Moon Shack has enemies among the stars. Appetites, as Mr. Hanson says. I feed 'em sight, from my doctorings, yeah?"

Hap starts to think of missing eyeballs on murder victims, and he doesn't have to wonder what was in that tin anymore... Dylan, the cop.

"He's here in this town, your town, and he knows everything? I thought you were alone?"

"I think, while I sleep, that maybe my dad left my mom here for a reason. Don' know him. I meet Hanson in Regensburg;

I learn small places are full. Only eighth time he does this, ever, cause of me. He's a man of books, till I show him my studies. He does not fear the Moon Shack, nor hate it, he just curious. Gives me, us maybe, a blessing, from the things the inhabitants of the Shack shiver at."

"What do you mean by that?"

"Some religions be made by man. Others, not. This one of 'em. All sorts of worship, lookit the olden Greeks with Pan and horns an' gods that make Christians invent the devil. Necessary evil."

Otis is shrugging away from Hap, travelling back down the tunnel and not casting a single glance back toward the dancing man. The twirling skeleton is mumbling gibberish words that make no sense even under Latin illumination.

Otis peeps through a crack beneath the stone circle before mumbling to himself and sliding it free. Eighth time, he said. How many murders have there been? Five according to the news and including Officer Dylan, but have there been killings undiscovered and not reported?

"Otis, this isn't working for me," Hap says, as the man slides the stone sphere back into place. "You're fucking with my head when what we need to be doing is getting some kind of evidence. I mean, no way the Moon Shack and the Miskatonic reach the FBI or even all of Rhode Island, right?"

"Not noon yet." Otis ignores the question, lurching back toward the cemetery path. He saved Hap, right? That should count for something. But what the fuck did he just show him down there? This is not forward progress; these are two camps of lunatics. Who's going to save Hap when Otis has a knife to his back...or eye sockets?

"When are we going to figure things out?" Hap asks.

Otis snorts and comes to a stop by a slab of stone with angels' wings engraved beside a name. "Well, we start fine and quick, soon as you spit out the name of every Miskatonic man an' woman you met." Otis smirks, showing off a glimmer of his yellow teeth. Hap could kill him.

CHAPTER 14
THE ABDUCTORS

Augustine, growing bored, runs a hand along the walls outside of Paul's apartment as she saunters over to the front door. One of the owners of the building is a citizen, and he gave her a key without the need for an explanation. At first, she thought Johan was playing another game with her when he said Paul was going to be the new face of the organization. She tries to keep her nose out of the citizens' business, with their mottos and rituals, but even without lying to herself over who they really are, she can't imagine her career ever taking her someplace else. Where to, after visiting Narnia?

She enjoys their unapologetic devotion for the same reasons Paul must. Nobody throws a better, more primal party than the freaks. Nobody treats you better than a weirdo does. She knew Paul before Johan suggested his importance, but before that, he was just another guy who was all talk with no game in bed. During that act, months ago, Paul wasn't even thinking of her. She was sure of it, so she had to do the same, and all she really remembered about him was how painfully old he was. Now, though, she sees a lick of it: the importance Johan always talks about. Paul does have something bright and shiny behind his eyes and around the corner of his smile, but it's nothing new, nothing dangerous. A relic. It's an old light that makes her remember the first boy she ever kissed, when her mother bought her a dress she had ogled in a magazine, and when the lights went off, and the stage lit up at her first fashion runway. She remembers leaving her first interview, excited, crying, shaking her resume folder in her hands because she was going to be in charge one day; she was going to have people want to be her!

The idea to ambush him came to her on a whim. It was a trick she'd pulled on an old boyfriend before she became a purple woman of the Shack. Of course, his apartment cost half the price of Paul's and had a fire escape to climb up instead of a superintendent's strings to be pulled, but it worked. In a few minutes, Paul will walk into his apartment, and she will jump onto his back. She will turn his panic into something fresh because now that she sees that special glow to him, it'll be like travelling to the past and reliving a greatest hit of sorts. She will feel all she has forgotten as she enters ecstasy. And if Paul already has a girl with him, then surely she'll be the sort that is willing to join in on the fun.

Humming, Augustine slides her key into Paul's lock, just as a sneaky someone appears behind her. She whirls around, ready to drive the one and a half inch key into The Eye Doctor's own eye socket, when she catches herself at the last moment. The tall black haired girl in front of her doesn't so much as blink. Instead, she slowly smiles.

"I'm Lacy. Is now a bad time to surprise Paul?" she asks, her eyes roaming up and down Augustine's body. *That's right,* Augustine thinks. She's got nearly a decade on this girl, but if anything, she's fresher, fuller, with all of this tall girl's silly youth plus the sophistication that comes with an extra decade in life needed to actually pull it off.

"It's actually the perfect time. Won't you join me?" Augustine flashes her teeth. She likes making the young girls do what she says. She's not into fucking women—she's tried more than enough times—but there are plenty of ways someone can please you without touching you.

She unlocks Paul's door, quickly surveying Paul's sparsely

decorated living room. There's a shining old clock on the wall, made of bronze, and there are photographs of—is that Federal Hill, back in the olden days when the brick on the buildings was still fresh? She ignores Lacy behind her, taking in the kitchen and the sink without any plates or half-eaten scraps of food lumped atop one another. Even Augustine's private room at the Miskatonic, separate from all the fun of the flesh, is dirtier than this place. Does his TV still have the plastic sticker over the screen?

Lacy takes a seat on the couch behind her. That's right, Augustine forgot about her. "So, are you here to fuck Paul?" she asks, relishing the discomfort the girl will feel. But Lacy doesn't react to her question.

"I wasn't planning on it," Lacy says, looking her dead in the eyes. Girl's young, but not young. Augustine grins. Of course, Johan knows how to pick them. What had he said about her?

"I thought you weren't allowed in Providence?" she asks, but Lacy only shrugs.

"I'm not much of a wanted woman by the police anymore. Nor anybody else for that matter," she says, looking to the harborside out the window. A runaway—Augustine's seen her type before. They always have their secrets.

A cough comes from Paul's bedroom, and Augustine grins. Could there be another girl in there? She walks halfway through the kitchen to his half ajar door before it opens. A tall, tall man in a wooden mask steps out.

Eyeing a knife rack on the kitchen counter, Augustine lurches forward, her hand draping across the handle of the biggest, closest blade, and the satisfaction of having reached it momentarily stalls her defensive strike. She pushes back, and Lacy's beside her. Good. Augustine reaches an arm around Lacy and pushes the girl toward the masked man. He'll attack her, Augustine figures, and then she can go in for the kill.

The tall man grabs Lacy's face, turns it left then right,

grumbles from beneath his mask, and then tosses her to his right with more strength than Augustine reckoned. Lacy's head smacks against the corner of the kitchen island, and Augustine has no choice. She lunges forward with her kitchen knife. The man hunkers down, thrusting his wooden mask toward her, the tip of her blade sinking uselessly into the wood. He kicks her feet out from under her.

The back of her skull bounces off the floor, and she is floating, swaying, swinging, hanging upside down, watching the floor swirl around her head. Lacy screams, dragging the block of knives to the floor in a serrated rain as she slashes the masked man across the collar with one of the knives. She's aiming for the neck, but he's leaned back. Those long arms of his grabbing her are a scrambled blur Augustine can't make out clearly.

"Not you," a warped voice grumbles. A knife punctures a windpipe, and from there, Augustine hears only wet choking sounds from the dying runaway girl. She's heard that plenty of times before. Upside down, the featureless wooden mask hangs above her head as the tall man peers down at her.

***

Back at Otis's house, they had been going over all the possible ways they could abduct somebody without getting killed or hailed down by the cops when Otis bolted outside like a dog hearing some kind of invisible whistle, only to return and slam a well-wrinkled newspaper down onto Hap's lap. "You remain nameless. Either good or very, very bad."

Never mind just what the fuck that means. There's no mention of any police slayings or suspicious Indian boy suspects in the news. The cult's web extends further than a corrupt sergeant or two.

The first name out of Hap's mouth, after Otis asked him who he knew at the Miskatonic, was "Paul Jones." When Otis shook his head, muttering he'd never heard of the man before, Hap asked him just who Otis *knew* was associated with the cult.

Hap then mentioned Augustine Sanfresco and the incident where he got stripped naked. But again, Otis gave him the shoulder shrug.

"You know the boss, good 'nuff. We partners—I know, you know, we know. A Miskatonic face all the same. We take him, peel his skull back, see what's beneath it. I'll show you how to take a man from his home." At the idea of actually abducting Paul, Hap's stomach started doing a series of flops, like he was a Lego piece being rearranged by an indecisive toddler. How many innocent people could Otis be talked into attacking as easily as Hap had convinced him to go after Paul? Then again, anybody who even so much as shines the shoes of the people who took Tiff probably deserves what's coming to them in the form of a crooked-toothed killer with an affinity for eyeballs.

It's Hap's shitty job to take point, making sure the hallway and back stairwell are clear as Otis takes Paul. When Otis appears with a woman slung over his shoulder, Hap knows everything has gone to shit.

Leading the way into the back alley, he sprints over to the Caddie's driver's side door, dropping the key that's oh-so-inconveniently lacking any sort of chain or grip. His knuckles scrape when he picks it up from the asphalt, but he manages to slide into the driver's seat and back up to the side door.

Beyond the two rows of parked cars, there's a rundown field that covers about four blocks' worth of uncut grass in front of the closest building to the apartment's back lot, a gas station. As far as operating in Providence goes, this is a nice place to abduct a cult-sympathizing wacko. The highway that extends through the East Providence Bridge is close by, but someone would have to be walking and peering over the sides of the bridge to catch a glimpse of them. Hap's heart beats hard enough to feel as if it's going to erupt out of his mouth as Otis lumbers out the door and his big legs pull him right to the trunk they left partially open. He dumps Augustine out of sight. Hap barely has a second to scoot across the front seat before Otis barrels into the car, grinning and panting.

Over the rock-and-roll-static remix on the radio, Hap can hear Augustine punching away in the trunk. Not for the first time, the thought of what's actually happening makes him want to hyperventilate.

Once they reenter the countryside, it's a relief that there aren't cops tailing them, but it's not the relief to end all reliefs. Given what Otis has told Hap about the Moon Shack's followers, any vehicle behind them could be the harbinger of their demise. Despite their caution, any number of eyes could have settled on them from the shadows as they fled Paul's place.

There's no doubt their victim is a living thing, as she continues banging against the trunk. Otis stands beside Hap with his knife drawn and watches his Cadillac shake. Globs of runny ink and Hap's blood still stain the floor. Having a burning, sore arm, inflicted hours before the most potentially perilous thing he's ever willingly done, goes to show that he has to sharpen his thinking because Otis will only encourage the dull mind to act first and worry never.

Before the abduction, Otis seemed proud when he showed Hap the simple white, wooden mask he was going to wear that vaguely resembled the tragedy and comedy theater icons. Then he started telling Hap all the options they had for abducting Paul; all the sneaky, wicked ways they could rip a man from his own home. With those thoughts swirling in Hap's head, Otis pulled out the tattoo kit; the drill was whirring before Hap could refuse. Otis said, "For Tiff," just once, as a loud grunt over the whine of the needle gun. The killer remembered her name. After a few minutes of agony, as if Hap stuck his wrist into the maw of a many-toothed reptile, a tingling sensation replaced the pain; it was almost like he was getting a new-age massage. If only it weren't for the blood that still dripped out of him.

Now that Otis has cast his mask aside, it's clear he has no

intention of letting Augustine go. Hap's not dumb. This woman who once grabbed him by the crotch and attempted to mate him with a masked female is going to die. Jeez, they haven't even let her out of the trunk yet.

Bumping Hap's shoulder, Otis seems free from any moral turmoil. "Women, 'specially pretty ones, can be more dangerous for boys like you and me than men, 'cause we designed in our blood and brains to be lil' puppets ta what reminds us of mum. How many women killers you ever heard about? At the drive-in? How many women wear a mask or swing a blade? There ain't less of 'em, just less that get caught. A woman in they group means she done more than the men ta earn her place. You ever hear of Lizzie Borden? Fall River gal, not far from Providence, by no coincidence. With an axe, she gave her mother forty whacks. When she looked at what she done, she gave her daddy forty-one. We can't be fools now." Hap wants to believe Otis's logic is for the greater good, but there's a hungry look to the killer's eyes, and all Hap can think of is that old Snickers candy bar commercial. "You're not yourself when you're hungry."

Following a creaking pop of the trunk, Otis's hand is a Kung Fu snake-strike that instantly grabs Augustine around the jaw, squeezing her mouth and cheeks as he hauls her out by her neck until her nose nearly touches his. "Your eyes is dim, but your tongue is fat." He turns to Hap with a dreamy smirk before grabbing her by the face and dragging her across the driveway and into the house. This time, Hap can't even pretend to help; he can't watch those squirming, long, pretty legs before they're slurped into the front door of Otis's own killing shack...which also just so happens to double as Santa's Workshop.

Now comes the part that Hap hasn't thought through. He follows the sounds of screaming into the small bathroom, where Otis is binding one of Augustine's hands to a pipe along the wall, forcing her to sit on the toilet as he does so. There's nothing she can reach except the ceramic back of the toilet seat that Otis preemptively picks up and tosses past Hap. The noise it makes when it clatters against the floor sends one of the cats bolting out of the house.

Hap's sensation of doing something irreversibly wrong is dulled by Augustine's lack of fear as Otis takes a step away from her. Her face is a frozen snarl, her words on the verge of hysterical laugher. "Are you a fucking hipster? Is that why you can't join the party, you evil fucking hypocrite? How could you betray everybody like you? You share the same dreams!" She's standing, turning as much as she can to face Otis, despite her arm being shackled to the wall. She cranes her neck just enough so her eyes catch Hap's stare. Her laughter, beyond ridicule, is a taunting flag of all the secrets she must know. Hap swallows and waits for Otis to make a move.

"I see a lot of little boys, but I remember your limp dick." The punctuation of her lips is heightened by her smeared lipstick, and Hap feels an old shame that comes with being spoken to as if he is indeed a timid little boy.

"I knew you wouldn't be the real hard cases because I'm friends with them and the things *they* do to people like you. You think taking eyes is some kind of message? Some kind of ritual, right? You fucking pagan losers." Otis reaches for her, and she spasms, her whole body convulsing as she shrieks, "Don't touch me! I'll pop my cherry, I'll fucking join them and bash your fucking head in. I'll bite your neck out and tear your prick off." She's screaming so hard her voice begins to crack. Hap is suddenly glad for Otis's presence.

"Boy, your teeth are pretty." Otis has a foot-long knife drawn by his side that Hap doesn't remember seeing at any point in the day. Could it have been on him the whole time, tucked away somewhere? Otis lunges, wrapping an arm around Augustine's neck while he plops down onto the toilet seat, cradling her onto his lap. His arm twists, and he points the tip of his knife on her forehead. Like dashing a checkmark, Otis quickly notches a backwards crescent moon into her forehead. Otis mentioned earlier that the backwards crescent is "to mock them," but now, even with Tiff potentially dead, Hap doesn't understand the need for cruelty. There's a need, and then there's desire. Surely, Otis derives his own sick pleasure from this ritual he's sharing with Hap.

"My skin!" Augustine reaches for her face as if to rub away her new scar. "You're the end of my virginity. Oh, you're the boys; yes you are. I'm going to feel your skulls crack. I'm going to feel your brains. They are going to welcome me in that pale hall, oh, you darlings." Augustine licks her lips and moans.

"Darling, threaten to hit me again, and I tear your straightened teeth out, press them into your eyes. Nothing wants to see what you see." Otis holds his knife against Augustine's throat, and she goes still. "We want information. You a blowup doll. Time to let out yer air. Who blows you up at the Miskatonic? Who's the boss?"

"The man whose apartment we were in!" Augustine shrieks.

"No, no, no," Otis coos and Hap has to lean against the wall because a rush of sudden vertigo seems to want to lift his brain out of his skull. Something awful is going to happen right in front of him, but he needs to hang onto this woman's words. He needs to get his say in, but there's no talking over Otis. "I need his boss. Come now, sit on my lap like a good girl and write me a nice little list." Otis giggles, causing those Christmas decorations in the living room to go from sad to vile. Otis, for all he has lost, is clearly enjoying this, and he hasn't even touched her eyes...yet.

Augustine snaps, "Names? What kind of pagan are you? You know names are useless. They can't even begin to sum up... you want names? Johan Weissbekoff, Elliot Sampson, Taylor McKinley, ha-ha, Charles fucking McKinley."

"The necromancer is dead," Otis snarls.

Augustine is cackling now, but it's a defeated sound,

not a joyful one. Is she okay with dying? Is she on drugs? Hap suddenly remembers, they are all crazy. This isn't a real person. This isn't just some woman.

"The old man lives," she says. "I've seen their grandfathers and great grandfathers, undying generations. Hah! You want any of them? Come on, all you've gotta do is ride that glass elevator and knock on a couple of doors. Some of the rooms at the Miskatonic have been checked out for almost a century. You're so tough, why don't you go do that?"

Otis turns to Hap but nods his head in Augustine's direction. "Hap, look it this girl, friend of man slayers. Look at her nails, done up all colorful." Otis puts his mouth to Augustine's ear, and is there even a point where this can go too far? "I'm gonna take um, put 'em in a jar on the windowsill over there, let you look at em."

"You think I haven't been tortured before? By men? By women? How about you take off my clothes and run your little knife over my scars?" Augustine moans and leans her head back to brush her cheek against Otis's, and Otis seems to go rigid for a moment. Hap isn't sure what the fuck is happening if they're about to kiss or not, but then Augustine's teeth are flashing toward Otis's neck. With his left hand, he throws her off him, and she's crying out, twisting the arm attached to the pipe along the wall to the point that something must be broken or dislocated because the waves that ripple across her vocal cords is that of a wounded animal, confused and bleeding in the middle of the road.

Otis tilts her head back, letting the knife negotiate gently against her throat once more. "Those are fine names, powerless and fake as they may be. Give me a place that's no hotel. Give me a place, and I won't carve up yer face. I'll leave it slick and just kill yer quick." Otis giggles, rhyming now, practically singing like a goblin from some *Brother's Grimm* fable. Hap tries to speak, but his throat is drying up.

"Sure." Augustine's spewing sarcasm, hunching up, leaning back against the wall as Otis moves away from her. "There is a church along a popular street. A hundred people walk and drive by it every day, and its doors are always closed to the curious. I've been in there, just like I've toured the Acropolis, the Pyramids, and the steps of Giza. You're the type of freak who likes old, dirty things, huh? Let me guess, I don't remind you of your mother enough?"

Hap feels the sledgehammer of memory striking Otis in the belly. The killer recoils and then delivers a fist to her face faster than Hap can turn his head to look away.

Hap keeps his eyes closed as Augustine goes on, telling them about a church that the citizens wish they could burn down but don't. She doesn't elaborate. "Looking through the ruins will be right up your alley, huh boys? You know what? I'm gonna tell you. Hey, limp dick! Open your eyes." Hap blinks in Augustine's swelling face, running with mascara and smeared lipstick. Her eye will be black before long. Otis is a rotten woman-beater, but she's sick and evil, right? "There you go. You're gonna find some kind of hope there, in the church. I want you to find it." She licks away some of her lipstick—or is that blood? "It's good you get some more of that in you because you know what's going to happen eventually when they find the two of you?"

"What do they do with the missing girls?" Hap asks quietly. He stands beside Otis; maybe it's because she called him a limp dick again, but he's feeling the hatred now. "There is a girl, Tiffany, tall with blonde hair. What did you do to her?"

Otis backs away, leaning out of the bathroom to throw his knife across the living room with a metallic crash.

"Aw," Augustine giggles. "Did somebody take your girlfriend? I probably watched her get fucked. We take names, though, we give them, and there's nothing I like better than dying hair, 'specially if it's all sticky with blood."

"Fuck you, fuck you." Hap can't think of a threat, only the

intention of scaring her into telling him where Tiff is. "Fuck," he mentions again. He wants a knife to show it to her, although he could never touch her with it.

Otis returns with a plate of mostly untouched chocolate cake. "Here ya are." He puts it on the sink out of Augustine's reach. "Ya want it when ya hungry enough. Maybe you get it." Otis puts a hand on Hap's shoulder but, no, not yet—he's gotten nothing about Tiff, just some starry church full of cult bullshit.

"You're gonna get hurt; you're gonna die. Where is she? What do you do?" Hap asks aimlessly, and he's trying not to cry. He has to ask questions; he has to get her to talk.

"You worked there, huh? You...." Augustine's laughing again to herself, "You sneaky snoop, you were looking for her at the Miskatonic? A regular detective. Try somebody's belly; inspect everybody's teeth for bits of her hair. Check all the bathrooms; maybe a pair of strapping boys with dicks twice the size of yours have shacked her up like you two have me. She's probably been handcuffed to a bathroom radiator, listening to you hoof bags down the hallway. How about it?"

Otis is pulling Hap's shoulder, leading him out of the bathroom as he slams the little door behind them. Hap can't cry anymore. There's a tingling sensation coming from behind his eyelids; he can't stop his hands from clenching, forming fists.

"There is a church I know. We shall pray and pry, and we come back and—sorry for the world, sorry for our souls— hurt her more and inchy inch ourselves toward knowing what we gotta know, to maybe save the people who are not her." A cat brushes by Hap's ankles, softly purring, and there is a heavy quiet from the thing in the bathroom.

"Need rest?" Otis asks as if that's possible after what they just did. Hap shakes his head, feeling the urge to pee instead. He stares at the bathroom door, and, yeah, he'll take a leak outside.

CHAPTER 15
THE THING WHO SITS, SMILES, AND ROTS

Parked outside of a boarded-up Providence church, Otis rambles on and on. "His fear made him tremble; mine had me doing something else. They were there, in a hole, whispering, almost like they saying my name. We had followed the drums like the piper pied, diddling his flute to steal the children. Old broken places sometime see more people than the new. Things live in cracks, ya see, in between; then ya have folks celebrating them ones moving about the muck of a bay, celebrating with they music, parades an dances, like ol' Mr. Hanson. Church's propped up, and what can ye say to they who worship tha' deathless?"

Hap can only listen to so much, but from what he can interpret, there is another cult in addition to the citizens of the Moon Shack. There are other pagan sects worshipping strange gods that the Miskatonic cult hates. Otis can't begin to describe these weird gods, which causes Hap to wonder if that means they're more complicated than this Moon Shack shit. The idea that there's somehow a worse cult than the Moon Shack carries with it more hopelessness than Hap is willing to tolerate.

Augustine said they would find hope here. They were forced to drive down a wonky series of side streets to avoid passing the Miskatonic, which acts as a prime spot hogging the nexus of Providence's limited roads. Johnson and Wales University is hardly six blocks away. Across from the church's thick doors, there's a long row of parked cars with their meters interchangeably flashing red and green. On a street corner beside a brick building with dark windows, it's less of a crumbly castle of belief than Hap imagined. Instead, it's compressed, its walls mummified and warped as if its foundation is coated in some strange preservative.

He raises his camera and snaps a picture of the church, forgoing all instinct to set up his shot. The church's spire, needling up into the eye of the sky, doesn't feature a cross like every other Christian house of worship. As if Otis's nonsense is slowly becoming fact, on both of the church's doors, there is the same five-limbed branch that's been stabbed into Hap's arm. *The Elder sign.*

Hap can see the familiar rooftop of the Miskatonic peeking from between a row of buildings and city hall in the distance. Otis turns in almost a full circle in his seat, squinting his crater eyes at every parked car along their row. He's looking for watchers, but how could he even tell them apart from, say, the beefy looking Hispanic dude coming around the corner of the church?

"How do we get in?" Hap asks.

"Find a loose spot and push 'er kick." Otis gives one last long look down the road before creaking open his door. Hap follows, wanting to crouch. It's hard to believe an hour or so ago, they left the city with a woman in their trunk. Between dancing creeps in crypts and Otis's knife disappearing in and out of Officer Dylan, will Hap be clawing his own eyes out by nightfall? Augustine said they would find hope here.

They casually disappear down the side alley between the church and the empty brick building with windows so black Hap wants to smash them just to see if anyone's hiding behind them. Picking their way through weeds, Hap is surprised to find beetles and even a few bees fluttering around the overgrowth, desperately looking for wildflowers. Where do the bugs come from? How do they creep into a little alley like this, surrounded by miles of concrete and asphalt?

Otis trails a hand along the cement of the outer wall, prodding his fingers into yellowed moss. There's graffiti behind it, long, snaking green tendrils intermixed with streaks of red. The artist's tagging of their name is more symbols than words.

Otis chooses a blank spot along the fading brown of the wall and presses his ear against the cement as if he could hear anything from inside. Hap wonders where he hides the knife or two he surely has on him; the pockets of the killer's jeans seem shallow. They must be under his sleeves, tucked along his wrists. Otis is like a grease-monkey mechanic, and a two-bit, sleight-of-hand magician all rolled into one homicidal lunatic. Otis crouches down, pulling aside clumps of yellowed grass, and there's a blackened basement window so sunken into the earth that the ground has begun to swallow up the glass. With a sharp kiss of his boot, Otis kicks in the window. There's a tink from the glass and a gasp of air as if the church itself is taking its first breath in years.

Swishing his foot in a circle, Otis knocks away the remaining chunks of glass before crawling onto his hands and knees. He pulls a little tube of a flashlight from his back pocket, shines it into the thick black ahead, shrugs once, and then sticks his head through the window. Hap imagines the window's glass suddenly reforming and slicing off Otis's head. If only he had his damn phone; he hasn't used a flashlight since he was a little kid exploring his backyard in the dark with his big brother Darren. He doubts Otis has a second flashlight; he should just stay outside… unless Tiff is down there.

Otis is muttering to himself as he slips through the opening, sticking his arms out straight and rotating his shoulders so he can fit. There's a wet plop from within when Otis disappears inside, and it's Hap's turn, isn't it? He already crawled through that tomb in the cemetery; what's a little old church? The sun's leaving. Will he be alive to witness its return tomorrow? He could just stay out here and watch it melt away.

Otis's face with a flashlight under his chin illuminates the black of the window, resembling a portrait of a coal miner. "Comin'?" Otis asks. Despite being fearless enough to abduct and murder, it sounds like he doesn't want to go any farther into the dark without Hap by his side. How much of Otis's life has he spent alone? How many other allies has he driven away? How many has he killed? Hap grimaces at the touches of dirt and grease pooling along Otis's face like war paint. Hap's already got the tattoo; he's part of Otis's tribe. Give Hap a couple of months, and he'll have a beard too. Who knows; maybe he'll be talking gibberish soon enough.

"Do I need to?" Hap remembers the bodies tucked into that crawlspace at the abandoned veterinarian clinic. He's lying to himself if he doesn't think, doesn't know, that there are dead things in this church. What if, by hope, Augustine meant she was giving him Tiff in an attempt to crush him? What if this is finally it? He doesn't need to see that. He takes back all those ideas of seeing her again if she's dead. He has his camera, all those pictures of her from the great before. He could just look at those instead and kill every part of him that isn't memory.

"I go alone, it easy for me not to come back. Up here, too," Otis taps his forehead. "Need ya." He whispers those last words.

Hap sighs and falls to his knees, holding the camera close to his chest as he crawls toward the old mouth of a broken window. Will it spit him back out or swallow him forever?

With his arm burning from his crawl into the dark, Hap is forced to grip the back of Otis's shirt as he swings his flashlight around a sparse, muddy basement full of broken tables and stacked chairs. A couple of life-size Jesus statues are propped beside the busted window and its trail of glass. Symbolism aside, Jesus on the cross is a dying body nailed to a piece of wood. Where does the line between religion and insanity begin?

Hap could use his camera's flash, couldn't he? His light soon engulfs Otis's, and the room is little more than a storage closet. The walls seemed farther apart in the dark. There's a drift and a whisper, almost like wind. The whisper becomes a faint whistle, and the stillness is comforting. Even Otis takes a moment to hold his breath and see if anything else is alive in here.

"What are you expecting?" Hap whispers and regrets asking immediately. Otis's madness will take on new life here in the dark. Whatever he talks about, whatever impossibility he hints at, it's all real here, like telling ghost stories while camping in the woods.

"Hope," Otis mutters gravely before pulling open a rusted sheet of a door. The ensuing screech of metal sets off a number of skittering noises that seem to echo from every corner of the building. Rats, surely. Otis stumbles, and Hap's stomach instantly starts hurting as he regains his balance.

"Do you have an extra, uh, knife?" As soon as Hap asks, Otis whisks around, pulling a knife the size of Hap's middle finger from his boot. He offers it to Hap blade first so that he has to pluck it with his fingers to avoid getting nicked. Otis ignores his reply of "Thanks."

"Let me see." Otis turns and grabs Hap's camera from his hands, pulling his neck along with it. Hap curses and gives it up as Otis exchanges his penlight. Those things moving around... rats? But don't rats squeak? No, no, they can be silent. They have to be; they must be. *There are only rats here*, Hap begs to himself.

Is "catacombs" the word for it? What may be coffins line the walls, and carvings are etched into the ovular passage around them. The carvings seem to resemble gargoyle faces, and some have wings seeming to sprout from their heads. The chamber slopes down probably another ten steps' worth, as Hap and Otis follow it to a barricaded door with a familiar symbol.

Whole tree trunks have been stacked and bolted over the entrance to a room that can only hold bad things. Under Otis's flashlight beam, the dust along the wood blocks becomes alive and wriggling in the air. Carved over four trunks of wood is that damned symbol of the star and its swirling vortex of planets. On the wood blocking the door in black graffiti are the scraggly words *Elder* = *Swine,* which makes no sense unless it's to mock the symbol bleeding into Hap and Otis's wrists.

"Couple heaves, we good." Otis rubs his hands over one of the old beams and pulls, groaning, expecting it to be as sturdy as it looks, bolted to the wall. With a pop that sounds like the accumulative burst of every twig Hap has ever stepped on, the beam snaps and a mess of skittering, black bugs gush out of the hollowed wood. Otis yells, crawling crab-like backwards, his knife never leaving his hand. The camera's beam of light dances wildly. The bugs, termites or roaches of some sort are vanishing into the blackness as Otis regains his footing, cursing to himself. He lashes out with his foot and kicks through the other twin beams. For the sake of Hap's jumpiness, only a smaller number of the black insects scurry free from the Styrofoam-like burst of the wood. "Citizens afraid of here," Otis says, and Hap can't tell if that's a good thing or not.

Otis hesitantly reaches his hand to the door without a handle, lightly pressing his fingers to the rust. The bolts in the stone line the frame of the door, still holding small chunks of the devoured wood in place. "Ready to run," Otis mutters before pushing into the room beyond.

In the center of the circular room, there is a well. Black candles, unlit, circle the rim of the hole in the earth, here in a church's basement. Around them, the hieroglyphs carved into the walls form a frenzy of dizzying images and illegibly curved words. Hap lets Otis walk ahead to peer into the well in the center of the room. When he sticks Hap's camera into the lower pit, he can't help but tell Otis to watch it. At Hap's words, more things scurry around them, fleeing to the cracks etched amongst the hieroglyphs. Otis mentioned, during his babbling earlier, something about things living in walls, in between the real places.

Otis picks up a stone and tosses it into the well, lowering

his ear to the hole. "Water," he mutters after a few seconds. "People I met, overseas an' in lower America, they think mister Roger Williams found somethin' beneath the city. Lies, I'm sure. Can't all be true. Hole runs deep, though. Plays they imagination, same as ours. You see Prospect Park? Statue? It lines with the moon, worshippin' it."

"I have seen it," Hap says, remembering pieces of his drunken delirium that night he hit the deer and trashed the hill house. "The water fires, they have anything to do with the cult?"

Otis chuckles and turns away from the well in a rush as if he's afraid something may drag him down into the unknowable depths. "Worshippers here is the reason man built the church, to hide they people in. They know some stars have appetites." Hap thinks Otis is trying to say the people who built this mock church had a religion they were ashamed of, which is funny, because wasn't Providence built as a city to embrace all faith?

There is something along the wall, along both walls, lined up with the well. Are those bells? Hap points them out, and Otis's smirk fades. "Rituals, two things every un needs, candles, a whistle, bells. Let's go. Don' think 'bout touchin' 'em." He grabs Hap's shoulder and steers him toward the busted entranceway.

Ascending to the upper floors of the church, they come through a pair of double doors leading to a familiar room of worship, if only in the shadow of memory. Rows of pews and ghostly, cobweb-covered candles on poles cluster around an empty, coffin-like altar. The altar's surrounded by disgusting statues that...wait...they are familiar carvings. That totem Tiff had...there are similar statues the size of large dogs scattered about the room. Perverted images, creatures twisted into mutants, monsters. There are things with wings and tendrils pouring out of their many-eyed heads, hunched over with twisting limbs that end in talons.

Aside from being larger, they are made of cement or some kind of sculpting clay, unlike the near obsidian stone that was

Tiff's totem. The ugly statues are surrounded by chunks of their crumbled brethren, scattered in heaps of mangled appendages. Pews are overturned. There is glass and graffiti tossed over everything as if there were a sudden snowfall of the stuff. Graffiti proclaiming "Fuck" and "Elder," along with other illegible profanity, blackens the church's insides like ash.

There is actual ash in the center of an aisle, a stack of it framed by the remnant bindings of textbooks. Otis crouches by it, picking up a charred page containing an inky red drawing of the same kind of ugly abomination as the sculptures. "Burnin's of the forbidden texts. Good and bad. Good 'cause wrong people won't know what they need to know to be wicked. Bad 'cause knowin' is only tool we got 'gainst the Shack."

Hap's little penlight comes across a torn-up banner on the floor. Its symbol is that of the Elder sign, stuck across his wrist.

"What the fuck is this?"

"What tha' Moon Shack is so afraid of." Otis tilts his head, and there are faint tears in his eyes as he pats a hand over a statue of a spidery thing with goats' hooves and worms for a spine. "Allies…." He laughs in a way that could mean he's on the verge of crying. "…hope."

CHAPTER 16
THE MAN UPSTAIRS

Otis pulls into a random side street next to a liquor store. The arms of a tree that has grown too fat to be rooted into the sidewalk scrapes against the Caddie's roof. Otis hums to himself, tugs at his beard, and repeatedly retightens his grip on the steering wheel. "Tell me again," he says, after a few moments, too many passes while Hap fidgets in his seat, matching Otis's twisting of his facial hair. With a great sigh, Hap repeats himself. He mentions the horrible totem Tiff brought home from the Miskatonic and how it looked eerily similar to the larger stone idols at the church.

"She got from the hotel," Otis says so slowly that Hap grinds his teeth and makes his gums throb as much as his head and wrist are aching.

"Yes!" Hap lets his frustration ring out while Otis remains silent, pulling at his beard with such frenzy that it almost seems sexual.

"Impossible." He waves his hands Hap's way. "Nazi flag in oval office. One," he holds up a finger on one hand and then a middle finger on his other. "Two," he says, and then he prods them against each other like opposing spears. "Not friends. Not swappers and renaming conquerors like Romans and Greeks. The totem, your girl...I must see it. Everythin' changes now. Yes, must see it." Otis shakes his head; is he crying or just angry? A tear trickles down his cheek and disappears into his stubble before he can wipe it away.

"Describing it's not enough?" Hap asks. Considering the fucked-up statues they just saw, how can Otis not imagine what a toad with human arms spawning from its back looks like?

"Girl's parents have it?" Otis taps the green digital clock on the Caddie's dashboard. A quarter to nine. "Early sleepers?" he asks, clearly not concerned with getting back to his home and the woman shackled in the bathroom. Hap remembers the first time he slept at Tiff's house and how they came back from a party at the end of her block. Both her mom and dad were up drinking wine and watching HBO until one thirty on a Tuesday; they're not early birds.

As Otis drives onward, Hap notices an Elder sign faintly carved into Otis's dashboard. Like many things, it was there the whole time, right under his nose. After what they saw in the church, just who or what would be protecting them from the Shack? Maybe the cult's beliefs can be used against them.

The woods of Coventry may as well be the same as those of Scituate, but from the way Otis paints the place, it's a different continent. "Is a woman, Mary, buried in a grave's yard round here, accused of being a vampire."

"Yeah, I've heard that one," Hap says, recalling a time Tiff and he took a trip to Coventry's infamous haunted graveyard one Halloween. It was anticlimactic.

"See? You can be one for lore. Pick out the truth like chicken from bone, and you got a meal, aye? Her accusers always monsters themselves, made her an outcast an' beheaded her. Accusing ones got secrets of they own. Always. Nothing special 'bout drinking blood anyhow. Sometimes ya gotta."

"If we go there, you're gonna stay in the car," Hap says. Otis becomes recharged, cackling as he guns the gas and pulls a U-turn in the middle of the street.

"Sure we don't gotta tie 'em up?" Otis asks when the Caddie's tires crunch along Tiff's parents' gravel driveway. Hap is pretty sure he's kidding, but he'd have to be a lunatic himself to think those words aren't harmless. Is Hap even capable of being around normal people? He's sweat through his clothes about three times over now, not to mention crawling through the graveyard and the church; his nails are black, and his teeth probably need a good brush. No matter what, he'll be a sight to see…and smell.

They arrive at Tiff's old house…the house to which Hap still holds a fleeting hope she will one day return to. Otis parks by a woodshed opposite the gravel driveway. Tiff's dad's Jeep is parked in front of a two-car garage. They won't be able to see Otis from the front door.

A moment later, Hap presses a thumb over the doorbell. If only he had Tiff's parents' number. Living in a woodsy neighborhood and having your doorbell ring past dark is sure to put you on edge. Plus, Tiff's parents already seemed to hate him the last time he heard from them. Maybe they've had time to realize he's done nothing wrong—aside from the whole helping Otis abduct a woman thing. Hap swallows as he hears cautious footsteps approaching the other side of the door. It's as if he's there to meet Tiff's parents for the first time. He imagines, for a moment, a reality where he is here to pick Tiff up for a date.

"Oh, Jesus," Tiff's mom says before the door's even halfway parted. How long did Hap have from Providence to Coventry to think of something, anything, to say?

"Hey, Mrs. Lorice, I'm sorry to be—"

"Jerry, Hap is here!" she interrupts him.

Jerry rounds a corner behind Mrs. Lorice, wearing a scarlet bathrobe and his reading glasses. When Hap first met him, he said to call him Jerry, but Mrs. Lorice never extended such warmness, so it's Mrs. with her even after dating Tiff for years. Mrs. Lorice puts her hand on her husband's shoulder, and they stare at Hap for a moment that extends for a small eternity.

Mrs. Lorice breaks the silence. "What the hell happened

to you?"

Hap's heart starts twisting around as he tries to come up with some excuse that explains all the grime, not to mention the fresh tattoo bandage on his arm. "I was on a photoshoot near that lake in Scituate, the reservoir." If only his words could reshape the world.

"Where are you staying? How did you get here?" Jerry's got his hands on his hips. They are concerned about him; they do care. Then why haven't they been here for him? Why can't he be staying with them instead of a crooked-toothed lunatic?

"I've been in the city for, uh, an internship that might lead to a job. I'm staying at the apartment Tiff and I were going to get...." And there it is; he's gone and mentioned their daughter. If anything, the Lorices' concern for him seems to grow.

"Oh my, you're staying where you two were going to...." Mrs. Lorice is almost on the verge of tears as Jerry pushes open the screen door.

"Come inside. We, we were wondering if we would hear from you again, after everything...." Jerry stops short. These are broken people. Hap feels Otis's sunken eyes on the back of his head as he's welcomed inside. "Why didn't you give us a call?" Jerry asks Hap as Mrs. Lorice leads the way to the kitchen.

"My phone's been busted. I've been working hard for the internship, distracting myself from.... Well...you know." Hap hopes they don't realize his face is growing hot. He hopes the dirt will hide the bruises from Otis's fists.

"Have you heard anything...anything at all?" Mrs. Lorice asks before Hap can even take a seat at the kitchen table. There are leftovers wrapped in tinfoil on the stove, and he remembers the taste of something not pumped out of a restaurant's deep fryer or fast-food window. Cidalia's breakfast this morning was a nice segment of a bad dream, but a dream all the same.

"No, no, I haven't." Hap trembles from the urge to tell them about his great and terrible search. How does he look if he says he has done nothing? Wouldn't they be impressed by the lengths to which he has gone to find their daughter, failure or not?

Mrs. Lorice notes Hap staring at the leftovers. "Want some chicken? It's still warm." There's a softly ticking cat clock on the wall, the kind with eyes that shift back and forth alongside a wagging tail; it's fairy-tale stuff Hap was impressed with his first time here. Somewhere in the house, there is an old sleeping dog called Snack, who's too tired to bark at strangers. The place still smells like the warm, soothing things that Tiff grew accustomed to her whole childhood.

Digging into a plate of mashed potatoes, corn on the cob, and hunks of grilled chicken seasoned with onion teriyaki, Hap experiences a tingling moment in which there is no psychopath lurking in a car forty feet away from the front door. It's not even that awkward that Jerry and Mrs. Lorice are silently staring at him as he eats as if he is some mythological Bigfoot that's walked into their kitchen. Before Hap can completely mop up his plate, though, he's struck by the sudden fear that Otis will barge in through the front door and make things happen with a snap of his fingers and the screeching of a knife against a wall.

Jerry asks Hap how he's been coping, and there's no better chance to get to the point than now. "There's something I've been looking for that was in our apartment before I had to move out." Hap stretches back into his chair. He can see a telescope, Tiff's telescope, positioned by the living room windows, and out of place with the room's décor. It reminds Hap of Otis's Christmas tree.

"Yeah, we.... I was aware of a lot of men's clothes, but you have to understand the way everybody, especially those girls, was feeling." Jerry's staring at his splayed hand as if he's trying to literally pull a proper explanation out of his head for how Hap was kicked to the curb.

"It's okay. I was...." Hap wants to say he was miserable

and difficult to deal with because it's true that he did just mope around that little bedroom, waiting. No, he won't belittle himself to set Jerry, or anybody else, at ease. "It worked out fine. I got everything I needed, really needed. Everything except this tote...this sculpture I actually wanted to use for a *Providence Journal* piece on heirlooms. Umm, one of the Browns, the Brown University Browns, owned it, if you can believe that. It's black and like a toad or a frog. It's an ugly little thing."

"I think I remember it. I didn't think it belonged to Tiff. *Providence Journal*, huh? You're taking pictures for them?" Jerry trails off as Mrs. Lorice stands by the sink with her arms crossed. Her eyes are misty; she doesn't see Hap or her husband anymore. She is off with Tiff in some sweet somewhere.

"It's in her room. Some of your clothes are probably mixed in." Jerry's biting his lip, standing above his chair with a hand clenching the frame of his glasses. "You can take whatever else you want," he says softly.

Hap notes that the TV is off. How much of their night has been spent in a cricket-framed silence? Or maybe they were just reading; maybe nobody's as miserable as Hap is.

"Thank you, this was really good. I've been living off wings and fries...." Jerry's hardly cracking a smile, but it's there, nevertheless. "I can go check?" Hap asks.

"Go ahead," Jerry says just as Mrs. Lorice seems to snap out of her trance.

"Oh, I never asked if you wanted anything to drink," she says like she forgot something on a checklist. Hap politely tells her he's fine, despite his throat and lips aching from their dryness. The leftovers went down fine enough. He has never responded well to pleasantries.

"Still taking pictures with that beaut?" Jerry asks just as Hap is about to head upstairs, noting the camera dangling around his neck. Hap has grown so used to the weight of it that it feels like nothing more than a tie.

"Ah, yeah, I bring it everywhere." Hap smiles. Jerry has always been a tech geek. He spent months planning out which telescope he'd buy Tiff.

"You have pictures on there of Tiff and you?" Mrs. Lorice asks, seemingly slipping back into their presence.

"No, not on here. Ah, they're on my computer in the city," Hap lies. Every photo he ever took of her is in the thing around his neck. He'll have to look if he shows them to Mrs. Lorice, and he can't stand to see Tiff's face. Not now. Not until he finds her.

"Would you send them to me? All of them. I would really, really love that...." Mrs. Lorice has given up. She is where Hap can't go. She is ready to pull the nostalgic trigger and leave her husband on the couch for the days, weeks, and years to follow before he too gives up and gives in to the suffocation of memory.

"Yeah, definitely, as soon as I get home. I'm just going to grab that sculpture."

Creaking up the carpeted stairs, Hap wonders if Tiff's dog, Snack, ran away or died in the last few months. She loved that little guy, a St. Charles like Ron Burgundy's Baxter from *Anchorman*. Old age hits the little energetic pups the worst. She used to kid about bringing him to stay at their new apartment "to keep out the mice," but most importantly, to eat up all the crumbs Hap would spill during his video game blitzkriegs.

Arriving at a familiar bedroom door with a Carl Sagan *Cosmos* poster plastered across it, Hap finds Tiff's bedroom to be both as it should and should not be. Everything is arranged the same way since Hap last saw it, save for one detail. There is a naked man in Tiff's bed, greasy with blood, and clutching a furry, shriveled up thing across his chest that is not a stuffed animal. Hap can only let out a single, hoarse shout that wants so desperately to be a scream, but his throat is too dry from the chicken. The man's blue eyes steal all the wonder from Tiff's bedroom, a ceiling covered in entire galaxies of glow-in-the-dark stars.

"I got really bored, so I had dinner too," the man says in a sickening whisper. He throws what's left of Snack onto the floor, perks up onto his knees, and grins at Hap with his tongue half lolling out of his mouth; it's almost as if he's pretending to be a dog himself. In his hand, he has a thin, wiry little knife: a stiletto. He is too groomed, muscular, and young to be anything like Otis. He is a murderous jock with a shaved head. Why the fuck is he naked?

Hap's hand settles on the half open doorknob. The totem is on the floor beside a pair of shoes and what must be the man's clothing; the naked man inspected it and cast it aside like a reptile's clump of skin. "Don't go!" the man begs, pouncing from the bed. He grabs Hap by the throat, forcing him to squeal as though he has not yet gone through puberty. Hap's jerked to the floor, banging his head against the side of Tiff's bedpost. For an instant, the glow-in-the-dark stars on the ceiling seem to be calling to him.

The blood-splattered man holds his knife up to the light, using his knee to press Hap into the floor. A yelling somebody stomps up the stairs. "You're with them, huh?" The man is moaning through gritted teeth as his face flares up with rage enhanced by the blood that seems to be fueling the fire in his eyes. "Your stars will blink, and your cosmic masters will weep and know us brave few men." The invader raises his thin knife to Hap's wrist just as Jerry bursts into the room.

"What the fuck!" he's screaming, barging toward the blood-splattered man just as the dog-eater pulls away from Hap, dancing on nimble feet. He meets Jerry, and there is a wet, popping sound. Swimming in through Hap's headache, he realizes he's becoming familiar with the noise a knife makes when it meets soft flesh and all those hollow pockets quickly filled by air beneath the skin. Turning his back on the butchery, Hap crawls toward the open window and the spiteful chill of distant autumn.

"Yes! Yes!" The blood-splattered man shrieks behind Hap

as the sounds of tearing meat, not unlike a T-shirt splitting in two, reverberate throughout the room. Mrs. Lorice is shrieking downstairs. Is she calling the police? Could the Coventry police be in on this too? No way the whole state could be corrupt, but with Scituate's reservoir and Otis's nonsense about a poor vampire girl in mind, greed and public anxiety create all sorts of loopholes for the cult's predators to operate. The killer was watching the house. He crept in from the woods, stuck to the shadows, and evaded Otis's watching eye. The Shack *is* looking for Hap. They want him quiet. They want him to disappear with as little commotion as possible; that's why he's not a wanted man....

There's a lower roof just below Tiff's window that she used to sneak onto when she was younger to watch for shooting stars. As Hap climbs through the window, his fresh tattoo begins to ache as his arms brace against the roof. He's sure the blood-splattered man will grab his foot at the last second. Instead, the man's glee-stricken face fills the open window frame when Hap looks over his shoulder.

"I see the moon. The moon sees me," the killer sings a lullaby, following Hap onto the roof.

Hap crawls to the second tier of roofing over the garage before rising on shaky legs to hop down to the garage gutter in hopes of lowering himself to the driveway. His camera dangles from his neck, and Hap wonders if the killer cracked it. The blood-splattered man's worn, white basketball shoes clunk onto the garage rooftop. In the time it took Hap to clamber across the roof, the man was able to slip on shoes and jeans, but still no shirt. Dog tags that Hap didn't notice before hang from his neck. Hap lets go of the gutter and drops to the gravel right before the man's shoes smash where Hap's departing fingertips were.

Someone who reeks of piss and grease brushes by Hap's side and Otis's stench has never smelled so good. Otis taps his knife against his thigh and tilts his head to meet the gaze of the blood-splattered man on the roof. Eye to widening eye, the mad killers smile at one another. Hap gets the distinct impression that, like two rabid dogs, these two may just turn on him in their frenzy and share the spoils. Hap takes a few steps back; the man jumps onto the hood of Jerry's Jeep before hopping to the driveway, holding his knife backwards.

"You could be my dad," the man says no less than fifteen feet from Otis. The dog eater's voice has the faintest Southern twinge to it. Hap is directly behind Otis, ignored for now. He can feel the chaos crawling through the air, ready to combust.

"Fuck moms after the fact, boy, with this right here." Otis holds his knife out like a badge. "Maybe I got yers?"

The young murderer is all smiles. "Well, congratulations on finding her. I'd do it myself, I could. My dad's the one I'd like to see, though. I been thinking — 'cause he's an outsider like you — I been thinking you know each other. You ever run into a man named David Woodbury? He's got a big ol' blue octopus tattooed on his bald head. Or are you not the servant of Yog-Shit-Sock and the hoarder of eyes?" The blood-splattered man then looks over Otis's shoulder and addresses Hap. "Do you know where my father is?"

Otis strikes amidst the dog eater's disjointed rambling, but the young man is ready. Like the mandibles of dueling insects they meet, and their knives immediately find soft bits and sink home. Interlocked and bleeding, Otis and Woodbury slide backwards into Jerry's Jeep. There are grunts and growls, though determining which man initiates each sound is impossible. They are conjoined into one snarling beast.

Otis is pierced in an ugly, blood-gushing spot along his breast while his knife has only sunk into Woodbury's bicep, which pumps streams of blood across Otis's clothes, filling the gravel beneath their feet like rainwater. Several flicks of the wrist, and the fight is already winding down. Both killers' movements are slowing. They're bleeding to death.

Woodbury angles his stiletto up through Otis's collar, slashing back down across his neck and chest, trying to dig deep into his throat. Otis, slower, pulls his fat knife through the rest of Woodbury's arm and into his ribcage. The stiletto clatters to the ground while Otis twists the blade, and the young man's startled cry gurgles.

"See the gatekeeper welcoming you in?" Woodbury moans. Otis coughs, birdlike. They both fall. Woodbury slumps against the Jeep while Otis, on all fours, presses a hand to his wound.

"Oh fuck, no." Hap is pulling his hair out, running to Otis's side as the big man struggles to get up. He immediately falls over Hap, nearly driving both of them to the gravel. Otis straightens himself up, taking a hobbled step toward the Caddie. Hap slings his arm around Otis's waist. The killer is so slick with blood that he nearly slips away from him.

"Couldn' even get the totem, couldja? Gonna have to drive now, gonna have to thumb the holes." Otis drools as he speaks. Hap half drags the limping goon into the backseat of the Caddie, and fuck it if he gets blood everywhere. Mrs. Lorice is screaming from inside the house. It sounds like she's talking to somebody, probably the cops. She's begging for help. Fuck.

Hap remembers Otis's insult and runs below Tiff's window. Tripping on the totem in the grass, he falls, hurting his own ribs. He grabs the ugly, damned thing and runs, wheezing, back to the car.

"Hospitals are where we die," Otis gurgles. "Cemetery man'll do um good."

"Not Cidalia?" Hap would much rather bring him to the old woman, but she's blind, shit.

"Hah, she no witch; he half a one at least."

Otis spits repeatedly onto the floor of his backseat. Hap brings the Caddie's engine to life, making thick tires grind away a sea of pebbles. Before them, the shirtless killer has curled into a bloody ball of torn, twitching flesh. Together boy and killer escape into the summer twilight, leaving both good and bad men dead and bleeding behind them.

CHAPTER 17
THE BRAIN FUNGUS

The man lives in a church, tucked away into a backroom the size of a closet; the place is really only one large chamber full of pews and a pocket of confessional booths. One door behind the stage, as Hap likes to think of the podium and Jesus on a cross, leads to a janitor's closet. The other goes to Mr. Hanson's room. The double doors are wide open, and candles are scattered among the pews. Hap never would have guessed that Mr. Hanson was actually a priest, but there's no way the guy is Catholic. Hap is surprised the freak doesn't actually live underground.

During the fifteen-minute drive from Coventry to Scituate, the still-conscious Otis begins to tear up his own clothing to tie greasy rags to his wounds. The one along his chest and collar seems to be the worst; Otis mutters that the blade touched bone, but it's the slashes along his neck that won't stop bleeding.

"Otis…Otis has been stabbed, hey!" Hap smacks his hands against the door to Mr. Hanson's room, hoping Otis was right about the man not being out back in his graveyard, dancing and piping all through the night for his mad rites.

"Otis has been stabbed before! He can hold on!" comes a reply before Mr. Hanson, clothed in sweat pants and sporting glasses, opens the door, scowls at Hap, and pushes past him. "Where is he, Mad Arab? Come on now; drag him out. I'll pull some stitching thread from the curtains."

Hap sprints down the aisle, realizing that Hanson hasn't

followed him outside to help carry Otis, who's lost enough blood at this point to have a proper excuse for being crazy. With much cursing and growling from Otis, Hap gets him into the church, sweating so profusely that if it weren't for the chill in the air making his perspiration run cold, he'd collapse from exhaustion. Mr. Hanson kneels down in the middle of the aisle; a messy clump of string, a stack of towels, tape, and a faintly gleaming needle in his hand. He's thrown a black sheet up over Jesus on the cross. Maybe Mr. Hanson is a little bit Christian after all.

Otis starts slipping in and out of consciousness. "Can I turn the lights on? Are there lights?" Hap asks, staring at the bulbs along the ceiling. More shadows than illumination pour from the eerily flickering candles scattered around the room. One sliver of burning is behind Mr. Hanson, but no way he can even get a good look at Otis's wounds. The priest jabs his needle in, sifting the curled-up thread through Otis's skin as Hap's opinion shifts to being thankful that the lighting is dim.

The process takes a good thirty minutes, as Mr. Hanson takes care of Otis's chest and neck. Hap asks if anything else needs to be done, but all he gets back is, "Maybe bleeding inside, maybe not. I'm not a doctor. I'm an artist of faith." Hanson grins at Hap as he says that. Hap wonders just how many visitors this lonesome graveyard church gets, especially with the bigger, better church in the center of town only two little blocks away. "I leave my stitching's all over the wood. Floating in the reservoir and sucked into the dam. Little reminders of what's waiting for all of us."

"Between you and this guy...." Hap gestures to Otis, who's blinking now but still seems to be out of it. "You talk like I'm supposed to actually understand what you're saying."

"You will wish you did. If only we could understand these forces, these living things right below, above and between. If you worship what you do not understand, you won't be disappointed, let me tell you."

Hap stares at the black sheet covering Jesus. The figure beneath that sheet could be anything. Masks conceal all.

Finally, Mr. Hanson mutters, "He'll live," and wipes his brow, trailing Otis's blood across his face. "Now, we bring him into the earth. Help me carry him." Otis's wounds are bandaged, the knife wound having severed what looks to be the tattoo of some kind of eel or weird fish wrapping around his torso.

"Underground?" Hap's not sure he heard correctly. "Can't he rest up here? Or I could bring him home to—"

"It's not about resting." Mr. Hanson sneers with a face so squinted Hap feels like he's being chewed out by an impatient professor because he didn't do his homework. "It's a rite. I will do my charms so nothing will spread to his mind. We will both shed our skin and dance and sing to the crawling—"

Hap stops Mr. Hanson's babble before it can really begin by waving his hand at him. "Stop, stop it. How about you help me carry him to the car?" Hap doesn't like how he sounds, as if he's about to totally lose it.

"He wants it. I give it." Mr. Hanson cradles Otis's head, and the killer moans and mutters something about cats.

"I'm going to get him home...home to his cats, so he can sleep and hopefully, you know, not die," Hap says, not wanting to imagine continuing on all alone without Otis.

"No right, not right." Mr. Hanson giggles, letting Otis's head fall to the floor. "Proud mockery of his father. His body will heal, but his mind will be taken. You don't do this, you will have chaos instead of a knife by your side."

"I'm not going into that pit out back. He's in no condition to crawl down there," Hap says.

"Don't make my efforts here be a waste of thread." From the tone of Mr. Hanson's voice, he doesn't seem to really care about Otis.

"We're not going down there into the dirt." Hap kneels by Otis's side and swoons, feeling the weariness from a shitty night's sleep and a long day's delirium. "Come on, buddy, can you walk at all?" he asks Otis, concerned about accidentally tearing his stitches.

"Chaos then, I salute it." Mr. Hanson kneels on the opposite side of Otis and whispers down to him, "Do you? Orphan?"

"Let tha' pipes fuckin' play. I see it in the field already, stealing the starlight to paint its door. Shack's behind me. Thank ya."

Whatever Otis is saying gets Mr. Hanson to grab his arm and nod to Hap, ready to toss him out of the church. Together, silent, they both carry Otis to the Caddie, and all the while, Hap can't stop shivering.

"I'll leave a memorial for you both, burning and floating in the reservoir. Something to remember you by."

Mr. Hanson's face is grim through the Caddie's window. Hap again takes control of the car that's twice as wide as anything he's ever driven, and it's no wonder Otis drove like a mad man.

Back at Otis's home, Hap struggles to walk him inside. The wounded murderer mumbles something about "sleep" and "bed." Two cats mull about their feet with affection and what Hap would like to think of as concern. That's when he remembers the woman in the bathroom.

"Did you find some hope? How high do your spirits soar?" Augustine taunts, giggling to herself.

Otis's bedroom is a teenage boy's den, complete with a water damaged *The Empire Strikes Back* poster against a wall. There's a fat TV attached to what Hap recognizes as vintage Nintendo SNES that has a stack of games piled on top of it. There's even a telescope, small and cheap, propped against the room's one window.

"Did you look into the well? Did you make a wish and pray to your forgotten, sleeping gods?" Augustine screeches.

Hap leans Otis down onto his twin bed, over Spider Man sheets and pillowcases. He heads to the kitchen, gets him a coffee mug of water, and is relieved when Otis manages to guzzle down some of it.

"How about whiskey? Get whiskey. The bottle. Gotta clean, didn' clean me." Otis spits some of the water onto his floor as he pushes Hap toward the door. That's right, infection — Hanson didn't seem to do anything about it. Otis's wounds are already dressed, fuck.

A voice flutters from the bathroom, calling softly, "Either one of you want to get sucked? Come on. Let me see you. Let me comfort you. I can be your whore. I can ease your broken hearts. You got me; you might as well use me. I won't bite."

Hap can't imagine someone sick and dumb enough to give into her. They'd deserve to have their dick bitten off. What the hell are they going to do with her now? That totem, too. Otis hasn't even looked at it.

Before getting the booze, Hap looks down at his hands and how sticky the blood trailing along his wrist is. He rushes to the sink, thankful, at least, that none of the red stuff is his. He then finds the sole bottle of booze easily enough. After that, it's a struggle, shifting through the garage — hell, finding the garage's light switch — before looking for duct tape. He walks past a big first aid box about a dozen times before realizing what it is. It's mostly full of Band-Aids, but there's antiseptic, gauze, and thick pads that'll work with duct tape. Otis is probably too out of it to inspect the totem but screw him. Hap retrieves it from the Caddie's back seat; maybe he can get some kind of answer on it before the night is through.

Hap notices his camera in the passenger seat and inspects it, only to discover that the lens cracked during his scramble along the roof. It still turns on, at least. He gently places the camera down and steadies himself by holding onto the steering wheel with one hand. He takes a deep breath before screaming out as much of his frustration as he can.

"It's nothing to do with the Moon Shack," Otis says of the

totem, staring at the whiskey with longing; he's too tired to get out of bed and take it from Hap, who stands just far enough away.

"But what is it?" Hap holds the totem up. Otis needs rest, but Hap's answers come first.

"Totem, like ya say. We may have an invisible ally in the Miskatonic. Why he gives a soon-to-be-missing girl a totem be a mystery to join the rest." Hap throws the damned thing on the floor, and he would never look at it again if he's so lucky. The man, Woodbury, he was already waiting outside Tiff's. The cult's organized; they managed to figure out the likely places Hap would go. Woodbury broke in, killed Snack when he saw Hap at the front door. But why?

Otis is all too happy to spare the whiskey while Hap washes away the ugly, red-and-black stitched oozing gashes that have already started bleeding through Hanson's bandages. The most he's ever done for somebody is put a Band-Aid on his little sister's foot. Now he's playing nurse. When the blood is out of sight, Augustine starts wailing about how they should hear her singing voice, so Hap shuts the bedroom door. He hears the cork popping on the whiskey bottle behind him.

"Could blame ya, but I won. One less of 'em. Two total, since me an you met. One for lova', one for motha.' Have a drink; we're livin'; workin', inchin' along, yeah?" Otis takes a swig, and Hap remembers the last time he drank right from a bottle. He feels nauseous from the memory alone. One of the cats begins mewing at the bedroom door.

"Little fella don' need to see this. You, me, drink," Otis says before Hap can let the beast in.

"I'm not a drinker. I'll puke on your rug," Hap tells him. Otis is a trooper. How many holes were slashed into him?

"Ya can only drink and upchuck so many times 'fore you're a pro…trust me." So Hap rips a shot and nearly pukes. Otis follows except he swishes around that burning shot like mouthwash. "Good enough," Otis says, propping the whiskey on a stand by his bed, closing his eyes. "Let light go. Morning, we start over."

Hap hopes that doesn't mean they have another day like this, but what else could there even be? What more must they do to bring Tiff closer?

Augustine is singing something nonsensical in a whiney, high-pitched voice. "Something else. Something else," she keeps repeating in her lyrics, reminding Hap of the sexless monster Otis babbled about, *The Else* that lives in the Shack. The cats linger by the bathroom door as if intrigued by the song.

Hap manages to find a few old clothes that sort of fit him in Otis's dresser beneath the TV. The weirdly orange T-shirt is too small, and the jeans are too long, but they're both clean. When Hap lies on the couch, and the cats curl across his chest, he finds sleep anyway amongst the melody of their purring. The sounds of Jerry's skewered, crying body resurface, and Hap's tears mesh with soft, feline fur.

***

Hap awakens with a throb from his bruised head. One of Otis's cats is on his chest, and the morning is freshly born, fading from the dark blue of night into sunrise. The thing in the bathroom is silent. Otis needs sleep and rest; he lost too much blood the night before. They are going to need food. Hap's stomach is so tight it hurts. He'll have to go back to Cidalia's.

Hap heads outside and stops when he's behind the wheel of the Caddie once more. The interior is like the bloody socket of a recently pulled tooth. Passing through town in this would be stupid, and Mrs. Lorice probably called the cops if they didn't kill her. There's a chance Hap is wanted now. She never saw Otis. Her husband is dead, along with a half-naked stranger outside, and her dog has been butchered and half eaten, while the boy who used to date her daughter who mysteriously disappeared is now missing himself. Yes, even if the Moon Shack's corruption extends beyond the point of reason, there is once again a good chance he is wanted by sane and insane cops alike.

He uses some rags from the garage to wipe down the interior of the Caddie, taking Otis's Boston Red Sox hat off the dash and placing it snugly upon his own head. It smells like aged sweat, but it'll do.

Driving through Scituate, Hap decides against going to see Cidalia. How much food could she make anyhow? Woodbury was watching Tiff's house because they knew about Hap. It seems like a massive leap, but maybe they figured he would run somewhere that would welcome him. Otis still isn't a suspect, but Hap, remembering what Jerry's hospitality got him, drives until he comes to the convenience store at a big Cumberland Farms gas station. He's about to use his credit card his mom pays the bills for to buy a heap of sandwiches before he realizes it could be traced. There are probably cameras outside, too, making sure nobody messes with the gas pumps. He has about eighty bucks in tip money he neglected to put into his bank account. What the hell is he going to do?

Hap scans a stack of newspapers by a bathroom but finds nothing mentioning the previous night's killings. Nobody's going to start noticing an Indian boy just yet. It occurs to Hap that this doesn't bode well for Mrs. Lorice's vitality. He returns to Otis's shack. As he walks through the front door, he hears Augustine singing while Otis is moaning in pain.

Hap creeps into Otis's room, where he's mumbling rhythmically in his sleep, repeating the same syllables of every incomprehensible word Augustine chants from the bathroom. It's as if Augustine really is some kind of witch, but that can't be. He can't start playing with superstitious ideas — not now, not when he's all alone.

Hap tries unsuccessfully to rouse Otis. His forehead is covered in rain droplets of sweat. His bandages have oozed through. Could it be tetanus? Woodbury's knife could have been rusty, or Mr. Hanson's needle could have been covered in all manner of graveyard muck. Fuck. Hap runs into the kitchen and gets a glass of water. He feebly tries splashing it around Otis's lips, pouring some of it on his forehead, but there's no response.

Infection. Otis needs to be in a hospital. His surely unwashed bed probably got him sick. Hospitals won't work, right? Rhode Island General is less than half a mile away from the Miskatonic. No, no, people overcome infection without doctors, right? Antibiotics, fuck. Hap needs to go out again. He remembers a CVS next to a soccer field across from that Cindy's Diner of alluring neon.

Making the trip through Scituate once more, Hap is wary of cameras as he walks to the pharmacy at the back of the store. When he asks for antibiotics, the pretty woman behind the counter, who's probably right out of grad school, gives him a frown. She then explains what somebody should've mentioned to Hap at some point in his sixteen years of schooling. If he wants antibiotics, he'll need a fucking doctor's prescription. He asks, "Is there anything like antibiotics? My friend doesn't have healthcare." He uses the worst lie he could ever think of, and the pharmacist tells him to fuck off in the nicest way possible. She talks to him like he isn't the sort of person to engage in kidnappings and befriend a lunatic who has since saved his life twice. That's what Otis has done, crazy or not. He's saved Hap's goddamned life, and now, Hap is too stupid to figure out something that'll return the favor.

There's got to be some method, some modern trick to help Otis. There is that library right next to the graveyard and Mr. Hanson's house and church. Even in college, Hap avoided the library at all costs, but when your phone's busted and there's nobody around to lend you their laptop....

An old librarian with classic-looking glasses looks Haps up and down, sniffs once to confirm that he needs to find a shower soon, and then points him to the computer section. Google solves as many questions as Hap can think to ask. He returns to the CVS and buys some Nyquil and a big bottle of Tylenol.

Back at Otis's, Augustine continues to chant and call Hap and Otis every dirty word in the book. As if she's a worthless seagull, Hap tosses two sandwiches into the bathroom without looking at her. There's an awful stench in there. Has she not been using the toilet? She'll need something to drink, too, especially with the muggy resurgence of August's heat. There must be a swamp nearby. It's as if the humidity is making the walls of Otis's house themselves ooze and stink.

Otis's fever has only increased while Hap was gone, and, according to Google, that's how the bacteria dies. If his body temperature gets high enough, that's how the fever paradoxically kills him. To keep some of the fever down, Hap pours a small cup of Nyquil between Otis's lips. He'll have to see how much the guy can take before pushing him further.

"I don't know if you can hear me," Hap starts to tell Otis, feeling corny. He's never stood over somebody's potential deathbed before. "Just wake the fuck up, man. You're going to get hot before you get better. You gotta boil before you kill this thing." Hap says "thing" as if it's more than bacteria making Otis loopy. He remembers that bullshit Mr. Hanson mentioned, but contrary to all talk of the Moon Shack and ancient gods from other dimensions, the superstition that disease is from an evil spirit is full on Salem-witch-trial nonsense.

"Been Egypt," Otis drools, his spittle creating a spider web through his beard.

"You can hear me...can you open your eyes? You, uh, want a sandwich?" Hap winces as Augustine's frantic chanting grows into a howling. If Otis manages to moan anything else, Augustine drowns it out. Hap wonders if that witch will melt if he splashes her with water. He'd be so lucky.

He has to slide apart the bathroom door to look at Augustine, and he doesn't want to feel bad. The idea that there is a woman in the bathroom slowly dying of thirst and maybe contemplating drinking toilet water is enough to make him vomit. This is a time for bravery, possibly revenge and even insanity, but he will not feel guilty. As Hap gets a good look at Augustine, the surprising sight before him recalls a multitude of feelings, but guilt is not among them. Nearly gagging before he can comprehend what he's looking at, Hap sees that the cats are dead and that they have pissed and shit themselves all over the floor in the process of dying. Cue the blood on the walls, sopping Augustine's skin and dripping from the jagged ends of raw, red bones — the cat's own bones, torn from their bodies — clutched in both her hands. Tossed into the sink are the mutilated corpses of both Otis's pets. She did this with her bare hands. The half-moon on her skull has been replaced with a bloody star, that familiar seven-pointed star with seven orbs spiraling from every point.

Hap vomits up his sandwiches all over the floor and partially into the mug of water in his hand, which he then drops, as he's consumed by a stomach-folding retching as Augustine's laughter seems to echo off the bathroom walls. She's throwing something that bounces off the front of his shirt and dribbles to the floor — a cat's eye. Augustine grins at him, and she spit it; she didn't throw it. There's another eye in her mouth that she clutches between her teeth as she sneers, spitting it up into the air.

"It came to me in my sleep. The Shack needs another purple queen. If your girlfriend isn't dead, then she'll do. They don't keep people chained up unless they have a plan. D'you have a plan, little boy? What do you want to do to me? Cause I've seen the moonlight. I've heard the ringing of the dinner bell." She smacks her fistful of bones against the floor, swings her arm around to the wall, and a seven-pointed star and its vortex of planets have been scratched across the tiles.

Hap hurls himself out of the bathroom, whimpering, slamming the door to that portal to hell as hard as he can. It's satisfying doing something with true force for once. He bumps into the fridge in an effort to get to the sink and rinse his mouth out a thousand times. The black ceramic cat on the top of Otis's fridge, a totem that in a way mocks and rivals the horrible toad sculpture, shatters across the floor.

Changing his clothes once more, Hap sits at the foot of Otis's bed and turns on the old TV. The Nintendo works fine, as a picture of Mario and Luigi fill the screen accompanied by their classic theme song. Otis starts humming in his delirium before saying, "They use storm damage ta cover 'em up, they do, civil wars an storms an chaos on hospitals," and then he slobbers back off into humming and moaning. Hap, unable to find a TV remote, presses the buttons on the screen to raises the volume as loud as it will go and begins level one. He will travel back in time, if necessary, to retrace every single step he's ever taken.

CHAPTER 18
THE PURPLE MOTHER

"It's a small mercy, at least, that he didn't get the chance to mutilate her face," Johan said over the phone as Paul knelt in the blood. She had been new among the Candle Lighters. Maybe that's why Johan seemed to not be too upset over her death. She had been so warm, kind. But beyond anything sexual, she seemed to want to make Paul comfortable. She wanted him to know that the Moon Shack wasn't so scary. And he believed that. The moment he walked into his apartment and saw her corpse lying in a Jack O' Lantern's grin of knives, he smiled. It felt like some kind of silly joke to him.

Johan had Paul leave the house before conducting his own investigation, which was his way of phrasing things, not Paul's. Augustine's purse was there, on the couch. Paul didn't notice it after discovering Lacy. According to Johan, Augustine had been taken.

Since Lacy's death, the drinking has gotten worse, as if there were an invisible strainer around him that has been broken. He's always been happy to have a few, but now he keeps emptying glasses until he pukes.

Johan has given Paul a room number. Four-four-four. The Moon Shack's priest mentioned on the phone that four is considered cursed in many oriental cultures, as the word for death in Chinese is the same as four. Just like the number thirteen in Western culture, many buildings in China go so far as to skip a floor, going from three to five. Johan mentioned that Augustine is "dead, surely." He told Paul, "Fittingly enough, in room four-four-four resides the woman she was to succeed. You will no longer have a wife, Paul. For the public, you will be a charming boy who makes appearances with his previously estranged mother: his best friend, mentor, and accomplice. We're gonna re-write your history, and we can thank your father for being a true gentleman and not publicly playing off your unofficial mother's death for political sympathy. I hope this is okay, Paul. Like the marriage, you won't have to play ball forever. You'll get what you want. Are you still listening? I promise, Paul, you will get what you want." Johan's words were melted caramel, and Paul, as if his lips were chocolate in the sun, met them and agreed. Why did he agree? Why can't he think straight? He doesn't even know what he wants. Where has he been this whole time? What the hell are they doing to him?

Paul doesn't ask questions because there are certain answers that will make him vomit, keel over, and look up at the stars for what they really are. He hasn't peered over the edge of the cliff where the Moon Shack sits below, but he has heard the sounds of what goes on down there.

The hotel is overbooked. Paul, even with his throbbing head and restless gut, has been forced to conduct several job interviews while assigning his leading employee, Cassandra, to interview another half a dozen. In droves, the citizens of the Moon Shack are checking in, staying a while. They've been coming from all over the country. Randal works around the clock, and being the machine that he is, he tolerates it with a smile. The bar is left nearly empty, as the kinds of people who drink and order room service are thinning out. It's gotten to the point that Paul feels sick sitting in front of the eternally bartending Randal, so he leaves the Egyptian to his room full of limitless poisons and his minimum wage.

As soon as Paul enters the Miskatonic lobby, he's pulled

aside by Cassandra's assistant front desk girl, Lindsey, before he can get to the elevators. "Do you know where Cassie is? Did she call out sick or something? She's not texting me back. I need help up here. Some of the requests I've been getting are weird. I called in Jamie and —"

"That's fine. Do what you need to." Paul realizes he's wearing the same clothes as the night before. Or is it two nights? He can't remember the last time he brought anything in for dry-cleaning. Hell, he can't remember the last time he went to the bathroom. He refuses to let himself wonder why the Moon Shack's citizens are filling the Miskatonic like a beehive. "I'm sure Cassie is just fine," Paul lies, not daring to think of the likely alternatives before he hurries off to the elevators.

The door to Room 444 is open, and when Paul enters, he finds himself bathed in the purple glow of royalty. The walls are violet curtains, the furniture a collection of antiques; this isn't a hotel room but some kind of apartment. The air smells of antiseptic and plastic. A shade of purple comes alive, elegantly approaching Paul like an optical illusion coming into focus. As his eyes adjust, a kindly old woman unbent by age beckons to him with a diamond-adorned hand.

"Are you my newest son?" She smiles, taking Paul's hand and hugging him. She tells him her name is Angie. She whispers in his ear, "Shame we never met at a wedding, no?" She pulls away. Angie's brown eyes show no senility. She places her fingers to her lips and says, "My life extends instead of ceasing, and I get to be a mother again. That means we should celebrate with a drink!" She goes over to an old-fashioned liquor cabinet built into the wall. Paul's still hung up on the word "mother."

"Were you Augustine's mother?" Paul asks. There is a hint of glamour to the woman while she pours him a brown burning something in a brandy snifter, matching his drink with a glass twice as full. As she hands it to him, he sees just how perfectly straight and white her teeth are.

"I am yours," she says, and there is life beneath those wrinkles. She is not his mother who lives in his head and who will remain in his dreams. "As far as the public will be concerned, the eyes of our citizens are already open to you finding a new wife. In the meantime, as I'm sure you've been told, I will be your companion, as unorthodox as it may seem. I will be your number one supporter. A man like you and a gal like me, we'll make all the citizens who are full of regret come to find relief."

"The purple's nice," Paul says, although he could care less.

"I don't need to tell you I love it," she says. "There is nothing more unique and special. Purple shows in flowers and gems, far from the common of red and blue. Purple is the miracle that comes from nothing. Why are you not wearing your tie?" Paul remembers that neck choker and how Johan gave it to him right before his first day at the Miskatonic. It was in a fancy box, the sort someone would use to stow a fine cigar or bottle of cognac.

"Who came up with this idea? I get the whole power-couple thing, even though this ain't Hollywood, but are people going to look up to me while I'm standing next to my mom? No offense, but name one successful man, name one leader who goes out with his mother."

Angie clasps her hands in front of her purple velvet dress, holding up her lightly-drained glass of brandy as she sits on a couch that almost looks like it's made of the same material she's wearing. "Dear, who put it in your head that you're a star? You're a sweet man, passionate and, from what I hear, primal." Angie licks her weathered lips, and Paul's loins shrivel. "I know Johan told you no such thing. Did Augustine give you this idea? May her spirit reside in the great hall within—"

"Johan said Augustine and I were a power couple. Exact words. I was thinking nightly dinners at The Capital Grille and front row seats at the old performing arts center." Paul takes a sip of the cognac and remembers being a boy who once threw up all over his father's kitchen floor after smuggling a single sip from the prettiest bottle left out on the counter.

"Your ambitions of being a cutthroat politician and the next Buddy Cianci fell short. It's a beautiful thing only made sad by how crushed you are. I know how you feel, Paul. I know what it's like to not get what you want. I was going to be a real star, the kind before a camera, but I had a son, a special son with a special appetite who needed me more than anything. More than any audition held at a rat producer's schedule." Angie gulps her brandy until it's no more than a splash. Her fingernails, trailing down to red knuckles, are purple.

"Listen, you want to know what I do with my time besides sit behind that desk downstairs? You and Johan keep calling me innocent; meanwhile, my dick is covered in ten kinds of skank, and I haven't been able to keep a solid meal down all week because of this right here." He thrusts out his glass, spilling its brown poison all over the black and blue carpet that Paul is surprised the old woman hasn't rebranded her favorite color.

"In my time," she says, "which is a healthy chunk of history, I have only heard urban legends of a mayor who was beloved, and those legends were spread by people with bonuses hidden in their front pockets. When a modern man goes to war, what does he have in his pockets?"

"Naked pictures of his girlfriend." Paul owes this woman no respect, no courtesy...she is Johan's, though. Of all the people he has met, she is a kindly old woman. A being who walks too straight and smiles with a suspicious sparkle, as if she swishes shots from the fountain of youth in her mouth and won't tell her secret to the decaying, walking dead around her.

"Perhaps." Angie smiles, and Paul bets she was a slut in her day. All you'd have to do to make a porn star a saint is have her become a soft old lady. "But it would be for more than just a pair of breasts to lust over. She would become something more than a nymph in his head. A soldier carries pictures of his family.

A soldier on the battlefield looks at an image from his dreams, from an alien world he fears he no longer recognizes. You're a living picture of what our citizens remember, flawed as you are, while they march ahead to make a stand against true evil. You're a middle-aged man partying like James Dean, and that desk you sit at below us is a throne."

"What do I do?" Paul asks, and he can't believe he's never made the connection before, but he's like a pig being fattened. A pig or a goat.

"Let us love you. When we find you a wife, you'll be happier. You'll have children. Children who will grow to both appreciate the Shack and understand it. You may even have a few on the way. Who knows. It's summer. Fertile season." Angie's mouth drops open as she dances over to Paul with raised arms, embracing him. The brandy goes from bitter to sour in his stomach. Where is the puke when you need it? "We're going to turn you into the human dream. You'll be that picture in the wars to come. Safely in the Shack, waiting for us to come in from the front lines. You and your beautiful wife and dutiful children will be the reason we persevere."

Paul sets the glass on the countertop beside the old-school liquor cabinet. He leans in close to Angie's perfect mouth. "If I wanted kids, I wouldn't have made my ex-wife get an abortion," he says—compliments of his first failed marriage, one month into their divorce negotiations. Angie doesn't even blink. What was that she said about war? Paul's nightmares are beginning to glow-in-the-dark.

"Paul, did you love Augustine? While everybody had hoped…we didn't expect you to fall for each other so soon into your arrangement. I'm sorry if you're hurting… she would have looked so beautiful, wearing purple down that aisle in the ballroom." The old woman's raising a hand to his cheek, brushing away a few tears that shock Paul into realizing he's crying. He feels nothing for Augustine, though. Lacy wasn't even twenty-five, he's sure of it. He'd never even gotten her opinion on Augustine.

"I have to get to work," Paul says, and more than anything, he has to sit down.

"We should talk more," Angie says. "You should come back and visit me every day to tell me how you're feeling. We'll make do with what we have, and we'll find you a new wife. The hotel's booked, after all. Our citizens will be impatient. This could be the summer our world ends, after all. But until you are situated, they mustn't raise arms against our foe." Angie folds her hands along the empty glass, standing like a looming purple specter as Paul wipes away his tears.

"I need to know one thing," he begins, standing, swaying. "And I know it's like I've been told, over and over. But the Moon Shack...I know the why, but what is it? Besides shelter, besides the afterlife for people like you...." Paul thinks of Hap, the boy who did nothing wrong and the thought, a submerged memory from the past week, sinks into his gut like a knife. "...and like me." The dread rolls off his tongue and numbs him.

"Isn't it obvious, darling?" the Purple Witch says, brushing her hands against Paul's cheeks. "*You* are the Moon Shack."

A dam breaks in his mind. As the flood begins, Paul steps out into the hallway. Just before reaching the elevator, he hears a scream from somewhere else on the fourth floor. It's a single short cry from a woman who goes silent before she can truly let it all out. He pretends that little scream doesn't belong to Cassandra. He starts crying again once the elevator doors close.

CHAPTER 19
THE DOOM THAT CAME TO THE DREAMLANDS

Hap is consumed by brown fur as he tries to lift himself back off the hotel bed. Pulsing along his chest is a spider with too many legs that all end in goats' hooves. Black lumps that are really eyes prod out and blink at him beneath the fur. "Momma," something croaks behind Hap. He can't pull himself out of the thing in the bed that's letting loose an erotic moan, like a running loop of orgasms. He tries to shake himself free. One of those hooves snakes around to his mouth, prying him back and bending his spine. The many-legged thing burrows its hooves into the back of his throat. "Us next, Momma. Us next, Momma," croak a number of pale and stumpy humanoid figures aligning the corners of the room.

Hap awakens in the dark with something crawling down his mouth. His jaw hurts. Is Augustine free and trying to strangle him? A squeaking sound comes from within his throat, filling his ears, scratching up the insides of his mouth. Something is scratching his lips, and there's what feels like a snake smacking his chest. A tail! A tail! He grabs at the wriggling end of the massive furry thing in his throat, and, gagging, he pulls at the creature trying to burrow into his gullet. He can't breathe; he's falling, knocking his glass of water off the coffee table. Augustine is laughing great, screaming peals from the bathroom. With a great pop and a burst of pain across his lips from the rodent's flailing teeth, Hap pulls the wriggling, squealing rat from his mouth. The little bastard jerks out of his hand and disappears along the floor.

Hap cries and screams and begs into the darkness, softly bleeding from his mouth. *Augustine really is a witch,* Hap thinks. Weary and half besieged by sleep, he spends the rest of the night in Otis's room. He sits in a chair by the sick man's bed with his head tucked into a pillow against his chest. The rats and their fellow creeping things have claimed the living room.

In the pale of the morning light, Hap watches as Otis pisses the bed, a wet stain slowly seeping through the covers. "Moon won't burn ya, will just lead 'em to you," Otis mutters.

"Hey, can you hear me?" Hap whispers. "That's good advice, bud. Otis?"

Otis remains silent. His twitches have become infrequent but, when Hap conducts the repulsive task of changing his bandages, Otis's chest wound and the slashes along his neck aren't covered in anything green; they appear normal, although a bit oozy. The stitches have held, and the bandages are mostly covered in yellow pus. There's something new, though — a rash along Otis's arm. A few bubbly blisters have formed as if he came into contact with poison ivy or something equally venomous. The rash forms a jagged spiral around his arm as if he were wrapped with rope — *a tentacle.* Maybe there's a simple medical answer for what it is, but Hap is too stupid to think of anything.

At some point, Hap will throw Augustine a wet rag and a sandwich because he can't just starve her, can he? Beyond tending to the madwoman, Hap hesitates to imagine leaving Otis's bedroom and finding something productive to do with his time. He is sure he hears rats scurrying in the kitchen and the living room, talking to one another, planning something. Maybe they're eating Otis's moldy notebook pages. They are in the walls. They want to be inside of him.

Hap spends the rest of the day at Cidalia's to avoid the ever-mumbling Otis and Augustine's presence. After telling her that Otis is sick, he asks Cidalia to put him to work, helping her out around her house and backyard in exchange for food for him and Otis. She asks him if he's not getting enough work at his job, and it's the easiest thing in the world to lie, to tell her that his hours had been cut. Just like that, an old lady was taking care of him. There has been no word in the news as to what happened to Mr. Lorice, or, more ominously, Mrs. Lorice. Hap stops by the Scituate library to browse its computers and finds nothing.

That night, while sitting beside Otis and reading an old issue of *Spawn* from Otis's boyhood comic collection, Hap hears, "Mercy me, mother above, mother below...there is a pharaoh," from up in the bed. He has never been more relieved to hear the sound of nonsense. He tosses the comic aside and leans toward Otis, his heartbeat quickening as the killer opens his eyes.

"Otis, Otis," Hap repeats, but Otis only blinks at him. After twenty minutes of blinking, Hap wonders if he has brain damage. Further brain damage. Hap tries again for nearly an hour, but the killer is wordless. When Hap brings him some leftovers from his lunch at Cidalia's, the killer, who has been propped up on a stack of pillows, gently raises his hands and takes a bite from the sandwich, chewing meekly.

"Take your time." Hap holds his breath as Otis finishes the sandwich and stares at the blank TV across the room. As the night draws on, Hap waits and waits. He resumes his usual sleeping spot, in the chair beside Otis, sitting up with the lights on. At night, the rats own the living room in this witch house; he's sure of it.

The next morning, Otis's bed is empty. Hap rushes to the bedroom window to get a good look at the Cadillac that isn't there. From out in the hallway, Augustine starts begging for him to let her go "before he comes back and lets out the thing in his head." Hap stares at Otis's bare driveway and the unfolding foliage of another beautiful summer day, wordless.

***

There's something Otis wants to remember about seashells and how they are just pretty skeletons dragged ashore. There's also something to remember about a mother he will never see again and a template for a father he has never looked in the eyes. *Daddy was a drunk; Daddy was a fool; Daddy didn't know how to handle his own tool.* He finally met his dad in that place where dreams grow, detach, and sail off. Mommy worked at the hotel his whole life, stealing toilet paper and soap to clean his bum. *She met a Miskatonic man, and he filled her with glee and then out hopped me.* Otis can't stop his thoughts from singing. He went to the place where all the eyes he's collected over the years are planted into the ground. They sprout songs that sing themselves into keys; in that dream place, he hung each of those many, many keys from his belt.

His most recent sleep was different, despite how familiar it seemed. That damned thing snuck into his blood. Before the plane of death, there was a second option, a fork in the road leading to a familiar shack that never looks the same, no matter how many times you see it. The Shack possesses all the abandoned shacks in the woods of the world, hopping from each one like an antsy devil looking for the right host. Otis resisted, still, that beckoning door and the strange pipes that played within; he has a code to keep. Otis could not resist peering in through the Moon Shack's window, though. He saw his father. He saw the dimly lit piss-stained mattress his mother was thrust upon while the early morning garbage trucks snacked and smashed their ways through the city streets.

His father tried to double-cross them. He didn't love Otis; he didn't love Otis's mom. But he loved life, and he didn't like what they did with their knife. He is choked, and then his heart bursts while two boys from two moms go their own way; one starts killing and learning his way up the food chain; the other boy goes about kissing the asses of things who could eat him. Funny thing is the Moon Shack isn't even mad it got the pussy instead of the ape.

Otis's beard is gone; he hacked it away while the boy slept, and the latest Purple Witch hissed at him and shrank into her corner of filth. He didn't deserve the noble creatures she gutted. They blocked his dreams, kept *their* rats away and gave him his sanity. What Otis needed all along was one final dose of delirium so that he could see why the pharaoh with a thousand faces has been so patient. Otis has seen a day when the Shack meets the sunlight in a public square, full of curious pigeons and a sea of spectators who have never had the blood of another between their fingernails. Otis has seen a well-dressed man and a woman, both teeming in color-choking purple, as they lead a ceremony in honor of a new religion that all must try for themselves, while people enter the Shack one by one and their screams are muffled by the applause as the whole world is fooled. The killers are waiting, idly drawing their knives over identical rooms. Otis has seen the face of their leader just as he has seen the face of the gate.

As a clean-shaven man dressed in rags, Otis parks in front of a No Parking sign across from the Kennedy Plaza bus station. In the park up ahead, there's a fountain of mermaids and fish faces etched in greening bronze. When he was a boy, Otis thought they were magical. Now he knows where they come from and that sometimes gargoyles fly.

He spits all over himself when he sees the Miskatonic's neon sign. He thinks of the seven-pointed spiral star, a mocking salute to the eventual constellations that will be the end of man. He misses his beard to pull, so he reaches up to his hair that has grown out of combat proportions, and he gives it a good tug, removing a few strands to rub between his fingers. The Moon Shack thinks the malice of man is so potent as to be regarded among the legions of the unnamable. The followers of the Moon Shack think that mankind can stand against the unknowable, vast cosmos and all the horrible things that lurk there. They think humanity is wicked enough to earn itself the respect of being spared when the doom inevitably arrives. There will be no war, just an execution. The problem with mankind in general, Otis knows, is that it clings to even the slightest lick of hope.

The lobby is so busy it could be mistaken for a French restaurant at quarter past noon. Otis remembers the elephant's dance of footsteps miles above his head as he roamed their crypts and followed a guide that specialized in the in-between places where secrets are stacked up on parchments of clay. Providence has its share of manholes with geometrically ordained covers. Holes are scattered across the earth where bodies are stored. A small line forms at the front desk, and it's full of summer tourists making funny faces as they are told the hotel is overbooked. The office in the back is empty, the door unlocked.

***

When Paul lifts his head, Randal is nowhere to be found. When he looks back down to the oak of the bar, he realizes he's been laying on a picture. It must've been slipped under his head after he fell asleep, but it's enough to make him not question why he's suddenly sober. The picture is a photograph of the rogue bellhop, Hap and a blonde girl. His girlfriend, Paul realizes, a numbness creeping through his chest. Front desk girls are disappearing. Nicky Namaste, his favorite bum in the whole wide world, hasn't been around in weeks. Paul didn't even notice at first, which made him feel even sorrier for the poor bastard, but Angie is right. A ceremony is on the way. He is the Moon Shack. Did that mean he was the only one among them with a heart?

He studies the blonde girl next to Hap in the picture. Blonde was her natural color. She was nearly a foot taller than him. He's never known tall girls to prefer shorter guys. Hap must've been something special to her. Once. He traces his fingers over the photograph. He remembers Cassandra's scream. A while back, he remembers seeing a face that might have been familiar on the news while he was at the bar across the street from his apartment. A grad student at Keane College in New Hampshire. A girl, one of those out-of-place guests who may have been at the Palace of the Komodo. Paul is the Moon Shack, but that's not entirely true, is it? He is the one who stands outside the Moon Shack, welcoming the citizens, the Candle Lighters, as they enter, but is forbidden from stepping foot inside himself. They think they can make him one of them without being one of them — what a joke.

Paul ignores the panicked stares of Lindsey and the new kid at the front desk. He needs his gun. Lindsey says out loud that she needs him, and he'll help. When everybody hears that shot ring out, they'll leave her alone. The crossing of the doorway threshold works its psychological charms on his brain. His darkened office is soothing in its emptiness. The old purple lady said his desk was a throne....

Paul takes his seat, and that gun isn't meant for him. Johan was right about that. There is a boy out there who believes his girlfriend is missing. Hap was not a college boy. He believes he is in love, and he fucking crept right into the Miskatonic, donned his disguise, and went about fooling Paul until the Candle Lighters caught on to him. Paul remembers his dreams, the nightmares from outside the universe, but the thing about them is that they don't go disappearing women. There is a killer out there; he is a soldier for the other side...the enemy of man, but more importantly, the enemy of the Moon Shack. Angie mentioned pictures you hold onto in war. Hap has one. Paul doesn't. Paul doesn't have anything. Paul has to take responsibility for the missing girls, and he can't do that by putting a bullet into his brain. He is still a man, a person. Murder is for the beasts.

Cool air blows behind Paul from the draft in the passageways between the walls, and he can imagine slender hands reaching around his neck. He can feel his mother stroke his cheek. What the fuck would she think of him? He has already betrayed her. She is with him, still. Ghosts and dreams, there is no difference. He can feel her arms around him, but if he turns in his rolling chair, there will only be darkness.

If Hap had come to Paul, if he had come right out and said what he was doing…hah, well, the kid wasn't stupid. Paul has been looking for a kid like him to do just that. To tell him he needs help. Angie, that old purple hag, she was right about kids. She was right about Paul needing to do something right for once. It is not too late. Hap, as lost and scared as he may be, needs an ally.

Paul flips his phone out, and it's nearly useless. The kid probably ditched his phone, but Paul scrolls until he finds Hap's number and clicks call. While doing so, he pulls open his top drawer. The gun is gone. From the thick shadows behind him come footsteps, perhaps from the hidden wall. A voice says, "Dear Abel." Paul whirls around in his chair as a tall stranger with a weak chin and sunken eyes raises his father's revolver toward him. The phone reaches a voicemail, and Paul lets it drop to the floor.

"I am the shepherd that imprisons the Shack. I will cut down all those who wish to enter, for the glory of innocence!" the stranger shouts, and before Paul can open his mouth in protest….

***

Otis shoots him in the jaw, and the lower half of the Miskatonic manager's face unhinges in a black mist made crimson by the light showing from beneath the office door. The Miskatonic man's body spins around in his chair, and he crashes over his desk as his back extends in a series of spasms. Not bad. Otis hasn't shot anybody since his return to the Island.

Taking in deep breaths of nostril-scorching gunpowder from the tip of his short barrel, Otis steps out of the office and into the diluted lobby light. He shoots through the eye of the first man he sees wearing the red and yellow décor of a valet attendant's uniform. Otis swims toward a floundering crowd of screaming fanatics, taking a shot at a bellhop who raises his hands in protest before falling to the floor a shriveled lump, clutching an arm as the rush of hotel guests tramples him.

A man in a Hawaiian shirt runs the opposite way toward the elevator, body slamming his way through the crowd. It couldn't be more clear to Otis that he is one of them, seeking the rest of the limp-dicked army that has booked out of the Miskatonic. He lets loose a shot that zips through a screaming woman's collar, and the man running in the opposite direction gets away. Otis raises his revolver high in an attempt to shatter the elevator's glass, but there is only a click from the empty barrel. He tosses the revolver to the floor. This is why he prefers knives. He disappears into the fleeing crowd of guests and staff alike, crouching to mask his height. He's decided that the only guilty mistake he's made is when he killed the wrong woman, but he'll make all of that up. All he has to do is make it home one more time before coming back with what it takes. The place will be well evacuated by then, save for the kings who hide at the top of their tower.

CHAPTER 20
THE PROBLEM WITH MANIACS

"You think I'm a bad girl? He's sold his soul to something much uglier than the Shack," Augustine moans from the bathroom. Hap hears the slam of a car door and heavy footsteps as Otis stomps through the living room. A monster has entered the house, and Hap is in a bedroom with a window too small to crawl out of.

"Otis?" Hap calls, cautious.

"You here, my mad, mad Arab?" A heavy metal thud reverberates from the kitchen countertop. Augustine is hunched over, cowering in the bathroom. Hap can't allow himself to forget where the dried blood on the floor and under her fingernails came from.

"None of these will do!" Otis lurches slightly, his hands on his hips. There is a faint spray of blood noticeable on his shaved, now alien chin. His wounds have bled through the white of his shirt. If his hair were trimmed, he'd look like some weak-jawed man from the nineteen hundreds, a professor or a librarian. On the kitchen counter before him, there is a blue duffel bag covered in dirt stains and small clumps of earth. Inside are what seem to be gardening tools: hedge clippers, an old-fashioned axe with a wooden handle, and some kind of saw. "This is a modern age. We need firepower. Bombs, all over the city!" Otis raises a hand in the air. Hap backs away into the refrigerator, and his sneaker cracks on one of the ceramic cat's shards he missed picking up.

This man seemed half crippled last night. "Where did you go?" Hap asks. For the past few hours, Hap's wondered if this was a miracle or delusion.

"To the Miskatonic!" Otis spreads his arms out, leaning toward Hap, who flinches and tries to burrow against the fridge. The clean-shaven killer hugs him, lightly patting both his arms, getting a smudge of blood along Hap's dirty shirt. "I ache yet, but I am free from feeding the worms below. You were a ghost in my dreams. I saw their clowns. They are real clowns with real red noses and real white skin and stripes along their faces. No make-up, no clown college, groundskeepers that roam and come with the Shack like the carrion in the sky that follow a pack of wild lions. The clowns came from the stars and formed an alliance with us—I mean, with the Shack." The fucking guy's brain is gone; there's blood on him....

"What did you do at the Miskatonic? Did you find something out? Who did you kill?" Hap asks.

"I am killing all of them—one big boom. I was a fool ta think we had to figure something out. Blow them up, over and over; that'll do. Then I die, enter the shack with a smile and poison them from within." Otis is talking differently. The hitch in his words is gone as if he can find them in his head clearly now. "We are going to rob a gun store. Walk in there and open up," he screams to the ceiling, and there comes a rustling from the bathroom.

"Oh yes," Otis smirks, reaching into his bag for the axe. "I forgot about her." Otis pushes past Hap before he can put it together. "Time to kill the right woman!"

"No, wait," Hap says, unsure of his suspicions. The crooked-toothed killer cautiously pushes open the bathroom door with the head of the axe. "There's a way we do this without becoming like them; we aren't going to hurt her."

Hap tries to make him see reason as Otis takes two purposeful steps forward out of sight. There is a stomach-wrenching howl of terror from the bathroom, followed by one cracking thunk after another, and the screams don't stop until the third. Hap hears an axe blade scrape against the tile. As he falls back against the hallway wall, he catches glimpses of a crimson bathroom and an equally crimson maniac coated in red.

"She was tied up," Hap says, and he is out of puke and tears and…. What just happened? What was he doing these past few days? Video games, comic books, playing nurse, and trying to ignore his dreams.

"You've gotta stomach up." Otis emerges from the bathroom. His mad, beardless grin is gone. "I won't fill you with lies no more."

Hap opens his eyes to see the red-rimmed blade of an axe hovering near his neck.

"You've gotta stomach up 'cause they'll get you. We will slaughter women and children and mothers and sisters and fathers and husbands and little boys who support the Moon. We have to fight fire with light, with a sun that burns it all out. That runs them to the maximums of what they think they are. We're gonna rend them exhausted by their own treachery, and then they will weaken and die. We're getting guns, and then we're gonna give them a massacre that'll make the front pages of every paper from here to fucking La La Land. We're gonna wear masks, and we're gonna sing while we do it. Come on!"

Otis shoots spittle across Hap's face as he presses the blade of his axe to Hap's throat, forcing his head back against the wall.

"What the fuck man, wha—?"

Hap can no longer speak clearly. Otis angles the blade, and Hap is looking into the bathroom at the Miskatonic witch, hacked up beyond recognition.

"Now I'm gonna write a map for us. A list and a map." Otis shrugs away from Hap and trails the blade of the axe along the wall as he walks into his bedroom. What happened to him in his sleep? What did he see?

Wandering into the bedroom after Otis, Hap picks up the knife from the floor. He thinks it's the one Otis had when they first met; he pokes his finger against the blade and realizes that it's sharper than he ever imagined.

"Your stomach's going to have to get thicker. Thicker. I want you to kill the man at the gun store. We'll have him lean over his display case and then pop. We'll have to stop anybody else there. We have to get to the city without the cops behind us. We'll then go into the hotel through two exits," Otis says, and Hap can't get over how clear his words are. Did he get an English lesson while he was asleep?

"You've got to calm down. We'll be worse than them if we do half of what you're saying," Hap says. Otis can't be so bad deep down; Hap's seen him be reasonable. With the knife held cautiously in one hand, Hap reaches for Otis's axe with the other. "Think of your mother. What would she say?"

"I have…I always think of her! I think of how they raped her! How they murdered her! How they did this to me! Calm? Drink a cup of tea, see their symbol at the bottom. Calm? Try and be calm, see what will happen to you!" Otis hefts up the axe, sliding his chair back. "I spoke with the Gate. A great old one visited me in my dreams."

Hap places a hand on the shoulder of Otis's arm where that ropey, tentacle-like rash appeared. A fly buzzes off and away into the house as if Otis is a rotting thing. "Listen, take a deep —" Then Hap is thrown to the floor, and he should've known: never, ever touch this man. The killer leans over him, his eyes now flashing different colors, even a trace of purple. A sun rises in Otis's irises, orange and red. "I saw the gate; I know the gate; I am the gate. I am the axe of Yog-Sothoth, and you will never understand me." Otis jerks the hand holding the axe, and Hap isn't sure if it's the dull backside or the blade that's pushed toward him. Hap thrusts his old knife into the babbling murderer's throat. The axe spasms away from them.

There is confusion across Otis's face as he slinks back and sits against the legs of his chair. The knife entered his throat at an angle. Hap has stuck kitchen knives into the pumpkins and pineapples, the sides of trees in his backyard as a boy. A throat is softer than fruit. Otis's hands go to the wound, and fresh, bright blood is pouring between his fingers. He was going to kill Hap, right?

"Moon makes the dark stronger, but we need 'er. She ain't the enemy, but some kinda hope they mock." Otis's mouth fills with blood, and he can't babble anymore.

"I'm sorry," Hap says. He sits at the edge of the bed, unable to move. Otis grabs the handle of the knife with one flimsy, shaking hand. Blood spritzes across the room, decorating the TV and the stack of comic books on the floor. He looks into Hap's eyes, and then his pupils roll up into his head like a camera without a memory chip. Otis falls toward Hap, holding out the knife to him like a final offering. An attempt to pass the torch that guided his poor ass for decades.

There is a time lapse, a gap in Hap's consciousness; when he awakens, he is stumbling through the woods beyond Otis's house, tripping over fallen tree branches. "I'm sorry; I'm sorry," Hap can't stop muttering as thorn bushes claw at his clothing. Eventually, he stumbles into somebody's backyard and encounters three little children running around a Slip and Slide. One of them, a little girl in a one-piece bathing suit, stares at him with wide eyes before crying out for her parents. Hap is a dead shambler from the forest. He flees, losing himself farther in gullies and dips in the earth. It is dusk before he finds Otis's house again.

Hap sits on the couch, staring at the piles of scrawled notes stacked up neatly across the table. He tried organizing them at one point in the days prior. It was impossible. What in the hell does he do now? He hasn't eaten all day. Fuck, he still can't. He can still hear the reverberations of Augustine's final screams and see that look in Otis's eyes as he died. Was he at peace? He needs to wash his brain. He needs weed; that makes you calm, right? He needs....he can't wander into Otis's bedroom and get the whiskey, comic books, or video games. Not without walking past the corpses. Ah, he is fucked all right.

The encroaching night brings with it the sound of drumming. What has to be a pickup truck or something pulls into Otis's driveway. There are no flashing police lights sprinkling through the windows. Whoever this is, they won't waste time putting Hap in handcuffs.

The pounding of the drums spreads between five seconds of pause. The sound of several car doors opening and slamming is accompanied by low murmuring and a clunk of boots in the driveway. The chills binding Hap to the couch subside as he crouches over to the window, peaking out of its corner panel. Two pickup trucks form a V, blocking the driveway and Otis's Caddie. There are half a dozen men, mostly in jeans and T-shirts. They wear cotton masks over their heads with black goggles sewn into their eyeholes. Some of the masks seem dirty like they've been worn recently. The men pass around flashlights. Lanterns come aglow in the beds of their trucks. Four of them have shotguns, and the others have bladed instruments. Behind the house, things creep and crackle through the woods. "Moonshuck" is repeated several times by several different mouths. No, "Moon *Shack*" is being croaked, froglike, by unseen things in the dark, things waiting for Hap to try and escape out a back window.

A crudely spray-painted seven-pointed star surrounded by dancing orbs is etched along the side of one of the trucks. One of the men holds up what looks like a big stick with a metal basket on top. There's a faint flicker of a lighter. A torch is stuck into the grass beside Otis's driveway. Otis could have saved Hap. Otis could be here right now, ready to knife these dogs down. Otis probably led these fuckers here and has damned Hap in more ways than one.

The drumming speeds up as the men begin to chant in low, murmuring voices. The croaking things behind the house join a chorus of crickets. Hap goes over to the coffee table and picks up a knife. They are all murderers; now he is one, too. Hap takes off his shirt. He's never so much as pricked his finger on purpose before. He focuses on a single image and begins to draw the knife across his skin.

***

A second torch is thrust into the ground as the drumming continues from within the woods. As soon as the tempo stops, the men will be free to speak, laugh, and taunt. Then, they converge. They swarm. The groundskeepers, sent from the Shack itself, will hold up the rear.

But before the hunting party can reach the front door, it slowly swings open, and a shirtless boy steps out with his hands raised. Shotguns, cracked, peeling, and forged a lifetime ago, rise to the ready position. The boy enters the torchlight before sinking to his knees. A knife slips from his hand as he spreads his arms and bows his head. A gleaming diamond wedding ring sparkles on one finger. His chest is crimson. One of his wrists is covered in a rectangle of ink. He has carved into his skin a dripping, seven-pointed star that trails up from his stomach and aligns with each of his nipples. The planets follow, crude and ovular along his ribs, forming a spiral from each point of the star. The symbol and the message are understood. There is a half-moon lightly etched into Hap's forehead, and on his wrist, a most dreaded symbol has been obscured by black marker. The shotguns lower, and there is an exchange of looks between unblinking glass goggles. The offering is accepted.

CHAPTER 21
THE INITIATE

Well past visiting hours, a trio of men arrive at Providence General Hospital in silence, their hats tilted low, lips grim. A dear somebody's son has pull at the building, so they enter through a backdoor and ascend a winding staircase to Room 2419. Currently, the room hosts two victims of the recent shooting spree at the Miskatonic Hotel. One is stable, the other barely alive. Both are fresh out of surgery and in no condition for visitors.

Mike Santalio removes his hat, a fedora, and places it over his chest out of respect as he enters. Call it old-timey, but the hat's a symbol and, as of late, a running joke, a testament to the days of old and the types of men who used to run Providence. Mike's business associate, Dino Marcello, bows his head. The Southerner smiles; not wanting to appear rude, he lifts his Red Sox cap. The Southerner claims that his affinity for Boston dates back to his childhood. Mike doesn't want to consider the kind of upbringing that makes a man like the Southerner become who he is today.

Propped up in his hospital bed, Politician Paul Jones lives, if only through the steady beeping of the machines by his side. Below his nose, a mess of gauze and bandages disfigure his face. Across the room, a boy no older than one of Mike's own nephews moans in his sleep. The kid's bicep is covered in gauze, and an IV is stuck into his wrist. From what Mike knows of his experience visiting hospitals, it looks like the poor kid had to receive a blood transfusion.

Approaching Paul's bedside, Mike mutters, "You should've told me you needed help." He places a hand on Paul's arm and mouths a prayer for him.

"And they haven't caught the guy who did it yet?" the Southerner asks from over by the window, spying on the city below. Across town, the edge of the purple neon sign bearing the Miskatonic's name is like a spy poking their head around a corner.

"No, the scumbag," says Dino, a big bastard Mike has been lovingly smacking in the belly for the last twenty years.

The kid across the room groans and mutters something, repositioning himself to sit up as best he can. "Who am I?" he says, sitting up partially. "Wait, I mean, who are you...?" He's drugged but somewhat awake, addressing Dino.

Mike marches over to the kid's side, trying his best to look like a bullish man of power to whom you spill your secrets, instead of an old man who's finding it harder and harder to urinate properly. "Did you see who did this? How many of them were there?" Only four people were shot, with one death and about a half dozen broken ankles and ribs from the poor bastards who got trampled in the mad rush out of the hotel lobby.

With his eyes closed, the boy tells Mike, "Eyes sunk into his face. Tall. Then dudes with knives while I was layin' bleedin'. Dudes looking over me. Thought they wanted to turn me into ham. Knife dudes talked to cops. One man wouldn't stop licking up the blood. I was trying to help people." The dope in the boy's veins begins to haul him back into the land of dreams. "People were running the wrong way, up the elevator, like they had nowhere to go...." He sings those last words before passing out. Mike forms a fist over the fedora.

"Hey, you," Mike says to the Southerner. The man's smile widens as he hooks his thumbs between the belt loops of his jeans. "It's a go. Do your best. I'm happy with a message, but do as much damage as possible. I'll be leaving town, but the money will find you." There's a vacation house in Sanibel, Florida, with Mike's name on it. It may be time to stay there and never come back.

The Southerner tips his cap and laughs. "Or I'll find it! Diggity. It's empty, right?"

"Empty of the good ones," Mike mutters, staring at Paul's face. Maybe the doctors will give him a new jaw. He'll never form words properly again.

The Southerner tips his hat and leaves. The door closes just as Dino sighs, glancing semi-nervously at the kid to make sure he's still asleep.

"You know," Mike says. "Pauly's mother was a great, great gal. I'm going to hell for suggesting he work there after what they did to her." Mike bows his head. He finds solace in the idea that, even if the Miskatonic curses its dead to wander its corridors, then the walls of their prison will soon be ash.

***

A sheet sticks to Hap's cuts, and he is wrapped up like a grand feast yet to be devoured. His abductors are gentle as they lift him over their shoulders. The burn from his wounds, pulsing with his heartbeat, is nothing new. After he sliced the first jagged point of the star into his chest, Hap was amazed at how easy it was to disfigure himself with Otis's knife. He is met by sirens and a light breeze as he enters the open air before being lowered between swinging hips and the gasoline-churned stink of his abductors. They are in downtown Providence, of course.

They burned down Otis's house. He smelled the first tidings of smoke as the last of his silent abductors loaded him into the truck. Though he still doesn't know whether his attempt to make himself a holy relic has actually worked, he has been spared the act of being pumped full of holes by those rusting guns. The determination of his fate has been delayed. He can feel the executioner slipping on his black hood. Maybe he'll die with one less question on his tongue.

A low murmuring reaches Hap as he's carried into an air-conditioned space that does little to unstick the sheet clinging to his wounds. He has become a willing totem of flesh and blood. A slow clapping of bemused applause begins from either side of him, and he imagines the grinning faces of the Moon Shack's lunatics.

Being suspended by the half dozen arms of his pallbearers makes the elevator seem like some kind of invisible string plucking him up through the atmosphere and into the gravity-defying damnation of space. With Hap's perspective infused with that of the floating cosmos, being dragged from the elevator is as pleasant an experience as Hap could have wished for. He is ready for death, to be reunited with Tiff in that eternal twilight cage.

Hap's pallbearers stop short as he sways in their grip. "Otis Lusk is truly dead," a nasally voice marvels; the speaker is some kind of man-killing snob, some intelligent and elitist asshole who uses his brains to ruin other people's lives. It's fitting, of course, that the people who run the cult aren't idiots, just assholes. They are more devious than Hap could ever hope to be. He has only acted out of emotion, but they act out of need and faith. If the cult consisted of merely dog-eating maniacs like Woodbury and sexual deviants like Augustine, there wouldn't be a cult worth maintaining in a redneck farmhouse in the middle of Vermont, let alone one that is capable of manipulating the vital heartstrings of an entire city.

"Cut his own throat. Drove this little jihadist up some kinda wall," one of Hap's abductors says, all too happy to add "racist" to his identity as a murderous fanatic.

"Please, please. He's Indian," a stranger with a kind voice says. The sheet is lifted, and a curious, slightly overweight older man with delicate glasses examines Hap's face. What looks to be a blind man grumbles from behind the kind man and walks out of view. "I couldn't be happier to learn you turned out to be special," the kind stranger says, pressing his hand against Hap's face. He is that peaceful, generic sort of old man who always seems to serve as the undying face of the Catholic pope. This guy must be the craziest one of them all. Behind the kind man and before the entrance to the Miskatonic's grand ballroom, Otis's body is crucified on a plywood cross. He does not wear a crown of thorns. Instead, he is bound by twisted strips of wire to the mocking lowercase "t" that is Christianity's answer to the seven-pointed star. The former eye doctor's gaping throat has congealed into an insect-like proboscis as if his rigid body has been frozen amidst some kind of strange metamorphosis.

The sheet is crumpled into a ball and tossed beneath a podium as the pallbearers carry Hap into the ballroom, setting him down on a giant old rocking chair three times as big as it should be. Before Hap is a grand ballroom full of empty, black, folding chairs. The thugs hold Hap down and use biting strips of wire to bind his neck to the wooden rung of the chair. Could there really be enough lunatics from the Shack to fill a room this big?

Johan rubs a hand over the side of Hap's chair and says, "It still remembers who it was. All things do." Facing Hap, Johan seems so gentle, like Santa Claus at the meet and greets at the Warwick Mall. "We do not honor a man who spills his own blood. You have made yourself a curiosity." Johan has an arm draped over the podium. His tuxedo is complemented by a purple bow tie. "On a day as horrific as this, a curiosity that will bring a smile to my citizens' lips is a blessing from the Else itself." Carved into the arms of Hap's rocking chair, as if by a crude pocketknife, are strange, companion symbols to the seven-pointed star and its vortex of orbs. Centipedes and other winged worm-like bugs also adorn the wood. Hap reads the word "family" and the phrase "plank by plank." The most detailed pictograph shows stick figures with their stick arms in the air, holding what look like little logs standing around a square hut.

"I have a girlfriend," Hap tries to say but only croaks. *Like those things in the woods behind Otis's. What were they?* Why did he waste so much energy running and weeping through the woods? Was he really so shocked at how easily that knife dug into Otis's neck? "She—"

"Yes, of course. Tiffany Lorice. A posthumous orphan. About that night, now, did Derrick mention his father before Otis killed him? He always mentions his father. David Woodbury, the son and father of killers, but not one himself. I was fascinated with what kind of being Derrick's own offspring would turn out to be. Shame I'll never find out. Now, Otis—"

"Where is she?" Hap smiles at the look of disgust on Johan's face; it's as if he yelled "shit-cunt-cocksucker" in the middle of a mass.

"No wonder you've been floundering about like a fish on a dinner plate. I was in the middle of telling you something you never would have known on your own. For a boy like you who tries too hard to understand, all of your mistakes come from your attitude. The least you could do is learn about the man who allowed you to last this long."

"Tiffany," Hap moans and sits up, nearly choking himself on the wire.

"Tiffany Lorice? You really want to know? You really haven't figured out the mystery by now? To be honest, the citizens go through a Tiffany Lorice every other week. I can't tell you what specifically happened to her, as in what order of horrific events she met before her fate, because I don't care enough to know. I don't remember her or who she may have become; I doubt anyone else will either unless you show them a picture of her when she still had ears and a nose and a little pink tongue. Maybe one after another, she was raped, cut, murdered, made to eat her own flesh as well as ours. I'm sure you've already imagined this. Maybe she saw the light and killed one of the other captives, or perhaps she gave up everything about herself to become one of us. We get a lot of new recruits, and by choice, I refuse to acknowledge who my brothers and sisters were before they gained their citizenship. Maybe she's with the group that escaped into the sewers. Wait, no, that was last summer…. Well, if she was with *that* group, then I can assure you, the things you aren't capable of hallucinating that got to them were much more cruel than any man or woman you will meet today. Now, Otis…."

A sob dies before it can clear Hap's throat. He's going to die at the end of a fishhook of a question mark.

"We are not concerned about your Tiffany. Today, we feel regret for that poor, misguided Mr. Lusk. Did he tell you of the old, undying gods that don't even deserve such a title? They don't create or destroy with any purpose. They are cosmic roaches that hide beneath what we can see and touch. They are bacteria that kill and give life at the same time. They are…horrible." A sheen of sweat glimmers across Johan's brow. He speaks with the same level of bitterness that Hap wants to spit across his face, if only his lips weren't so dry. "They don't care about us; they will make girls and boys like you kill themselves if they so much as twitch in their sleep. We citizens fight to be recognized. Otis could have been one of our best and most wicked. You see, it takes us fighting against our nature to stand out to them. It takes us becoming more than human compassion, more than empathy and revenge, much, much more than love. People, when they're dead enough, forget the love. No matter how much a wife remembers her sick husband, after she is dead, after her children's children are dead, love goes away like the end of a long blink. The cancer is the victor. Cancer is to be worshipped. We wield death. I wonder, did Otis try and train you? You carved our emblem into your chest; do you know what it means? It is our solar system. It stands for all that we are, as mankind. All that we will defend as death's disciples."

"Otis is dead because he…because you took his mom,"

Hap spits out. It's getting harder to breathe; the wire around his throat is slowly strangling him. There are several men and women scattered throughout the sea of folding chairs. More are coming, slowly, clicking into their spots as they sit with their backs firm and their eyes burrowing into Hap and Johan.

"You think we don't understand vengeance? You think we wouldn't let Otis duel with the man who killed his mother? Sure, we'd pick a citizen at random. We wouldn't remember who it was in a million years, but we respect revenge. We would've lied to him so sweetly. We have the utmost compassion for line-crossers, except when that line happens to cross into the unnamable. Otis sold his mind to the atomic bomb, and he couldn't take it anymore. That's why he cut his own throat. He didn't give up on his pursuit, you see. He imploded." They don't know Hap is a murderer. Maybe…just maybe, that's the card he can play here.

"He would have killed you," Hap says. "He would have killed everybody here."

"I would have told him it was one man who did it, and he would have believed it. Knock, knock, common sense makes it plain that revenge causes you to become blind. Speaking of which, are you seeing clearly? Have you been looking closely? Maybe the answer to your beloved's fate was right in front of you." Johan shakes his head because Hap doesn't seem to be learning. "You know, we humans aren't engineered to kill one another. Soldiers get PTSD for a reason because we aren't created to kill. It's not a natural thing. We have to adapt. Man is best at adapting. That's what makes us different. That's what makes us the next step in evolution. If you can slit your fellow man's throat and do the same to his wife and kids, then you can face the *true* darkness with a thousand faces. Let me ask you a question before the ceremony begins."

Johan is going to talk no matter what Hap says. The silent crowd is building, washing ashore from a strange tide. They aren't all dressed up; some aren't wearing shirts. For the most part, they look just like people. Save for an unusually high count of long, tangled beards and tattooed faces, nothing screams murderer about them. Speckled across a city, even one as small as Providence, these people fit in easily enough. Hap imagines that the members of the cult form a line outside the ballroom doors that must snake around the entire eleventh floor. Cult members bow, one by one, before Otis's cross with their fists over their hearts. What about the other hotel guests? How can it be a sure thing they'll avoid the crucified man and roomful of lunatics on the eleventh floor?

"Hap?" Johan says, and Hap flinches as the demented priest rubs a hand along his cheek. "Good, stay with me; you're not bleeding that badly. You're not on anything, are you? I don't know what Otis's false religion led him to consume, but it would be a shame if you were poisoned and neither of us knew it."

"I don't do anything," Hap says. He reaches a hand to the wire, and Johan doesn't stop him as he begins to try to loosen it from his throat.

"I was asking you, now, whether you think it's funny that there are so many different breeds of just about every animal there is, but there is just one human. I'm not talking monkeys, certainly not race. We come from those that slaughtered the Neanderthals." Johan laughs, looking to the crowd. The front rows are filled. The room is growing smaller, hotter. The Moon Shack's lunatics are too silent. Their stare makes Hap want to shrink into the cracks of the rocking chair. If only it wasn't so big. His feet don't touch the ground. He is made small like a child.

"We.... Hap, come on now, listen to me. This is fascinating." Hap knows it's all in his head, but his efforts to remove the wire are useless. He can feel the wire growing tighter, drawing fresh blood. "Neanderthals were one of many, many other subspecies of early humans. Not monkeys. I repeat, much different from monkeys. There were lots of variant types of what could still be classified as man. Some of them were giants compared to us. Some of them were like little leprechauns, I imagine. You want to know what happened to the rest of them? Everybody but us? It wasn't the eldritch fungus, and it wasn't a meteor. Our version of humanity was born because men were able to overcome their compassion, their trauma, by killing all the others, by massacring all the competition. By killing and beating and ruling, we prevailed. We are superior now, Hap. Mercifully."

There is a loud click as the ballroom's doors close, and the last few citizens find their seats. A silence sweeps across the room like a crinkled piece of paper that's finally been smoothed out. Not a single one of these people so much as rustle in their chair; aren't they supposed to be lunatic killers? It's as if the idea of a community mellows out their uncontrollable twitches. Johan nods at the audience and then pats Hap's cheek. Hap tries to draw his head back as far as the wire around his throat will let him. Slow smiles grow across the faces of those in the front row. Johan stands above the plain podium, tapping a microphone and causing the room to thump as the speakers hidden along the walls reveal their presence.

"You are all brought here today because we have experienced what some would call a setback. Our nuptial celebration is ruined." Johan looks down at the podium as if he is reading from a notecard, but Hap can see there is nothing there. Johan lifts his head, and his eyes are different. He's molding them with tears that may as well be flames for his audience. "This saddens me, but it will not break me. I would like to thank our dear purple mistress, Angie, for all the work she did preparing the bride and groom who will never be." An old woman stands up too quickly for her to be considered fragile, and she is made of purple; like an insect's shell, she is completely shrouded, with her face hidden by a veil. The citizens applaud, offering a controlled and calculated response as if every clapping hand falls to meet another at once.

"I would like to say farewell to Providence, but not to all of you. Stars be damned; come tomorrow, there may be a new speaker for our group. Part of me wants to hold on...the selfish part of me." Johan walks over to Hap and plops a hand upon his head. He shouts now, wrenching his point home. "The citizen in me wants our message to be clear. No matter how much longer the other forces knock us down, we will continue to grow. We will continue to influence, to expand. Soon, very soon, we will, at last, go to war. The final war. If I am to die tonight, I hope I can die for all we believe in." Hap squirms as Johan squeezes the top of his head. "I will see you all in the Shack. I will greet you all as we find shelter together. Now, what else?" Johan says, before taking a bow.

"The Else!" booms the ballroom as the citizens' voices become that of a titan.

"What Else?" Johan screams into the microphone, gripping the podium as tears mix with the sweat dripping from his brow.

"The Else!" The same synchronized clapping follows, creating galaxies in the space between every smack. Johan points to two men in the front row, and they run toward Hap while the crowd keeps up its clapping, its chant of Otis's fairy tale thing who lives in the Shack.

The two henchmen slice away the wire, and a bald-headed bastard in a jean jacket, riddled with blue tattoos all over his face, grabs Hap by the arm. Other men appear on either side of him, motionless, waiting to participate. A razor catches the light, and the crowd's unified voice is booming to the point that Hap's screams are drowned out. His arm, with the still-healing five-limbed branch tattoo of the Elder sign, is raised in the air as the other men hold him to the ground. The Elder sign, along with his skin, peels off in ribbons. There is more blood, more of that familiar fire: the rubbing of coals against his nervous system. The tattooed fucker in the jean jacket is holding the light strips of Hap's wrist to his mouth as he prods the flesh with his tongue, slurping the strips down like sushi.

Released, crawling along the floor, Hap attempts to make his way down the aisle between the folding chairs. The men are returning to their seats, resuming their shouting. Johan helps Hap to his feet, throwing his arm around him as the two of them make their way to the elevators at the back of the ballroom. "The Else! The Else!" the crowd shrieks from behind them.

"You tried to cover it up. Maybe you should have done the same to Otis. The Elder sign...the Moon Shack doesn't deserve the disrespect. When you see it, oh, when you walk inside, Hap...you'll be thanking me." Johan has something in his hand obscured by his side. The elevator dings, closing them in together. Even as the steel doors fold shut, he can still hear the crowd's frantic cheering. A long dagger appears in Johan's hand, like a massive silvery toothpick.

"Where are...?" Hap begins as the elevator begins to rise. They're already on the top floor, though—they're going to the roof? Is Johan going to throw him off the side of the building?

"It's waiting for us. The Moon Shack is here. It showed up after the evacuation. We are all that's left, dear. You are the only unblessed virgin in the building now that the old witch has popped her cherry, but you deserve a chance; you've earned at least a chance. Here, hold this, would you?" Johan hands the blade to Hap, offering the handle first. It's pale, like a sliver of moonlight made solid. He ignores it; he doesn't understand.

"You and your girlfriend were so young. Do you even know what happens to a relationship after five years? After ten? What are you holding on to? I had a wife and daughter, and I'm not ashamed to say I killed them. I spared them from what's coming one glorious evening after the sunset."

If what Johan's saying is true, then why couldn't Hap have just let Otis go on his mad killing spree? These people are so much worse, and they'll continue to do worse. One man could've exterminated them, innocent casualties and all, and Hap had to go and stop him. Johan draws on.

"I killed them because I realized I had allowed them to become my everything. But when I took a step back, I realized I had lost myself. I had traded in my soul to them. If that sounds crazy, it's because I was for a time. But the Moon Shack was there to redeem me. A great man, Charles McKinley, was waiting for me beside the door. He welcomed me in. He introduced me to his family. I liked them—I loved them. You're going to deliver me to them. Whenever you feel it—whenever you want to drive that little nail file into me—do it, boy. I'm ready. Then you get to go inside. Then you get to dine with the Else and all the others who have come before you." All of this shit Johan has been talking it's not just insanity. It's a sales pitch.

Johan prods the handle toward Hap's arm; his wrist feels so ruined he can't raise his hand, can't grasp the handle. Johan lets go, and the blade slips from Hap's weak fingers, clattering to the elevator floor. "Come on, like what you'd do with your woman. Get a grip! Stick it in; come on!" Johan grabs Hap's left hand and places Hap's own fingers around the blade. The door dings open, and the Providence skyline, lit up for the evening, sprawls out before Hap. Before him is a dirty rooftop speckled by great columns of air conditioners. On the far side of the roof sits a squat, ugly little shack. Drumbeats, the same maddeningly monotonous kind that he heard at Otis's house, echo from all around him.

"You know, if you kill me, you get to live. We'll find out if Tiffany saw the moonlight, too. Maybe she's in there. Maybe she killed for us. Maybe she's waiting. Come on, I'd prefer to look at the city while you do it. I love it here, you know. Everybody always underestimates Rhode Island. You could push me off the roof if you'd like, but you need to put some effort into it. If I subconsciously jump, then you won't be a killer."

Johan is holding the elevator doors open, and Hap is still confused. Hap's also holding the knife. They want him to be a killer amongst killers and kill 'til the days run red. His legs are shaking. They don't know he killed Otis, that he's already a killer. They don't know anything about him. What does this even mean, then, about the Shack? About what it expects from him? About what it wants from him? The Shack. It's real now, isn't it? It stands beside a series of rusted cages stacked upon one another. Did they keep people up here? To look across at the city? He killed Otis. He can kill Johan.

Hap lunges forward as Johan steps back reflexively, but not before the blade rips through the fleshy part of his leg above the knee. The fake priest crashes to the rooftop just outside the elevator's threshold. The Shack, in the distance on the far side of the roof, seems to glow. It has pale walls with splotches of brown, and there's a backwards half-moon carved into the door. The Moon Shack. Its wooden walls are filled with jagged carvings too far away to identify, though Hap recognizes the rough outlines of the symbols the citizens like to wield. Two windows on either side of the door exist as black portals to another world.

Johan chuckles to himself, devoid of pain or fury. "Won't let a doomed man have his last wish. Oh, you are evil. Go on now, the chest or the throat. You can make it slow, but make sure I'm not breathing when you're done. A man can survive the strike of a hundred knives. I've seen it. Women too. Make it count. Go for the arteries; make me bleed. Come on; you're doing so well, better than I thought you would. I'm thankful you're drawing this out, but come on!"

Johan's chanting, leaning back, not clamping a hand over the gushing puncture in his leg. Hap turns, staggers back into the elevator, and jabs a hand at the button for the first floor. Johan can't scramble to stop the doors in time. "The Else! The Else will punish you!" He's shouting from the other side of the steel doors as Hap repeatedly jabs the "Close" button until there's a click, and he starts to descend. The last thing Hap hears is a distant howl from beyond the doors, beyond Johan. It could be anything.

Why would it have to be coming from the Shack?

The elevator descends to the eighth floor before it begins to shake, and the little beams of light overhead start to flicker. Like the song of a whale, except broken and formed by moss, something begins to cry mournfully from above. Hap isn't sure if it'll work, but he jabs at the "Open" button for the elevator's doors. Of course, nothing happens for a moment, but then they peel back, and the elevator begins slowly pulling upward. The square threshold leading to the seventh floor corridor becomes jagged, like a closing mouth, as Hap lurches himself forward, stepping onto solid ground. Some great force is slowly sucking the elevator back toward the upper floors behind him. There's a crying thing who sings a song that's at once both beautiful and capable of making Hap want to jab nails into his ears.

The flickering lights transform the hallway into an eerie strobe. Behind Hap, there begins the sound of gnawing of metal that reminds him of those goddamned garbage trucks that would tear down America Street at four in the morning and cause him to think the world was falling apart. The Else. The Moon Shack was real enough as a hut on a rooftop beside a collection of rusty cages. Otis said it travels, but Otis was insane. The Else, though. Maybe he wasn't that insane. Man is worth fearing more than any boogeyman. The Else. Something sings like no living beast Hap has ever dreamt up; as it does so, he realizes the sounds he's hearing are something eating its way down the elevator shaft. He takes off running for the stairwell; God save him.

CHAPTER 22
THE PLACE WHERE BAD MEN LAY THEIR HEADS

The Southerner's lungs are used to smoke and chemicals of all sorts, but he finds himself hacking as he leaves the Miskatonic. The back of the Parks Department pickup truck is now empty of its treasure trove of flammables. There is some thermite, too, that's meant to ensure the structure will collapse when the fires grow hot enough. The Southerner's got two partners with him, a pair of boys from a crazy city along the Massachusetts border called Woonsocket. He's taken to calling one kid "Woon" and the other "Socket." The Southerner likes to make his job as fun as possible.

They've each got brand new handguns with the serial numbers scraped off. The Southerner was told he'd get to keep his if he didn't use it; right now, it's looking that way. Hotel's been evacuated since the shooting. The Southerner was told there were people who live here full-time. The special kind of criminals that operate alongside this pathetic city's idea of a mob, which is more like an underground network of associates, nothing like the genuine gangs the Southerner grew up around. The Southerner was told to expect resistance of some sort, but nothing. They went up as far as the third floor without seeing another soul.

This fire might just be The Southerner's best yet. There was nothing more satisfying than tossing his Red Sox cap right into the thick of the flames as the hotel's golden embroidered walls started to melt around him. Whatever city he's called to, he always wears the local team's hat; in New England, go figure, it has to be the mortal enemy of the Yankees, the team the Southerner was raised loving. It won't be long now before the fire really starts popping. Best to get a move on.

"Hey there," an unfamiliar voice says from behind the Southerner. The roundabout in front of the Miskatonic is just far enough removed from the city sidewalk that the Southerner figured parking in front of the black sphere erected between the grass and purple flowers at the center of the roundabout was enough. The man addressing him looks like he's covered in mud. Three more filthy fools are behind him, and one of them is a chick.

"You been inside, yeah?" the woman asks.

"Yeah, turned out it's locked down, so we gotta go." The Southerner acts out of logic first. They've been seen, so it's time to get a move on. Won't matter these rats know his face, given how little he operates on this side of the country. The hotel's security cameras are troublesome, but there won't be much tape left after the flames are through. Instinct comes last, as he recognizes just how filthy these people are. There's an open sewer next to the parking lot of the closest building. Something is wrong.

"Moon Shack," one of the trio says. Then the other two join in with a unanimous "Moon Shack." The man, wide as an ox and at least six-foot-five, with skin that appears bulletproof, says again, "Moon Shack?" and the Southerner realizes it is a sort of question. A code word meant to gauge the Southerner's reaction. It is a familiar name to the Southerner, one that he has often woken up muttering. A dream place, though the Southerner's never been one for clubs or gangs. Just cash from the closest buyer.

The Southerner draws his gun just as the big man lunges. He's wearing a long-sleeved shirt in the middle of summertime, and he has something long and sharp up his sleeve. The impact from the pike, the freaking vampire-slaying stake that's jabbed through the Southerner's chest, hurls him backwards to the ground, but not before he completes his draw and puts a fat bullet into the fatter man's skull.

The Southerner bleeds while a woman shrieks. They are warriors, lunatics. One of them has a sawed-off, which he fires at poor, terrified Woon and Socket. "Aim true, Minnie, aim true!" The madman is talking to his gun. Woon and Socket begin firing back, and time slides back to the fireworks of the Fourth of July. The approaching opposition is cheese-grated with bullets as they run and duck around the pickup truck. Either Woon or Socket, the Southerner can't remember who is who, is knocked over the hood of the Park's Department truck, and a gleaming knife wielded by the wild woman goes in and out of him. Either Woon or Socket fires a bullet through the woman's skull before they begin screaming, choking on their own blood. The Southerner looks to the sky as a dirty man leers down at him.

"Let it ooze out, brother. I could smell the killer in you. I am true."

The stench of a fire burning more than wood and paper consumes the Southerner's nostrils. The sky into which he helplessly stares grows hazy from smoke before becoming black. And then there is a distant glow. Silver, like the moon.

***

There is a chance Hap can live. Tiffany is gone, dead. He will never forgive himself for everything he's done, but he wants to live. He wants to continue eating and breathing and drinking. He wants to keep enjoying little things despite how crooked they have been bent.

Hap slips on his own blood that runs sleek and thick from his butchered arm, and he sails above the last three steps his foot would have otherwise contacted. The almost thrilling sense of free fall ends just before the elbow of his raised arm connects with cement. The slivery knife Johan gave him goes sliding away, rendered useless against the dissolution of reality that seeks him. With his arm paralyzed and throbbing, it only takes Hap receiving a new wound to make him forget about his previous injury. He is beyond wishing for sleep and rest. Hap is alive, with a rapidly pulverized body by his hand, that of others, and his own stupidity. From somewhere above comes the sudden pop and drawing crackle of organic fireworks as something comes for him.

The banister along the stairs is there for a reason, as Hap puts as much of his weight on it as he can. He makes it halfway down another floor, and the numbers are mixing up in his head. Each doorway leading to each hall is numberless, and he is remembering Randal the bartender and his talk of the hotel being a maze that could trap spirits within eternal loops. Maybe this is the fate that awaits him. Maybe Hap's throat has already been slit, and now he's damned to flee the Else for eons in purgatory. In the stairwell above, he can hear footsteps. Something is creaking as it descends upon steps made of cement.

The approaching thing is rendered inaudible by the screwdriver down an eardrum blare of a fire alarm that seems to come from the very cement walls of the staircase itself. Hap's nostrils begin burning, and it takes him another half a flight of stairs before he registers the pungent, sense-flaying aroma of smoke. This place will burn to the ground, and Hap is cool with that. If only whoever started the blaze hadn't forgotten to let him out. He can no longer hear the Else or tell how close it is. The smoke-poisoned air, at first imperceptible in the dull grey of the corridor, billows like a black cloud. He heads into the smoke, his lungs giving out instantly, and the tears won't leave his eyes; he can't catch a deep breath. He lurches toward another set of stairs and bursts through a set of double doors, emerging into a corridor that immediately brings a soothing blast of clean air across his face, into his lungs. He's collapsing onto his hands and knees across a familiar carpet embroidered with flowers that seem to form a pair of eyes that stare into him.

The alarm owns him. It is a mask the Else has slipped on.

Ahead of him, toward the end of a hallway, a window is open. If there is a fire below and a legion of murderers above, then he's going to have to jump. Maybe those bastards will burn. Maybe, slippery as they are, there is a way to escape. He will not stay for the flames or teeth of something, some *Else* that he doesn't understand.

All at once, every single doorway in the hall before Hap slowly opens at the same time. Where there were once panels of brown, there are now portals of black, and Hap can't even jump out a window with ease. Who, or what is waiting for him in those square portals of blackness? Hap digs his foot into the floor and tries to form a runner's pose. Moving was easier with a banister to brace his weight. The lights begin to dance on and off, and Hap runs and screams through his scorching lungs. His own voice becomes a fuel of sorts as he hobbles and barely surpasses a jog. Something moves in front of the window, shifting down from the bend of the hallway out of sight. It's a mist, a dust cloud with something in the middle, lightly blue and stretching to the very ceiling. A song of humanity cries from the hulking, humanoid thing before Hap. He gets a glimpse of hideous skin made of ice, flaking blue pigments of flesh mixed with moss, and it is as if the farthest depths of a sentient cave tried to give its best impression of a human being.

Hap turns and flees into one of the open rooms, embracing the arms of the looming boogeyman he doesn't know as opposed to the devil before him. The lights within the rooms flicker for just a moment. It's not a guest room, but one massive chamber, an entire hallway's worth of rooms connected and disguised by doors that give the illusion of singular domains. The massive chamber holds a scattering of couches and beds and gleaming things displayed along the walls that are puffed out with soundproof foam padding. Strange masks and colorful helmets sit waiting in storage cubbies. If they kill people here, what do they do with the bodies?

Like an S&M dungeon devolved into the land of snuff, there are shackles and whips and old-fashioned stocks. Ropes dangle from the ceiling with half-tied nooses. Hap stomps on a fluff, a red clown's wig. This hidden series of rooms to which he never delivered baggage is a Halloween store of disguises and playthings. Swords, scimitars, battle-axes and spears, and then military-grade cutting dispensary. There are cattle prods and barbed baseball bats next to stone mallets and what looks to be the entire power tools section from Home Depot scattered along the floor. This is where the Moon Shack's citizens went to unwind with their victims. A separate side of interconnected rooms lies just beyond this one. How many other torture chambers are there?

The Else has doubled around, cutting him off from the floor below, moving faster than Hap thought possible. Is it toying with him on the staircase? Is it even a solid thing? Half mist, half an abomination of appendages. Hap will have to venture down below into the smoke and growing pockets of carbon monoxide. Will he just fall asleep? Will death come so easily?

In an instant, he is running too fast to stop before he's turning, slamming his flailing arm into the back wall by the door closest to the staircase. The Else's miserable song cuts through the alarm. *It is the alarm.* The wall into which he has collided seems to sink and slide, and as he squeezes through the tight, black space, he begins to understand rats and roaches in a way he never thought he could.

He finds a smaller staircase within the walls, and the smoke has not yet tainted this hidden place. Instead, he's assaulted by mold and mothballs. He walks and slides his way down narrow steps until he comes into a circular pocket of a room with its walls formed of black mirror. Hap sees different versions of his mangled self frowning and shivering. From the carvings along his chest to his arm being more blood than flesh, he is equally as haunting as any emissary of the Moon Shack.

Fearing he is trapped in the bubble of black glass, it takes Hap a moment to snap out of the illusion and realize the sliver of dark space that doesn't have his worrying reflection peering back at him is the way out. As he enters a narrow staircase once more, he feels something pressing on the walls around him. Tap, tap, tapping. The dark is pure. There is only the siren and the Else following him along the walls. It has found him. The secret places are just for fun. He hears the faint whale song of the Else just before its claws tear through the dark, and Hap is pulled into the flickering, ailing hallway light in a burst of bending limbs and crumbling plaster that sneaks up his nose and fills his mouth.

He has made it down another floor, maybe to the fourth or fifth. If this were all a test to race to the bottom, then he gets a D, which is still passing. Good enough. The Else bends Hap's body back, and he squeezes his eyes as tight as he can. The heat from the looming fires disappears. The Else, above all things, is a void. Hap's wounds stop aching for just a moment. It's a hand around his throat, as rough and bristled as it feels. It's just a hand. Neither man nor woman, Otis said. The Else was once a human. This is still recognizable, just like the groups of masked men who march along a road of beheaded heretics in some godforsaken desert or the backroom trumpeting of modern-day slavers, tugging along naked starving things addicted to opiates they can't get on their own. Hap won't open his eyes to get a good look at the Else's face, both because he doesn't need to see and because he realizes, now, how true everything Otis said was. Don't look the Else in the eyes. Otis never told him why not that it matters. Otis wasn't as crazy as he sounded, so with all Hap's heart, he trusts that son of a bitch.

The Else, while bending and twisting and inspecting Hap, spreads its hand to the back of his head. The hand is rough, almost like sandpaper. It tilts Hap's neck back, and despite the bruises along his face, he's using every muscle he has to keep his eyes shut. Maybe this is the trick, a simple trick to survive an encounter with the Else. Like a fairy tale, keep your eyes closed, and the monster will go away.

The Else presses down the edge of its thumb and pries open one of Hap's eyelids. It cocks its pale head, enshrouded with long frizzled black hair that drags on the floor. Mist rises from its body like that of a vampire smoking in the sun. Its eyes are glazed blue, and its fingernails are impossibly long and curled up like a *Guinness Book of World Records* nominee gone wrong. Beneath the sagging skin lies a sex that belongs to neither man nor woman. In its open maw lie rows of backwards teeth.

Hap makes out an image, a waking dream of something singing to itself in a cave, holding a bloody stick that pokes a pile of humanoid corpses with primitive, deformed faces. Something beneath the earth is screaming, reaching up, pushing through black walls to reveal a multitude of stalk-like arms. The song turns to a scream as the primitive human runs out into a lightning-streaked sky before falling to its knees in the rain and mud, utterly alone and lost. The Miskatonic crinkles to black; all Hap can see with his single eye is fading, searing white.

He's unaware that it has let go of his eyelids as he falls to the floor, blinking and staring at the carpet as the wispy presence around him is sucked away. That mournful song of the Else rises above him before fading. His nose burns from the pungent odor of rising smoke. There's what sounds like rain on a rooftop, bringing to mind the vision, the hallucination of that person all alone in the dirt. It's not raindrops but the crackling of the fires below. The Else has left him. Hap sobs and buries his face in the carpet. He's blind in one eye. His sight will forevermore be halved. The Else has left with a part of him.

He lies on the floor, listening to the crackling flames, wondering if he'll pass out from the cloud of looming carbon monoxide or if he'll somehow find the strength to escape through a window. An elevator dings, and before Hap can stand up, Johan is sticking his head out of the metal box and giving him a gander. "Hap? You hear me? You're alive." He staggers from the elevator, leaning against the open doors. Elevators and fires, isn't there something about that? Then again, Johan wanted Hap to kill him. "Your eye has gone white. Who…who did you kill?" Johan raises a hand to his chest as he limps toward Hap, his mouth hanging open.

Hap moans, and he wants to either cry or scream, which is a good want because he still wants to feel. He is still human. He is still alive, and he wants to feel. He wants the pain to end.

"It doubted you…challenged you. I…in all of my years…. Oh Hap…." Johan's smiling, reaching to help Hap stand. From the staircase at the end of the hall, Paul Jones comes barging forward in his usual black shirt and purple tie. Hah. Hap knew that pathetic son of a bitch was in on this.

"No!" Johan turns, his face growing pale, the last of his priest's demeanor bursting like a bubble. He reaches into his tuxedo for something while lurching back toward the elevator. Paul Jones is suddenly twenty feet closer than he was half a moment ago. A part of his arm becomes an inky black tendril that extends and retracts in a single blink of Hap's last remaining eye.

Johan falls, plopping wordlessly across from Hap. Something has happened to his head. It doesn't fit the rest of his body; it's been crushed and twisted. "I do hate to use anything but words." Paul's face shifts and melts to form that of another as Randal leans down over Hap, his lips grim. He extends a hand, and Hap reaches for it, hoping to be helped to his feet. His own pain is an anchor. Randal's hand instead seems to grow as it slowly closes over Hap's. "I would offer you a trip to a place you cannot dream of on your own," Randal says, "where the mad pipes will have you dance and laugh around and around. You will get there, however, in time, in your own way."

"Who are you?" Hap cries.

The familiar face of the bartender is changing, warping ever so slightly again. At first, the skin ripples like water. The nose is growing and then shrinking, the cheekbones realigning. Something like a crown — no, a pharaoh's headdress molds out of Randal's skin to become an inky black accessory.

"I am merely the abdicator of coincidence. I met the female you seek. I gave her the stone idol that brought you and the Moon Shack denier together. I am pleased with this outcome, so I'll tell you something you are not to repeat." Randal crawls closer to Hap and whispers in his ear. "Your children have playhouses. You know they are plastic and false, but children believe them to be real, and they are never told this is not so. They go on believing until they forget, or they become those that live on street corners, in tents, believing what is not. Have no worries for the Moon Shack because none of those who exist both outside and in between fear it. Some, like me, are amused. You have your playhouses. Your Moon Shack. You men have given me a new joy to prod and poke, just when I thought I was done with you."

Randal seems to grow taller than ever before. His skin grows blacker than his crown, blacker than mere melatonin in the skin, and blacker than strange metals locked below the earth. Hap backs away on his hands and knees as Randal, a many-faced thing worshipped by old, rotten cults, strides toward him. The crown of a pharaoh appears across his skull as if forged by the smoke itself. Done with Hap, Randal walks past him, disappearing around the bend of the corridor. Hap doesn't get a chance to wonder an almighty "What the fuck?" The Shack has appeared in the hallway as the flames begin to trickle up from the floor below.

Tiffany's face distracts Hap from reading the words carved into the half-moon door. Tiffany's face exists, pale and unharmed, beyond the pane of the front window. She raises a hand, pressing it to the glass. The ghostly Moon Shack sits amidst a hungry fire unscathed. Behind her, Hap can see the shadows of other people. One of them flickers, and Hap recognizes one of the men who held him down in the ballroom. An old man with a white beard steps out from the shadows behind Tiff, placing his hands upon her shoulders as he leans forward to whisper something in her ear. He smiles and looks at Hap as he does so.

From Hap's seared eye, there is only the pale glow, which is a step beyond the blackness. *What they made her do*, resounds in Hap's mind as he stares at Tiffany and that blonde hair he wants to run his fingers through. He's already paid the price of entry. Oh Tiff, what they made her do....

Hap rolls over onto his stomach, and it's as if a bubble has broken, and the smoke is eating his insides as he sees a thousand twinkling stars. The Shack has vanished if it was ever there to begin with. If he closes his remaining good eye tight enough, maybe he could fall asleep. That's what dying is. He's sure of it. Like going to sleep. Tiffany wasn't a killer; no, she's dead. Hap begins to sob. He hopes she's dead. He remembers the night he checked into a room here. He remembers Tiff's ring moving. There was something else, a shadow, standing over him. That was her ghost. Another spirit to wander the haunted hotel. That's what she is. What she *has* to be because he refuses to accept the alternative. He can feel her right now, yes. Her ghost. Her ghost standing over him while he curls up to asphyxiate and then burn. Her ghost, prodding his shoulders, caressing his cheek, whispering in his ear that he can't give up.

Haps pushes himself to his feet. With his eyes closed, he can see Tiff standing beside him, crying yet happy, happy that they got the chance to love one another. Yes, that's how this story goes. Hap runs as fast as he can toward the window at the end of the hotel hallway. He doesn't break the glass when he runs into it and instead bounces off, bruising his body once more. He slaps at the windowpane with weakening hands, and he swears he hears Tiffany calling through the fire behind him. Fuck it. Hap smashes his head forward, shattering the glass as he swings his legs through. For a few brief seconds, he flies.

EPILOGUE
THE GUN-IN-YOUR-MOUTH SELFIE STICK

They have shipped him out of Rhode Island and dumped him on the outskirts of Pittsburgh. When he hears the train most mornings, he imagines his dad sitting on it with his legs crossed, reading a newspaper while everyone else holds tablets. The walls of Hap's special hospital for special people aren't padded, and Hap's arms remain free from any straitjackets. Regardless, he is still forced to dress in the ceremonial white scrubs of the soulfully ill.

Hap hasn't been a good patient. He bit a nurse on the arm and told her there were stars in her tummy. After that, they put him on medication they said would calm him down, but all it did was make him sleep more. He dreamed and dreamed and eventually saw the Moon Shack; its door kept opening like the smile of a Cheshire cat that continued to grow wider, although it never quite showed him what was inside. It's as if the Shack were telling him he has to get out of the hospital and find out for himself. For the rest of his wretched life, he will always be welcome behind that ancient, half-moon door.

Sometimes Hap imagines that he sees Otis, if only because the other guests of Wilbur Sanitarium are allowed to grow their beards as long as they want. Hap keeps feeling the urge to tap those unshaven patients on the shoulder and tell them he's sorry. Sometimes the doctors will suddenly have Randal's face, and eyeballs will start appearing where their shirt buttons are. Hap tells them he won't go to that place where the pipes play, and the old undying things dance without rhythm.

Hap's mom visits, and he hugs her and tells her he loves her. His dad visits and he shakes his hand and tells him he's trying his best to get better. His siblings cry, and automatically he becomes the youngest, not by age but by special needs. His big brother Darren gives him *One Flew Over the Cuckoo Nest* to read in his room, and before somebody ends up stealing it, Hap feels as pacified while reading that thing as he used to be while playing video games.

He doesn't walk so well anymore; he needs help getting his food in the cafeteria because, with the crutch in one hand, it's still too much for him to get used to, but he's trying. When he jumped out of that window, he landed on a firetruck. He didn't break his back, which makes him a lucky Jack. Sometimes Hap wakes up reciting a poem he once read on a bathroom wall, except it's complete in his dreams, and he knows the right way to sing it.

Providence is an empty city. The doctors control Hap's access to the news, which means no Internet, but during those first days, at the real hospital, he heard everything. The reason why people were moving out of the city and why government funding was being drained wasn't because some hotel caught fire the day its manager and a few people were shot. It's because, after the place partially burned down, they found a mass grave of charred bodies somewhere in the basement, a basement that connected to a bunch of sewers that fed into the ocean. Hap tells everybody that Tiff is one of those burnt beyond recognition. He tells so many people that they believe him. People say Tiff's mother killed her father before turning the blade on herself. Hap says they are wrong there, too, but there is only so much the good people of the world will believe from the lips of a lunatic.

The *Providence Journal* initially wanted to interview Hap, but his mother wouldn't let them. She was also confused as to why they didn't already know him through the internship.

Lucky for Hap, after seeing the condition he was in, his mom didn't push the issue. That was around the time when he started telling everyone as much as he could about the Moon Shack. Corpses were found, but not enough to match the body count of killers in the ballroom. Most of them got away. Hell, aside from Johan, Augustine, and that Woodbury sucker, they all got away. They are still out there, doing what they do best. If the Shack, like a phantom, can appear anywhere its worshippers choose, then it could fit a lot more people than its squat, crumpled walls would indicate. The Miskatonic was burned down by the mob. That's what the papers said. Some guy with a too-Italian last name was arrested, who then killed himself that very night. Hap doesn't want to read between the lines to see how suspicious, how deliciously shady that is. The heart of the cult has left Rhode Island, but dig and dig as inquiring minds might, and there are surely lesser organs that remain.

By rambling on about the Shack and its guests, Hap got the cops to question him in his hospital bed. They wanted to know how he knew about Otis's house burning down with a woman's body chained inside. They asked, and they asked, and Hap broke down and told them everything.

"You have been through a lot," they said, which is true; he has. "You have the rest of your life ahead of you. This small handicap won't hold you up," they told him. There may be surgeries for his eye because the doctors, with their many hard-earned degrees, cannot figure out what went wrong with his sight in the first place or how fire could scorch a single pupil but leave the flesh alone. There are surgeries for his leg: more metal to join the stuff they already had to place in his arm and along his ribs. He's got a good brain, they say, and a college education to boot. Tiff has a gravestone somewhere he would like to visit. He would also like to get dinner at Cindy's Diner in Scituate and then pay Cidalia a visit to cry for the boy who Otis was. For now, though, Hap needs to focus on getting better.

The doctors are steering his therapy in the direction his heart was always pointing. Eventually, Hap is delivered his pictures from Otis's Cadillac. The actual camera is still held up in evidence, but some kind detective goes through the trouble of uploading the pictures to a USB that he then gives to Hap's doctor. On a day when Hap is inconsolable and filled with memories of the Miskatonic, he is presented with a gift: a new digital camera with the pictures already uploaded. The ones of him and Tiff and... four years. Their four years.

In his room, Hap waits for the first light of a full moon in order to see out of his new, damned eye. Hap has discovered that moonlight makes his eyesight good as new. In the face of endless suffering, there are strange miracles to be discovered.

Hap begins with the most recent pictures. He remembers instantly when the first photo he sees is unmistakably that of the Miskatonic ballroom, where it is empty of people and decorated for an Astronomer's Ball. Models of plants, glow-in-the-dark stars, and rocket ships intermingled with cutout displays of the meteors and the Moon. The next photo shows one of Tiffany's coworkers. Another is a selfie of Augustine, Tiffany, and a man... no, Woodbury, the naked killer now wearing clothes in the photo. All of them appear to be helping to set the Astronomer's Ball up. More photos. More people Hap can almost remember from his final visit to the ballroom. He totally forgot that he let Tiff borrow his camera the day before she disappeared. He tries to tell himself that the evidence on his camera wouldn't have mattered anyway, but boy does it leave a bitter taste in his mouth.

Hap knows he has done everything he could, as he hunches over the warm glow of his camera, interchangeably crying and laughing. He looks at the picture of Tiff trying on her graduation gown. He sees his and Tiff's last birthdays, both spent at their favorite wing restaurant, Boneheads, in Warwick. He relives their trips to the White Mountains of New Hampshire and that famous Massachusetts beach town, Silverport, with its magical beach that sparkled. He can't help but smile over the snapshot of Tiff's former fake ID that she wanted a visual memory of in case it got confiscated. On the ID, she gave herself a fake name for shits and giggles: *Lacy Miyamoto*. There's a photo of the day Hap first moved in with Tiff and had all of his junk spread over the floor. Pictures of lakes, the woods, birds, Newport, Tiff's dog Snack, a dozen chicken wings for a dozen restaurants, the starry night sky, and, with every passing month for nearly four complete years, a picture of the full moon, through fog and the cracks of tree branches with every scar of a crater visible. Through hundreds of pictures, Hap knows he can still become free, free to be lost in the 1,347 days of memory logged between the first and final picture. He will look back, both over his shoulder and through time, until his neck snaps. There are no more moves left to make.

Nick Manzolillo's short fiction has appeared in more than 60 publications, including Thuglit, Red Room Magazine, The Terrifying Tales Podcast, and Wicked Witches: A Journal of The New England Horror Writers. He currently lives in Providence, Rhode Island, with his wife and two well-read cats. He currently spends most of his time growing a beard and hiking. Learn more at nickmanzolillo.com.

www.ingramcontent.com/pod-product-compliance
Lightning Source LLC
Chambersburg PA
CBHW030125180626
46812CB00002B/558